CROSSWIND

A Novel by
Patricia Valdata

Pat Valo

This book is a work of fiction. Names, characters, places and incidents are either the product of the author's imagination or are used fictitiously. Any resemblance to actual events or locales or persons, living or dead, is entirely coincidental.

ISBN: 1-879630-41-9

Published by

Wind Canyon Publishing, Inc.
P.O. Box 1445
Niceville, Florida 32588

Layout/Cover Design: Becky Jaquith
Cover glider from slide provided by Chuck O'Mahony

First Printing, 1996

Wind Canyon Publishing offers other book titles. **Wind Canyon** offers software applications work related to book publishing, including converting titles to multimedia CD-ROM discs and other computer formats. For further information, including details regarding the submission of manuscripts, contact the above address.

Printed in the U.S.A.

ACKNOWLEDGEMENTS

I must especially thank Jim Beckman, who by taking me for my first glider ride made me realize that dreams can become reality, and Nick Warner, my glider instructor, who showed me how. I am also grateful for the assistance of Catharine Cookson, Esq., and Gary Hoagland, Esq., for their advice on New Jersey probate laws; Doris Grove, Maria Grove, and Rosalie Grove Keene for their information on ridge soaring flights; Chris Noël, Andrea Freud Lowenstein, and Mark Doty for their kind but firm criticism; and of course, my husband, Robert Schreiber, for his patience and understanding and love.

Chapter Five of this novel appeared in abridged form as the short story "Just Like a Hawk," published in *Soaring* magazine in July 1993. That story received the Joseph C. Lincoln Award for 1993-94.

For Dad, who loved airplanes —

he'll always fly with me.

Chapter One

I was drunk when my father died.

While he lay dying on the bathroom floor at home, his skull fractured and his blood and urine seeping into the grout between the floor tiles, I was 900 miles away, lying on a different bathroom floor, cold sweat on my face and a vile mix of 7-up, gin, and cold pizza seeping into the grout between the floor tiles. I blew my nose to dislodge a piece of mozzarella cheese and started to cry. Had I moved a little more quickly, I would have gotten to the bowl in time. Had my father moved a little less quickly, he would have seen that the floor had just been washed, and he would not have slipped on the wet tiles. Had my mother been able to sleep that night, she would not have scrubbed the bathroom floor at 1:00 in the morning; some people drink warm milk or read biographies to cure insomnia, my mother cleans house. When she finished the floor she dumped the rinse water down the toilet, leaving the seat up. When my father slipped and fell, his head hit the unyielding porcelain instead of the deluxe padded plastic seat. Later, when I learned the details, it was a comfort to know that my father and I had lost consciousness at very nearly the same moment; at least we had done something together.

I was in Chicago for the Labor Day weekend. Cathy Molnar, my best friend from high school, went to college there, and she invited me for the first party of the semester. We drove out there together, and I was to have gotten a ride back with a friend of her roommate's who was going to school in the East. It was Cathy who took the phone call about my father, and got me sober and clean enough to fly home. She took me as far as the correct gate at O'Hare and gave me a couple Dramamine tablets before going home to clean the bathroom floor. I owe her one — maybe more than one — that floor was a mess.

I can't remember much about my first airplane ride; I must

have passed out again. The last thing I recall was wondering, as the front of the jet tilted up, whether we were taking off or whether I was losing it once more, and the next thing I knew my head was pounding and a disgustingly cheerful flight attendant announced our arrival at Newark.

It was 7:00 in the morning. The New York skyline was semi-visible in the smog. Mrs. Pulaski, our next door neighbor, was waiting for me. She cried when she saw me, and sniffled intermittently all the way down the turnpike. I stared out the window while she filled me in on the details of last night. As the grieving daughter I guess I wasn't expected to say much, which was fortunate, not that Mrs. Pulaski needed more than an occasional "mm-hmm" to keep talking. She was one of those old ladies who lived for life's major events. A birth was like Christmas, a wedding as good as a World Series, and funerals were the Super Bowl to her. She read the obituary column in the newspaper each day, more often than not finding someone she knew or at least had heard of listed there. I think she actually enjoyed going to wakes. She compared flower arrangements, noted how many mass cards were given, counted the mourners. My father's accident would keep her going for months. I couldn't begrudge the relish in her voice as she talked about it. I sighed and looked out at the familiar landscape, if you can still call a landscape something so altered by man and machine.

Heading south on the turnpike we passed through Linden, a hellhole that Dante would have recognized. Linden was an unending stream of tank farms and cracking plants, the reason for all the jokes about New Jersey. It was inconceivable to anyone passing through the state that people actually lived here. How could anyone survive next to a huge grid of stinking pipes and towers, with flames coming out of some and clouds of yellow-gray smoke out of others? People always drove by with the car windows rolled up and the outside air vent off, even in midsummer. You wanted to hold your breath and close your eyes and floor it to get by, always wondering what would happen if one of those tanks blew up as you drove past only yards away. The sight was so revolting that no one seemed to notice a few miles down the road when the turnpike passed through acre after acre of farmland. It was as if Linden left its nightmare image permanently burned on the retina, and all anyone saw of the rest of the state was a heavy framework of iron and flames.

Today the view suited my mood — the refineries, the trash blowing along the 12-lane highway, the sulfur dioxide and God only knew what carcinogens I was inhaling. My father was dead, I was hung over, and I had no idea what would await me at home.

Home was Hardenbergh, New Jersey, a town of 30,000 people on the shore of Lake Lenape. Hardenbergh was settled more than 300 years ago by the Dutch, and a Dutch last name still was the key to making it in Hardenbergh high society, what little there was in a working class town. After 300 years, Hardenbergh was still trying to find its identity. It wasn't North Jersey, it wasn't South Jersey; it had old money in one ward and Spanish groceries in another. It advertised itself as a college town, since it was the site of Hardenbergh College, a two-year county college and my alma mater, but it was dominated by the offices and factories of Van Dyke and Son, the world's leading manufacturer of personal care products, a company dedicated to wiping out body odor in the armpits and crotches of the U.S. Almost everyone in Hardenbergh worked at V.D. If your last name was Dutch, English, or Irish you worked in The Home Office. If your last name was Italian or Hungarian or Polish or Spanish you worked in The Plant. My father had worked in The Plant. He was a day shift foreman, and it had taken 20 years to get there.

My parents were both born in Little Hungary, on the east side of town. Although Catholic, both their families had been small. My mother was an only child and my father's only brother had been killed in Vietnam. None of my grandparents were still alive. During high school my mother had hung out with the north side crowd, kids with names like Frelinghuysen and Campbell. Their families lived across the street from Lenape Park on the south shore of the lake, not in anything you'd call a mansion, except for the Van Dykes, of course, but in colonial-style homes on quarter-acre landscaped lawns, with three or four bedrooms, paved driveways, and detached garages. My mother was smart and pretty but her parents couldn't afford to send her to college, and when her crowd went to Princeton or Da Nang she stayed behind and got a job at The Plant, as did my father. He had flunked the Army physical but not V.D.'s. They were married in 1966.

By the time my mother's old boyfriends came back — the few who did — my parents had had me and two miscarriages. My mother's old boyfriends went to work in The Home Office.

Mrs. Pulaski finished telling me the gory details as we reached our exit. She wouldn't let me pay the toll. A few minutes later we were driving over the Wheatstone Bridge, which spanned the narrow end of Lake Lenape, near the dam that created it from Lenape Creek. A couple minutes later we were in our own neighborhood.

Mrs. Pulaski turned onto our street and parked. It was quiet, presumably in deference to our family tragedy. We lived in the center of town, where the main ethnic neighborhoods met. On a Saturday afternoon you could walk down our block and smell Central Europe making dinner. I was raised on the three P's — pasta, pierogies, and paprikas. I chose my friends based on their Grandmother's cooking. I could always bum a hot garlicky meatball from Mrs. Bongiovanni, or some pungent stuffed cabbage from Mrs. Pulaski, or a savory piece of strudel from Grandma Nagy. She wasn't my grandmother: she was the neighborhood's. An old lady when I was a kid, she still tottered around the neighborhood, bearing gifts of palascinta or cabbage soup to the needy, which was anyone with kids.

The neighborhood wasn't much different from the way it was when I was little. The porch steps sagged a little more, maybe, but they were just as clean, and the old ladies still hosed off the sidewalks on summer mornings. The Spanish and black neighborhoods to the south were a few blocks closer. They would blend with ours in a few years. Pretty soon you would be able to smell the paella on Saturdays.

Our house looked just like the others on the street. It was narrow, only a room and a hallway wide. If you leaned out a side window and your neighbor did the same, you could borrow a cup of laundry soap over the narrow alley between the houses. The houses were mirror images of each other; our front door was on the right, the Pulaski's was on the left, and so on down the street. Each house had a full front porch, not a suburban stoop. The hall ran the length of the house from the front door to the kitchen, where it met a side hall leading to the basement stairs and the side door. The front room was the parlor. Behind it was the small dining room, and behind that the smaller kitchen. A half porch led from the kitchen to the back yard, a few steps down. Upstairs were two bedrooms and the bathroom, and above them the attic, which many families finished to make a third bedroom.

My mother was upstairs, lying sedated on the bed. She was already dressed in black, except for fuzzy red slippers.

According to Mrs. Pulaski my mother had found my father sprawled on the floor, his head slumped against the toilet pedestal. My father, who was a sound sleeper, never heard my mother's nocturnal cleaning binges. He had woken to pee, as he did every night about that time, the natural result of knocking down a few Buds before going to bed. My mother, after scrubbing the kitchen and bathroom floors, was sufficiently tired to fall asleep. But she was a light sleeper, and when he didn't come back to bed in a while her busybody alarm went off and she got up to look for him. Thinking that my father must be having a digestive problem to stay in the bathroom so long, she knocked on the door to see if he needed the Kaopectate. When there was no answer she pushed the door open, which she did with difficulty because my father's big flat feet were up against it. A few minutes later the Pulaskis were awakened by my mother, who was hanging out our bathroom window and banging on theirs with a damp mop.

I gave my mother a kiss on the cheek and she stirred but didn't wake up. Just as well. I walked into the bathroom. It looked like any other bathroom in the neighborhood: white fixtures, white half-tiled walls with a border of black tile at eye level, a particularly hideous wallpaper with green and yellow eagles on it that my mother had chosen when I was ten, a green shower curtain, yellow towels with daisies appliquéd on them, a framed drawing of a mouse sitting on a toilet, a plastic mushroom with solid air freshener in it, a crocheted house hiding the spare roll. The floor was made of small white hexagonal tiles. Next to the toilet the grout looked pinkish, but it may have been only an afterimage of the shower curtain. I hoped so. I noticed that the toilet seat was down, and the lid closed. I lifted them up, half expecting to see a patch of dried blood, with a few dark hairs stuck to it, but the porcelain was clean, the water clear and blue.

I felt queasy again. I went to the sink and rinsed my face, then drank a glass of water-flavored chlorine. It was a mistake; my stomach lurched and the running water made me want to pee. I looked at the toilet, and at the pinkish grout between the floor tiles. Not the most dignified way to go, was it. Not the way old man Van Dyke would choose. How the hell were they going to handle the obituary on this one?

I walked out of the bathroom and down the stairs, past the print of John and Bobby Kennedy, into the kitchen and out the back door. Then I went over to the Pulaski's to use their bathroom.

My mother woke up about an hour before the viewing. I was shocked when I saw her face in the harsh fluorescent light of the kitchen. She looked exhausted; her long, drug-induced nap had not erased the dark circles from beneath her eyes. Her hair, usually as neat as the day she leaves the hairdresser, thanks to a complicated turban of toilet paper and netting that she slept in, was disheveled, but she hadn't bothered to comb it. She had lines in her forehead I'd never noticed before, and a grim set to her mouth that made her look old to me for the first time. I could picture her twenty years from now, white haired and tight lipped, frowning at nothing in particular, the way she frowned tonight at the odor of stuffed cabbage, as though puzzled our kitchen should smell of it. I walked over and gave her a hug, awkwardly; we weren't much of a hugging family, and she seemed frail.

I helped her sit down at the table, where Mrs. Pulaski was dishing out the stuffed cabbage Grandma Nagy had dropped off earlier in the day. I mostly pushed mine around on the plate. My mother spent a lot of time concentrating on cutting hers into small rectangles with her fork. Finally she just put the fork down and pushed the plate away, despite Mrs. Pulaski's gentle arguments that we needed nourishment no matter how we felt. But my mother sat there, looking at the tablecloth, and twirling her wedding ring with the fingers of her right hand.

I watched her twirl the ring, and then I put down my own fork and asked, "Ma, why did you marry him?"

"What?" she said, coming back to the kitchen from wherever she had been.

"What made you decide to marry him, out of all the boys you went out with?"

She kept twirling her ring.

"You never told me," I said, "why you chose him, in particular. I just wondered."

"Because," she finally answered, "when I first came to this country, he was the only one who didn't call me a refugee." She said the word with contempt, the way some people say the words "nigger" or "spic."

I could imagine the ridicule she endured when she arrived in 1956, with her accent and European clothes and pierced ears, and I could picture her years later, a high-school beauty and a tease to the boys who had once been cruel, saving it all for my father, who had been kind to her in the third grade.

"Did you love him?" I asked, putting my hand lightly over hers.

She withdrew her hand and looked back down at her plate. "You ask such foolish questions," she said. "It's time to get ready." She stood up and walked to the stairs, slowly, like an old woman.

A few minutes later we walked to Barone's Funeral Home, only a few blocks away. Mrs. Pulaski went with us, although the viewing for nonfamily wouldn't start for another hour. Since my mother and I were the only family it seemed silly to have a special viewing for the two of us — the whole idea of a viewing was pretty disgusting when you thought about it; personally, when my time comes I hope someone stuffs me into a space capsule and shoots me out of the solar system — but my parents are nothing if not conventional and so we have the viewing tonight, and the funeral tomorrow morning.

Unlike Mrs. Pulaski, I had very little experience with wakes. So far it felt like waiting for a root canal, only worse. I felt ultra-alert, the way you are while you sit in the dentist's waiting room.

I noticed every crack in the sidewalk. A neighbor was watching MASH reruns on TV. A cool breeze started to blow, carrying the fragrance of spaghetti sauce and chrysanthemums and car exhaust. My bra strap fell over my right shoulder. I listened to the pattern of our shoes, my flats scraping, my mother's spike heels tick-tacking, Mrs. Pulaski's sturdy black orthopedic soles clumping. I started chewing my Lifesaver, feeling the peppermint scorch the back of my tongue.

Joe Barone was standing next to the door of the funeral parlor, waiting for us. He was stocky and balding, with the unmistakable schnoz of the southern Italian, and a complexion that should have been olive but was pasty from spending so much time in the basement stuffing stiffs. Dressed in a dark suit he reminded me of a dorky little vulture I'd seen once in a Saturday morning cartoon. I suppose that was appropriate. Maybe it was a reflection in his glasses, or maybe it was the last of the hangover, but as we walked past him I could swear his pupils were shaped like dollar signs. He inclined his head and motioned us in with his left hand.

"Mrs. Horvath," he whispered. He always whispered. "Mrs. Pulaski, Ellen."

"Ms. Horvath," I snapped. I was not in a good mood.

He apologized and led the way into a corridor whose walls were covered in flocked silver paper. Candle-shaped lamps flickered on the walls. He stopped before a doorway marked with a black-edged card in a little holder at eye-level. It read "Horvath."

Mrs. Pulaski said, "I'll be in the lounge," and walked off sniffling. Then we walked in, my mother leaning on my arm and me looking at the floor. I didn't know where else to look. I didn't want to look up ahead, at — it. My mother, who had been sniffling since the Valium wore off, began crying in earnest, muttering "Sandor, Sandor, Sandor." When we got up to the casket she grabbed the satin-draped kneeler and thudded quite ungracefully to her knees.

I took a few steps back, still staring at the paisley carpet the color of Gulden's mustard. The smell of carnations was not helping my touchy stomach, and my mother's moaning and wailing, honed by years of attending neighborhood wakes, was adding to my headache.

It was time to look at Joe Barone's latest achievement in mortuary art.

This room, I saw as I looked up, was papered in gold flocking, which clashed with the yellow mums of the neighbors' arrangements. One of the more garish, a heart-shaped cluster of pink carnations, had a white satin banner across it reading "In memory of my beloved father." I wondered if my mother had ordered it for me. I half expected someone to send an American Standard in white carnations.

On either side of the display were flickering candles, actually candle-shaped light bulbs in plastic holders. Barone spared no expense when it came to setting a mood. In front of the floral tributes was the casket, with brass handles and an ivory satin lining that must have cost a fortune. I wondered who picked it out. Maybe my mother and my father went casket shopping one day, just in case. They probably would consider that a fun way to spend a Saturday afternoon. They probably did dinner and the movies afterwards.

The casket lid was half open. The closed half was draped with an enormous spray of gladioli and mums and rosebuds, with a gold banner that read "In memory of my beloved husband." Judging by the cheery colors my mother must have chosen it while in the first throes of a Valium rush. Inside the casket was something that looked more like a store window mannequin than the remains of a human being. It was dressed in my father's best grey suit, a pale-blue French-cuffed shirt, silver tone cuff links shaped like bowling pins, a pale blue handkerchief folded in the breast pocket, and a dark grey tie, several seasons too wide. It was wearing too much makeup, with too much orange in the foundation. And lipstick! Christ, my father would be pissed if he knew about that. He wouldn't even wear men's cologne. His hair looked as though it had been moussed. His lips and eyelids were sewn shut, which looked better, I suppose, than tying the head with a rag and putting coins on the eyes, but I would have preferred a less barbaric technique.

Even odder than the makeup was the stillness — not a rise of the chest, not a twitch of a finger, not a flare of a nostril. Those hands should have been dealing a hand of pinochle, opening a beer, punching the air with every swing of a Mets bat. That chest should have been rising with the excitement of a double play or a bowling ball knocking down an eight-ten split. That face should have been full of expression: the adolescent grin on the night his team won the bowling trophy, the glower when the Mets lost. Even his poker face showed vitality as he leaned back to look at the hand he was dealt. He was a man of motion; he mowed and nailed and shuffled and bowled and drank and carried and threw and danced. When he had to sit still, in a doctor's waiting room or in church, his left eye twitched a little and he tapped his knee with his right hand, driving my mother crazy.

My mother had graduated from muttering my father's name to chanting, "It was my fault, my fault, my fault," over and over. I probably should have gone to her and tried to comfort her, but I thought it had been pretty asinine to scrub the floor at that hour of the morning, especially when she knew my father would be getting up a few minutes later to use the room; you could set your clock by him.

Maybe, in some deep, dark coil of her brain, a part of her had wanted it to happen. On the other hand, maybe she was just reacting to years of Catholic guilt training. Maybe, in some way I sure as hell couldn't understand, she really had loved him. I sat down on a green chair, wondering if my mother was crying real tears, and waited for the neighbors to arrive.

Toward the end of that very long evening, I stepped into the hall for a few minutes alone. I stared at the flocked wallpaper and tried to remember how my father really used to look. It was already hard to picture him; the image of that orange-faced mannequin kept intruding on memory. By concentrating I had almost gotten it right, when I was startled by a hand on my shoulder. It belonged to a woman I didn't know. She was a heavyish, middle-aged women dressed in a beige knit pantsuit, and she wore her hair in a bouffant flip, probably the same hair style she wore in high school. It probably looked just as bad on her then. She had tears in her eyes, and although I was getting used to seeing that, something about her manner made me realize that she was truly saddened by my father's death. She was so moved that, if I didn't know my father, I would have thought she was his mistress, or at least ex-mistress. Maybe she was an old flame. I smiled as she took my hand.

"I was your father's bowling partner," she said. I wasn't sure what to say to that. Before I could think of an appropriate reply she added, "He was such a good bowler!" Then she walked away.

I turned back to the flocked wallpaper and started to laugh. I tried hard to stop, holding my hands over my mouth so no one would hear; I hoped anyone who looked out and saw my shoulders shake would think I was crying. It was so inappropriate to laugh tonight, and yet that was all I could do, so I laughed and laughed until I really did cry.

After the wake, we walked home, my mother and I, escorted by Mrs. Pulaski, Mrs. Bongiovanni, and Grandma Nagy. My mother went straight to her half-empty bed, and I made the ladies some coffee. I supposed they were going to stay and keep some sort of vigil. I couldn't handle that so in a few moments I excused myself, went into the kitchen, and grabbed a beer. I opened the back door quietly and tiptoed out to sit on the back steps. The night was cool and windy, the first hint of fall. The sycamores had already begun dropping their brown leaves. I leaned my head against the balusters and closed my eyes.

I felt tired and guilty. Tired, because it had been such a damn long day, and guilty because I probably should be with my mother. We hadn't said much this evening. We'd hugged each other briefly when she went to bed, but it felt forced, almost as though we hadn't really touched at all. We were each isolated in our private emotions, unable or unwilling to break through. I had no idea how she really felt. Who ever knew what parents really felt? I took a sip of beer.

I heard a minor commotion in the kitchen and got up to see what was going on. I poked my head in the door. My mother was filling a bucket, and Mrs. Pulaski was trying to get her to stop and go back to bed.

"But I can't sleep," my mother said.

"Mrs. Pulaski," I said wearily, "let her be. She does it all the time. Let her get it out of her system."

Mrs. Pulaski shrugged her shoulders and went back to her vigil in the parlor. My mother schlepped her bucket upstairs, muttering again, this time about the stain in the bathroom floor. She was a neat freak, my mother. Our carpets had plastic runners on them, and our furniture had plastic slipcovers. She did fall and spring cleaning three or four times a year. I was becoming a slob out of reaction.

I went back outside and took another swig of beer. It really was cold; I'd have to go inside soon. I looked down at the steps. They were clean. It really wasn't her fault, I thought; any more than it was my fault for being away, and at a party to boot. My father was a known klutz. If it was anybody's fault it was his. It was a goddam stupid accident that left her a widow and me freezing my ass off on the back porch to avoid being in the house with three old biddies and Lady MacBeth.

So there I sat, sobbing and angry and terrified of tomorrow. I'd never been to a funeral before; I had been too young to go to any of my grandparents' funerals, so I didn't know what to expect. I couldn't sit still anymore so I went for a walk, half hoping to be mugged so I could avoid this funeral as well.

When I walked back up our street I could hear the noise from several houses away. I ran through the alley and up the back steps, wondering what else could go wrong today. I opened the back door.

Mrs. Bongiovanni was crying and talking on the telephone; Grandma Nagy looked bewildered and kept asking questions in Hungarian. Mrs. Pulaski walked over to me saying "Oh Ellen, oh Ellen, oh Ellen," over and over again. Everyone was repeating things today. Life was repeating things.

"Mrs. P," I said, forgetting to watch my language, "What the hell is going on?" She put her hands on my shoulders. "It's your mother," she said. "I think she's dead."

Chapter
Two

"What do you mean, there's no money?" I asked Tony Dimeo, my parents' attorney. We were sitting in his overheated office, less than two weeks since my father fractured his skull in our bathroom, and my mother asphyxiated herself trying to wash imaginary bloodstains out of the floor tiles with a mixture of ammonia and bleach.

"What this means," said Tony, "is that although your parents' will stipulates that they left you everything, they really had nothing to leave. They had no savings. Your father cashed in their life insurance policy last year." He paused. "I'm afraid all they really left you was a substantial debt."

This was not what I had expected. My father had made good money as a foreman. We'd been living in the same house for years. The mortgage payment was only about a hundred fifty a month. There were no new clothes, no new jewelry, no big purchases. Same old couch. Same old car. For vacation, we rented a house down the shore for a couple weeks. The same beach house every year, in Lavalette.

"Pardon my French, Mr. Dimeo," I said, "but what the hell is going on? What debt could there be? What do you mean by 'substantial'? How much can a mortgage payment be?"

Tony looked down at the file on his blotter for a moment, then he sighed and looked me in the eye. "Ellen," he said, "Haven't you looked at your mail? Didn't you notice the bills that were coming in?"

"Some," I admitted. "I've been meaning to go through it all, but I wanted to wait till I talked to you and found out how much there was to work with. I guess I've just been putting it off. There were so many decisions to make, right after, I mean about the funeral and all. I don't know. I never expected this."

"Ellen," he said, "I know this is a very difficult time for you.

And I'm truly sorry to give you more bad news. But for your own sake, you've got to understand the situation. Obviously, your parents didn't want to worry you. Now you've had quite a shock. Maybe you should go home and think it over. We can discuss the details in a day or two."

"No," I said. "I'd rather hear it all now."

"Very well. Your parents' original mortgage payment is quite low, as monthly payments go. But they took out a second mortgage five years ago, when interest rates were sixteen, seventeen percent. They should have refinanced, but they didn't. So."

"Why did they take out a second mortgage?" I asked.

Tony said, "Would you like a cup of coffee or something? I'll ask the secretary."

"Why did they take out a second mortgage," I repeated.

Tony looked down at the file. "They took out a second mortgage to try to pay your father's gambling debts," he finally said.

I stared at him. "Gambling debts? What are you talking about? What gambling debts? Besides," I added stupidly, "What bank would do that?"

"Ellen, I'm sorry, they probably told the bank it was for a new kitchen, or college tuition or something. Instead, your father used it to pay some of his debts, but mostly he used it to finance his gambling. Unfortunately, your father was not a lucky man."

"No shit," I said under my breath. I looked at Tony, who slumped back in his chair, a bead of sweat rolling down the right side of his pudgy face.

"How do you know all this?" I asked him.

"A lot of people knew this, Ellen," Tony said quietly. "In addition, I happen to know who was your father's, uh, contact in these matters."

"My father's bookie, you mean."

He nodded. "A relative of mine. A distant relative."

"What kinds of things did my father have your distant relative bet on?" I asked.

"You name it," Tony said. "Football, baseball, any ball, the casinos, the horses...." He spread his hands.

I thought of the time my father had taken me to Monmouth Park. I was sixteen, just old enough to get in, and we'd spent the afternoon at the two-dollar windows. I picked horses by their name, or the color of the jockey's silks. My father read the racing form. One of the horses I'd picked won us ten bucks, the rest were losers. But we'd had fun, until the seventh race. The horse my father had backed came in next to last, and we left right after the race. My father was tense, and didn't say a word the whole way home, which puzzled me — after all, the outcome of that race wasn't much different from that of the preceding six. Now I remembered that he was speaking to someone just before the race. I came out of the ladies room and saw him, shaking hands, I thought, with a man I didn't recognize. My father told me it was a friend of his from the plant, and I didn't think anymore of it. Now I understood.

"So how much is it?" I asked Tony.

"There's ten thousand dollars left on the first mortgage, and thirty-five on the second. Another ten for the funeral expenses, and the gambling debts, well, the bottom line looks like a hundred thousand," Tony said. "I'm truly sorry."

I must have stared at Tony for a full minute. A hundred thousand! A hundred thousand smackeroos, my father would have said, a hundred thousand clams.

"Mr. Dimeo," I finally managed to say, "I have about fifty dollars in my purse. I can't even afford to pay you for this, this office visit or whatever you call it."

Tony waved his hands. "Don't worry about it," he said. "Here, have a tissue."

"Thanks," I said, and blew my nose. "Where am I going to get so much money? How soon do I have to have it? I mean, is someone going to come to my door in a couple days and threaten to break my kneecaps or something?"

"No, no, Ellen, it's nothing like that. Everyone understands your situation. And remember, the firm will do what it can to help out."

I took a deep breath. "Okay, lawyers are supposed to advise people. So advise."

"Very well," he said. "Supposing we could arrange some sort of payment schedule, we're looking in the neighborhood of a couple thousand a month. Even if you had a fancy degree and made forty grand a year, that's a hefty sum. I think the only realistic thing for you to do is sell the house and its contents and use the proceeds to eliminate the debt."

I started tearing the tissue into little bits. "I don't know what to say, Mr. Dimeo. I just don't know what to say."

"This has been a shock for you," he said, reaching into a desk drawer. "You need a little time to think about it, absorb it all."

He handed me a business card. "Here," he said. "When you're ready. She's a good realtor, my sister-in-law. I swear I don't get a penny from the referral. She'll take care of everything for you. You give her a call when you're ready."

The card read "Jersey Realty. Bernadette Maiorano, Member, Million-Dollar Club." I put it in my pocket and stood up.

"Thanks, Mr. Dimeo," I said, "I'll give it serious thought."

I walked home slowly, kicking a small rock around the damp yellow and brown leaves that littered the sidewalk. I felt hollow, like a wind chime my mother had bought at a flea market. She didn't notice it was cracked until she brought it home. The only sound it made was a dull thunk. That's how I would sound if someone tapped me, I thought, as I buttoned my jacket. Thunk. A chilly breeze blew the dry leaves down around me, and they spun past my feet in patches of dun and faded yellow. What changes a couple weeks had brought, yet everything around me was the same. The sidewalk was still old slate cracked and heaved up by oak roots; the twelve o'clock whistle still hooted each weekday; church bells still tolled every Sunday from the steeple of St. Elizabeth's; September drifted toward October, just like any normal year, but this was no normal year for me. By now I should have been in classes at Trenton State College, going to football games and parties, meeting guys. The college had given me a partial refund on the tuition; I just couldn't deal with school so soon after my parents' — accidents. The money gave me something to live on for a while but it was going fast. Now here I was, stopping at the corner store to buy a newspaper so I could look at apartment and job ads.

It was the same corner store where I'd bought Batman comics only ten years ago, the last store in town to have wooden display cases filled with penny candy: coconut watermelon slices and dots of colored sugar stuck to paper strips, Mary Janes and black licorice, jawbreakers and root beer barrels. On top of the cases, Mrs. Kowalski arranged cardboard displays of cheap sunglasses, pocket combs, cigarette lighters, aspirin packets. Behind the counter Mr. Kowalski made sandwiches. The shelves were filled with canned goods, toilet paper, small boxes of laundry detergent, things you'd need in a hurry but didn't feel like driving to the supermarket for. The newspapers were arranged in a rack, each regular subscriber's name penciled on the upper left corner. When I was a kid it was my job to retrieve the daily paper. I'd be given a quarter to pay for it, and with the nickel change I'd get some candy, or horde the nickels until I had enough to buy a comic. It seemed pathetically naive to think I used to be satisfied with a box of pumpkin seeds when kids today used their allowance money and then some to buy crack.

I bought the evening paper and headed home. I'd never lived any place else. I had been thinking about getting my own place but apartments in town were expensive, and I didn't have a car of my own. So I lived at home, as did a lot of people my age. I didn't know anyone who might have an apartment to share; I had only a couple of really close friends. Cathy was in Chicago at school; Doreen had gotten married, and hung out with married friends now. She had come to the funeral, of course, and we promised to see each other afterwards, but I knew we wouldn't. We'd talked after the service at the cemetery, back at the house, when all the neighbors came bringing food. Mrs. Pulaski, bless her, had taken charge and I didn't have to do a thing except pretend to eat. Doreen had just found out that she was pregnant, and talked of the baby and invited me over for coffee. Coffee! When she and Joe were just living together, they'd invite me over for beer and pizza. Once they'd gotten married it had changed to dinner with wine and now we were down to coffee and dessert. We'd lost whatever we'd had in common, and we'd keep in touch for a while out of politeness or nostalgia, and I'd buy a present when the baby was born, but the real friendship was gone. Maybe it was never there; I couldn't tell anymore. I felt out of touch with the rest of the world, somehow, folded inward, cocooned. I wasn't totally alone; neighbors invited me over for dinner about once a week, or came over with a plate of palascinta or a bowl of stuffed cabbage, but I wasn't about to start going to Wednesday night bingo with Mrs. Pulaski. People in mourning weren't supposed to have much of a social life anyway.

I stopped in front of our house — it was hard to think of it as my house — and tried to look at it from a buyer's point of view. It was in good shape on the outside. My father had repainted it last spring. The front steps were a little saggy but none of them creaked; hardly anyone used front doors around here, except to come out and sit on the porch on summer evenings; only the mailman used the steps. The side gate was dull but not rusty, and the back yard was well kept, or it had been until recently. I hadn't noticed before today how dismally overgrown and weedy it looked.

I walked into the kitchen and draped my jacket on the back of the chair. No one would yell at me for doing it, and I had to admit I enjoyed these little freedoms I suddenly had. The kitchen needed paint. I could do that myself; it would give me something to do. I'd spent the past two weeks sending thank you cards and watching TV, Phil Donahue in the mornings and Oprah Winfrey in the afternoons. Mostly I slept a lot. I looked in the refrigerator but nothing was appealing. Something in the back right corner on the second shelf was getting fuzzy. I decided to let it go for a while to see how many colors it would grow. I walked aimlessly around the kitchen, touching things, until I came to the sink, where about a week's worth of dirty dishes festered. I knew I'd have to clean the house before I could let a realtor look at it; might as well start with the dishes.

I couldn't believe I was seriously planning to sell the place. I waited for the sink to fill. Above it was a dusty knickknack shelf with a set of Precious Moments on it, some spare keys, and a small picture of the three of us at Lavalette, taken when I was ten years old. We squinted into the sun, dressed in bathing suits and thongs. I remembered how the sand was so hot it burned your feet, and the water so cold it turned them blue. We'd spend the whole day on the beach. At night, we'd go to a movie, or play miniature golf, or drive to Seaside to ride the Swiss Bob and the Himalaya. My father always tried to win me a stuffed animal at the wheels; once in a while he actually did. Maybe that's where it started, trying to win a panda for his little girl, or maybe it was the poker game after a dinner of spaghetti with crab sauce that we'd have with the Bongiovannis, who rented the beach house next to ours. Mr. Bongiovanni had taken the picture.

Why didn't you tell me, I thought, as I started on the glasses. Why the hell couldn't you have let me in on it? It would have explained so much — the lectures on how much pork chops cost, the fights over the gas bill being paid late, why it was so bad when the Giants lost again. I blinked, and tears made little craters in the suds. Maybe I wouldn't have understood, when I was little — Christ, had it been going on that far back? I had no idea. The whole damn town knew, but I didn't. "I didn't even know," I said out loud to the picture. "Look at us! Was it going on then? When you talked to each other in Hungarian, is that what you were talking about? You pretended everything was fine, when all along it was lies, and everyone knew except me! I had a right to know. I had a right to know what you did, and to know who you were, and now I never will. I'll never know!"

A soapy glass slipped out of my hand and shattered against the faucet. "Now look what happened!" I shouted. "Just look!" I picked up the picture and threw it against the wall. The glass and frame broke apart and fell to the floor. "You had no right, you had no right!" I screamed until my throat hurt. "You had no right!" I picked up another wet glass and threw it, too, and then another, and another, until I'd smashed every glass. Then I started on the plates, brown stoneware my mother had spent a year collecting at the supermarket, one plate a week. Plate by dirty plate, they went flying against the wall, to shatter in a mess of shards and dried food, until only the pots were left, and they just bounced.

That night I drank an entire six-pack of Bud Lite. I slept so soundly I didn't even have to get up to pee. It took all morning to clean up the kitchen. Afterwards, I took a long nap. When I woke up, after dark, I cleaned the rest of the house. Like mother, like daughter, I thought, as I shoved the couch aside to vacuum under it. After I dusted and vacuumed, I took down the curtains and washed the windows and hung up the drapes. Then I cleaned out the kitchen cabinets and washed and waxed the kitchen floor. I finished scrubbing the bathroom floor, and when I was done there was no pink stain in the grout between the floor tiles. It took all night to do the fall cleaning for my mother.

I slept through the next day, and that evening went to the big hardware store south of town, where I bought spackle and paint and brushes and rollers. I spackled the kitchen, especially the one wall that had gotten pretty dinged up, and then I painted it. The kitchen looked so clean that the rest of the house seemed dingy, and so I ended up painting every room. I liked the precision of the work. I spent a whole day just putting masking tape on all the windows. I liked the consistency of the spackle; working with it was like frosting a cake. I liked the smell of the paint and the glossy thickness of it, the wet squeaking sound it made coming off the roller. After the whole interior was freshly coated in off-white, I worked outside. I raked leaves from the lawn and mowed it and pulled out the dead begonias and the ragweed, but I left the mums, which were still blooming. When I couldn't put it off any longer, I called Bernadette Maiorano.

Our house, which my parents had bought for $23,000 in 1968, was sold for $102,500 three days after it went on the market.

The day after the contract was signed I headed for the employment office at V.D. The V.D. corporate headquarters building occupied an entire block in downtown Hardenbergh. The Plant used to be next to it, but when it got too big they moved it to what was then the country, and what is now an industrial park on the outskirts of town. Headquarters was an old-fashioned looking thing for the first two floors, with a steel and glass cube rising above it for a total of ten stories. The personnel offices were on the third floor. I'd been there before, when I applied for summer jobs during high school. I'd gotten the usual kind of jobs, inspecting cans of deodorant as they glided past me on the assembly line one year, packing cartons another. This time around I hoped to avoid the assembly line.

Although I had called for an appointment, it was forty-five

minutes before anyone from personnel would see me. While I waited I filled out the application form. That took five minutes. Then I flipped through the latest *People* magazine. That took ten minutes. That left thirty minutes to sit and wonder if I was dressed for success. I didn't know where to go if V.D. didn't give me a decent job.

Finally, I was escorted into a cubicle. The third floor of V.D. was organized on an open plan. People worked in cubicles that were orange, brown, beige, or yellow. Each one was just wide enough for a small desk, a built-in bookshelf/file cabinet, and two chairs. The cubicles were only five feet high, so if you stood up you could look over a whole square block of cubicles.

The cubicle I was shown to was beige, and so was the woman sitting in it. She wore a beige suit, a light beige blouse with a high collar, beige shoes, and beige makeup. Even her hair matched her cubicle. I bet she didn't even know it. Maybe she'd been working here so long she blended in naturally. She looked about fifty years old.

"My name is Edna Staats," she said. "You may call me Mrs. Staats. I've reviewed your application, and I think we may be able to help you. May I express my condolences? Your father was a valued employee for many years." Here she paused to look at me, and one corner of her mouth stretched upward about an eighth of an inch. I assumed that was her version of a smile, and I wondered how she managed to do it and keep her lips pursed at the same time.

I smiled back and said thank you.

"We have several openings in the assembly line," she continued.

"I had hoped to work in The Office," I said quickly.

"The Office?" she asked, raising her right eyebrow. "Do you have a degree?"

"I have an associate's degree in liberal arts," I said. "It's there on my application."

She looked at the application as though she'd never seen it.

"I plan on going to night school as soon as I can," I added helpfully. It was a lie.

"Well," she said, making it two syllables, as she reached for a Rolodex.

"I would consider any entry-level position you have," I said. What did I know about entry-level positions at V.D.?

"Well," she said and sucked on her front teeth, "our entry-level clericals usually start in Reproduction. Have you ever used a photocopier?"

"Sure," I answered, thinking of the ones in the Hardenbergh College library. Insert a dime and they gave you a copy. Easy.

"Well," she said again, tapping one of the index cards, "When could you start?"

"Tomorrow," I said. "Today."

The other corner of her mouth turned up a fraction. "Monday will suffice. I'll type up an employee card for your file, and you'll report to Medical on Monday at 8:00 a.m. for your company physical. Barring any unforeseen problems there — you are in good health, I presume?"

I nodded enthusiastically.

"As I said, barring any unforeseen medical problems you'll come back here to complete your W-4 and J-9. When your forms are filled out completely and correctly, you'll proceed to Reproduction. Medical is on the first floor and Reproduction is on the first below-ground level. Any questions?"

"How much?" I asked.

Mrs. Staats looked puzzled.

"How much does the position pay?" I clarified.

She raised her eyebrow again, as though I'd asked something vulgar.

"The starting salary for clericals is $6.00 an hour," she said. "You are paid every other Thursday. Van Dyke also provides medical insurance, dental insurance, life insurance, and parking decals for the company garage. You get one sick day every two months and one week's vacation the first two years. Have you any other questions, Miss Horvath?"

"No," I said quickly. "Thank you very much, Mrs. Staats."

I left the cubicle and immediately felt like a rat in a maze. I could see the Exit sign, but not the path to it. I wandered up and down until someone in an orange cubicle noticed it was the third time I'd passed that particular orange cubicle and led me to the exit. Once I was off the elevator, through the revolving doors, and on the street I took out my pocket calculator. When I factored in taxes, typical rent, utilities, and food, I was looking at a disposable income of minus ten dollars a month. I decided to worry about it later; I didn't have a whole lot of choice.

Finding a job was easier than finding a place to live. Apartment complexes were out of the question; the minimum rents at those things were $550 a month, excluding utilities. I was hoping to find something for under $400, which would be about half my take-home pay. The closing was less than a month away before I found a roach-free place I could afford. It was in an old house near the Hardenbergh College campus. The first and second floors were full apartments; the third floor was half attic and half furnished studio. The tiny bathroom was tucked under the eaves and must always have been rented by women; it was impossible to stand and use the toilet — even sitting, you'd be tempted to duck. The kitchen was a miniature two-burner stove, a half-size refrigerator, and a lavatory-size sink arranged along one wall. The apartment was painted in semigloss the color of my mother's chocolate butter cream icing. It was furnished in early yard sale with a plaid sofa bed and a flowered wing chair over a threadbare oriental rug; an art deco floor lamp, white plastic end tables, and a French provincial coffee table completed the living area. A dinette set straight out of the fifties sported turquoise plastic seats, chrome tube legs, and a fake marble Formica table top. The studio would be cold in the winter and hellish in the summer, but it was clean, apparently bug-free, and only $350 a month. I paid a month's rent and a month and a half security and it was all mine.

There was nothing left to do but sort through all of our things, the furniture, my parents' clothes, the dented pots and pans, the garden tools in the basement. Mrs. Pulaski helped me tag everything for the sale, but when we got to the attic, I asked to be left alone. It was odd enough for me to rummage through my parents' memorabilia, let alone Mrs. P., even if she was a neighbor. I found stuff I never knew existed. Albums of Hungarian violin music, my mother's prom gown, her mother's prayer book, which had an ornate cover and gold on the edge of the pages, and the prayers in Latin on one side and Hungarian on the other. A brandy decanter with tiny snifters in green, blue, and red glass. My parents' high-school year book. In his senior picture, my father's sideburns were long. Under the picture were the words "Sandy. 'I'd bet the ranch on it.' Sodality 1, 2. Pep Club 3. Hardenbergh bound." My mother's hair was teased. Her caption red "Eva Gabor. 'Frodo lives.' C.D.A. 1, 2. Pep Club 3, 4. Prom Committee 4. Future kindergarten teacher." So she wanted to be a teacher, and he was going to Hardenbergh College, but they got married instead. She read Tolkein, and he was already betting what he didn't have. I put the book in the "keep" pile, and looked on. Soon I found my mother's wedding gown, high waisted with a short train and puffy sleeves. She had saved the shoes she wore that day, and even the underwear. I left the underwear in its box, but I took the gown and held it up in front of a dusty mirror. After a minute I tried it on. She was thinner then, and it almost fit, although I'd never have her bustline. I stood in the gown for a long time, feeling the material, listening to it swish as I walked back and forth in front of the mirror. I had thought it would be an emotional time for me up here, among the memories. But the memories I found here belonged to them, not me. Sure, my old Monopoly game was up here, and report cards and Little Women, but most of the attic's contents were theirs. Many items I hadn't even seen before, and didn't know where they had come from, or whose they were. I had thought it would be hard to sort through these things, but they stirred few feelings in me. I wasn't feeling much of anything, anymore. It had all happened weeks ago, and besides, how long can you mourn for strangers?

On the day of the closing, after paying off all my parents' debts, and Jersey Realty, I was left with $750 in cash, our car — a faded red '68 beetle, my clothes, some books and personal belongings, and the contents of a strong box I had found in the attic. It contained my birth certificate, a ringlet of baby hair, presumably mine, and one other very interesting piece of paper: my parents' marriage license. They had told me that they were married on June 20, the Saturday after they graduated from high school. But according to the license, they were actually married on September 20, and I was born the following March.

Chapter Three

"This is a rush job, hon," said the client who always brought me rush jobs and always called me hon, as she dropped what looked like a ream of paper on the counter. I had only been on the job a few weeks, but I was learning fast. Paper came 500 sheets to the ream, 10 reams to the carton, and I handled carton after carton of the stuff every day. I added her rush job to the stack of rush jobs I had to finish before lunch, and fed more paper into the maw of the Kobiyashi-Maru 9000.

The KM9000 was a monster of a copier, designed by Japanese engineers who had seen too many Godzilla movies as children. With a flash and a whirr the KM9000 would copy, enlarge, reduce, collate, and staple any report, memo, printout, drawing, or proposal you fed it. The finished product spewed out of it faster than human hands could grab. Each time I pressed the PRINT button I stepped back, afraid to get too close to the vortex of whirling paper that lay beneath its automatic feeder.

The KM9000 had a control panel with more buttons than a computer, and a liquid-crystal schematic diagram that would pinpoint a paper jam anywhere in the guts of the machine. I was not allowed the luxury of a few minutes peace while I searched for the mangled sheet that caused — or resulted from — the paper jam; a little electronic voice announced "Paper jam, area 4" until I removed the last shred.

I was trapped with the beast in a square, windowless room on the fourth floor of The Office. Clients — I had been instructed to call my coworkers clients — dropped their work off on a small counter in front of a two-foot by one-foot cutout in the wall. Most clients dropped their work off on the counter without a word to me; a few would stop a moment to shoot the breeze, which was difficult to do above the din of the KM9000.

Those brief encounters were my only contact with other

humans during the day, except for break and lunch hour. During break I'd put a little sign on the counter reading "Back in 15 minutes," and then I'd hustle to the ladies room, climb two flights of stairs to the nearest vending area, grab a soda and candy bar, dash down the stairs, duck back into the ladies room to wash the chocolate off my hands, and go back to my cell, where a new load of work would already be piled on the counter.

At lunch hour, which was only forty-five minutes, I'd meet a few other repro clerks in the cafeteria, where I ate my one decent meal of the day. Chris, who was seventeen and had a figure like Kim Basinger's, always had a boyfriend story; Nina, who was in her fifties, ate a quick salad and spent the rest of the time knitting something for one of her children; Jose, who was twenty-one and worked in the big repro shop in the basement, flirted with Chris and griped about work.

"Man, this place sucks," he said to no one in particular, "I could make more money at McDonald's, you know?"

"No, you couldn't, and the benefits are better here," Nina said between counting stitches. She and Jose had this conversation at least twice a week.

"I should be a supervisor by now," he grumbled. "So Chris, when I get to be a supervisor, you'll go out with me, right?"

"Sure, Jose," she answered, "Just be prepared to buy me lots of champagne."

"What are you making today, Nina?" I asked.

"A sweater for my youngest," she answered, while swirling teal yarn on and off two slim knitting needles.

"How is she doing in school?"

"Just fine," she answered with a smile. I smiled back, wishing more than anything that I, too, could be at school right now, instead of counting the minutes that were left before I had to shut myself in a little room with a big copier. I'd begun to hate that room — the copier I'd hated the moment I first saw it — and hate the job I had wanted so badly a few weeks ago, and still needed, no matter what I felt.

This is what it's all about, I thought after lunch, as I shut the copier room door behind me, and looked again at the paper I'd taped up there. I'd written "Huis Clos" on it, only my second day there; it hadn't taken long to see that I was as stuck in a dead-end job in a dead-end town as my father had been, and his father before him, and anyone else in Hardenbergh who didn't have the luck or the money to get out. After a few years I might get promoted into a word-processing pool, but my future at V.D. loomed long and clerical and it wasn't much different from the assembly line. The days dragged by slowly but the weeks passed alarmingly fast, with a rhythm that I slipped into too easily. Monday was awful, Tuesday bearable only because it wasn't Monday. Wednesday was the hump day; at lunch time someone was sure to point out that the week was half over. Thursday was good because it was only a day till Friday. Friday was the best, the day we woke up sighing "TGIF," but the day that the clock hands seemed sure to freeze at 3:45 in the afternoon. This monotonous world view was reinforced by the repro staff, as we copied and passed along little cartoons showing smurf-like creatures dragging themselves up a flight of stairs marked by the days of the week, or laughing themselves silly at the thought "You want it when?" We copied snide comments about bosses, mildly risque cartoons, puzzles to work on while waiting for big jobs to finish. I wondered how long it took a new bit of repro humor to travel from coast to coast by copier.

Finally, the big hand was on the 12 and the little hand on the five. I pushed the red "off" switch on the KM9000 and grabbed my coat. Fridays the wait for the elevator seemed interminable, so I walked down the four flights of stairs, through the employees' entrance, to the parking garage. It was always a shock, after being cocooned in the copier room, to get in the car and drive out of the garage into downtown, to see so much texture, so much color. The dusk seemed darker than usual, after eight hours under the glare of fluorescent lights, and the traffic lights glowed brightly even through the foggy windshield. Plastic evergreen boughs and silver tinsel stars fluttered from the street lights, and the store windows were full of color — red and green, silver and gold; Santas and reindeer, snowmen and angels, and occasionally a menorah. Every pedestrian carried packages; every shopper had a purpose.

I did, too; I was going to the laundromat. Friday nights were the least busy times there; everyone else was getting ready to go out. I rarely had to wait for a machine or a dryer. After laundry I'd go grocery shopping, and by the time I'd get home, Friday evening would be Friday night. I'd make a light supper, then watch TV until I was able to fall asleep. That took care of one date night. Saturdays were harder.

The laundromat was in a strip mall on the south side of town. The grocery store, a liquor store, a pharmacy, and a video store filled the rest of the mall. I parked the VW and grabbed the black plastic trash bag that was my hamper and laundry basket combined. The contrast between the cold air outside and the near-tropical humidity in the laundromat made it hard to breathe. I filled two machines as quickly as I could and stepped outside again, watching my breath puff out in a grey mist. I went browsing in the liquor store, looking at the wines. I'd never had wine that hadn't come out of a cardboard box. I wanted to tour the world with wine — Argentina, Australia, France, Germany, Italy, Spain. I wanted to speak the vintner's language — Pouilly Fuisse, Chianti, Cabernet, Bardolino, Bordeaux, Chardonney. If I'd had extra cash, I would have chosen my wine frivolously, by its name or the colors on the label. As always, I bought my usual six-pack of Strohs.

By the time I put the beer in the car my wash was done. I loaded it in the dryer and watched the clothes tumble in colorful swatches. The only other person in the laundromat was an overweight woman whose hips looked like saddle bags. Her salt and pepper hair was held back with a rubber band, except for short strands that stuck to her neck and the sides of her red face. She was folding clothes, perspiring in a faded blue sweatshirt. She was so heavy that her grey knit pants rubbed against her thighs, and the material rode up in folds, exposing her white ankles, sockless above men's faded black sneakers. At first I thought she was washing for a huge family, because all of the dryers were full, but as the last load, except for mine, tumbled to a stop, two young women came in to claim it. They were around my age, wearing fashionably thick down jackets, which they took off as soon as they were in the door. I watched them as they emptied three dryers and began to fold their laundry, laughing and talking.

Both wore faded jeans, so tight they probably had to lie down to zip them up. They had no hips, like French women, and slim, small bones. The fat woman walked out the door without a glance at them, waddling under her load of wash and breathing heavily. They waited for her to pass, then looked at each other and began to laugh.

I sat unobtrusively, embarrassed for the fat lady, while the two women giggled and folded their little bikini panties and their boyfriends' underwear. Not that size 14 was obese, but in these days of Richard Simmons and Jane Fonda my figure was straight out of the fifties, big framed and full hipped. I'd inherited my mother's lovely high cheekbones and tall frame, but what looked statuesque on her was just ungainly on me. My looks were non-descript, nothing special. My plainness must have disappointed her when I was younger, but probably was a comfort as she grew older, since I was not and would never be any competition. She had aged beautifully, if a tad plumply, and would have been a striking old woman, if she had lived.

It was a relief when the two sweet young things gathered up their clothes and left before I began to fold my own unfashion-able, plain white cotton *gacies*.

By the time I finished the laundry and grocery shopping it had begun to snow, a light, pleasant dusting that sparkled in the street lights. I hated carrying everything up two flights to my attic apartment but told myself every step was two calories and got it all upstairs in just two trips. I hadn't added much of my own things to the melange of styles in the furnished apartment; all I really had were a few books, a couple of pictures. I put the groceries away and put a frozen macaroni and cheese dinner in the oven. I was putting away the laundry when someone knocked on the door.

"Who is it?" I called.

"Me," answered Latanya, my downstairs neighbor. She was a sophomore at Hardenberg College, studying fashion design, to the chagrin of her father, a doctor, and her mother, a high-school vice-principal with a Ph.D. According to Latanya they were the Huxtables with no heart, a self-consciously upwardly mobile black couple with a son already in medical school and no sympathy for Latanya's desired career. I opened the door.

"Tonight's the night," she said stepping into the room with a small-boned elegance I envied, all perfume and matching accessories. "No arguments, either."

"Fine, thanks, how are you?" I said. "Would you like a beer?"

"No, thanks, we don't have time," she answered.

"What's this 'we' stuff?"

"We're going out," she said, in a very determined voice.

"You sound like somebody's mother," I said, "I'm too tired to go anywhere, and I have dinner cooking."

She walked over to the oven and looked in. "Yum, nouvelle cuisine. Looks lovely but it'll keep," she said, taking out the macaroni and cheese. She tapped it with a polished fingernail. "See? Not even thawed. I'll wrap this in foil and put it in the freezer while you get changed."

I groaned.

"Girl, you need to get out of this place and I need to get out of this place. We are going to get out of this place together. It's only 8:30, the night is young, we can be out of here by nine. That gives us hours and hours to meet men."

"Latanya," I said, "Don't you have a boyfriend already? Kareem or Abdullah or something?"

"Fareed, and that was last month. Now there's Wayne and there's also Darryl, but he doesn't know about Wayne and vice versa and I like it that way. Unfortunately, Wayne has to work tonight and Darryl has some kind of family thing going on, so I am available. Now, you said the next time I'm available we'd go out, so get your butt in the shower then put on something sexy — if you have it. Besides, I got you a present and I'm not giving it to you until you're ready."

"You got me a present?" I said, surprised.

She pulled a small package out of the pocket of her green silk slacks. "Not till you're ready."

I showered and brushed my teeth, gargling twice, and looked in my drawers. "Latanya, I don't have anything to wear," I said.

She came over to the dresser. "Sure you do," she said, rummaging. "Here. Black slacks. Anything goes with black. And they're very slimming. You just did laundry. You must have something that doesn't look it came from a Sears catalog. What do you wear to work?"

"My work clothes are covered with toner," I said. "I'll wear this."

I pulled on a royal blue shaker-knit sweater.

"You'll be hot when you dance," she said doubtfully.

"I won't dance," I said, brushing my hair.

"Don't you have any makeup?" she asked.

"Makes my face break out," I said firmly.

"A little blush won't hurt," she said, just as firmly. "You look washed out. We'll use mine — it's hypoallergenic. I'm light enough that it won't look too dark on you."

She put the blush on me and said, "Not bad. You look nicer than you think you do." Then she handed me the package, with a smile. "It's no big deal, but it's cute. I got it today at Lingerie 'n' Lace."

I pulled off the bow and gift wrap. Inside was a little cloth purse, about the size and shape of the folded handkerchief I used to carry a dime in when I went to kindergarten. It was made of blue paisley, and the little triangular flap was trimmed with white lace.

"It's sweet," I said, "But what's it for?"

"Look inside," she answered.

I looked inside. It held a condom.

"Latanya! Are you crazy?"

"These days you're crazy not to," she said. "Isn't it cute? They're called 'Coverups'; I got one for myself in hot pink."

"You've got to be kidding," I said as I put my coat on.

"Why not?" she said. "Besides, you never know. I'll drive."

"I'm really hungry," I said as we walked down the stairs.

"They'll have food," she said. "It's happy hour."

"It's after 9:00!"

"On Fridays, happy hour lasts till midnight at this place."

"This better not be a polyester palace," I warned, getting into her car. The snow had stopped and it was getting colder.

"I swear, there's not a leisure suit in there. I promise."

As we walked in the door of Orgazzo's Gym we were assaulted by more noise than an office full of KM9000s. A live band was playing somewhere in a haze of cigarette smoke that changed color as different spotlights passed through it. The first floor was a gigantic dance floor, made of hardwood like a real gymnasium; all the tables were on the cantilevered running track that circled the building upstairs. I could see a scoreboard, lit up with the score 69 all, and basketball backboards. Around the perimeter of the room were pieces of equipment, horses, bench weights, chinning bars; the walls were full of nautilus posters and neon slogans like "No pain, no gain."

"Where's the food?" I shouted after we checked our coats.

"In the boxing ring," Latanya shouted back, pointing to the right.

We made our way slowly around the edge of the dancers. Fortunately, the designer of Orgazzo's wasn't too authentic; the ropes went around only three sides of the ring and a short flight of steps led up to it. We got on line and got plates of typical happy hour food: stuffed mushrooms, little meatballs in brown gravy, chicken wings, tiny hot dogs wrapped in pastry, cubes of swiss and cheddar cheese. Latanya just picked but I piled my plate and immediately got back on line for seconds before walking over to the bar, which was on the other side of the dance floor. Instead of bar stools it had a row of stationary bikes. Latanya bought drinks while I tried out one of the bikes. That lasted all of fifteen seconds and then I got off. At the end of the bar was a pedal and flywheel arrangement, like a stationary bike for the hands, where a group of sweaty young men were staging a loud endurance contest.

"Latanya, this place is full of jocks," I screamed.

"Better than paunchy old dudes in leisure suits," she screamed back. "Go meet somebody. I'll see you back here in an hour."

"Latanya!" I started to shout, but she melted into the dancing crowd and I was alone, as alone as you can get in an overcrowded bar, which is pretty darn lonely. Not that I had gone out of my way to be with people these past few weeks; I'd even avoided passing through the old neighborhood ever since I moved out, preferring not to see my old house with some strange family living in it. I just didn't know what to say to people, after they said they were sorry to hear about my parents.

I sure didn't know what to say to anyone tonight, assuming you could have any kind of conversation over the music of "Heavy Decibels," a most appropriately named band which was playing under the scoreboard. I ordered another beer and tried to find a relatively quiet spot. I went upstairs and leaned my elbows on the railing to watch the dancers. In a moment someone stepped up to the rail next to me, so close our elbows touched. He was tall, with curly blond hair, and wore a polo shirt that stretched tight across his biceps.

"So where do you work at?" he asked me.

"V.D., in The Office," I answered, shifting a half-inch to the right.

"No, I said where do you work out?"

"Oh," I said, and took a sip of beer while I tried to think of a good answer. "No place, really. I climb stairs a lot."

"Wow, stairs, bitchin," he said. "That's good exercise."

"Uh-huh," I said out loud, while I thought to myself, "Bitchin?"

"Name's Scott," he said, holding out his hand.

"Mine's Ellen," I said, shaking his hand. He didn't let go after we stopped shaking hands.

"You have nice hands, Ellen," he said. I looked down at my left hand, which was holding my beer. I hadn't been able to get toner out from under my index finger.

"Thanks," I said and drank some more beer.

"You know," Scott said as he stroked my palm with his middle finger. "I've been sort of, well, frustrated lately. You know what I mean?"

"I probably can figure it out," I said, pulling my hand from his.

"I mean, frustrated, you know. Sexually frustrated."

"I thought that's what you meant," I said, turning around to look downstairs for Latanya. He moved closer, brushing my leg with his.

"I like you, Ellen. I like you a lot."

"You don't even know me," I said, looking harder for Latanya.

"I'd like to know you better," Scott said, turning a little so his crotch pressed against my hip.

"Well, Scott, I tell you," I said, moving away, "I'm sure deep down you're a really nice guy, but I came here with someone."

"Ditch him," he said, moving his head down. He'd had onions for lunch.

"Well, I can't exactly do that, Scott," I said, leaning back. Then I spotted Latanya. "In fact, there she is."

"She?" He took a step backward. "C'mon, you're shitting me, you're not a dyke," he said, doubtfully.

I just smiled and shrugged. "You never can tell, Scotty. It's been real."

I put my beer on someone's table and moved quickly downstairs. I lost Latanya again and spent a determined fifteen minutes searching before I caught up with her near the ladies "locker" room.

"Latanya, either we leave together right now, or I'm borrowing your car," I said. "You know I can't afford a cab."

"Oh, come on," she said, "It isn't that bad."

"It's worse," I answered, grabbing her arm to steer her towards the door. "And if we pass a muscle-bound creep named Scott on the way out, feel free to give me a kiss — on the cheek."

Latanya dropped me off and went back to Orgazzo's. On the way in I passed the first floor tenant. The name on the mailbox was S. Pilecki, but Latanya and I called him the Wraith, partly because he was so thin — he was well over six feet tall but I was pretty sure I outweighed him — and partly because we saw him only at night. He was some kind of computer programmer, according to the landlady, and he kept the strangest hours.

"Hi," I said, as he loped down the front steps two at a time.

"Uh, hi," he mumbled, looking down at his feet. That was the longest conversation we'd ever had.

I went up the stairs wearily. It seemed I always felt tired anymore, but I still had trouble getting to sleep. I'd be up until two or three in the morning, then sleep until early afternoon on Saturday. The same thing would happen Saturday and Sunday night. I'd wake up on Monday after only a few hours sleep, and begin the work week already exhausted. I went inside and changed into my robe, made a cup of tea, and sat on the floor near the front window. It was peaceful, sitting there, sipping tea, looking down three stories to the street below, watching traffic or people passing by. I was beginning to like this feeling of being hidden away from the rest of the world. It didn't seem to matter whether I was here, or at work, or in a crowded bar. I felt out of step with everyone around me. I didn't care about the holidays. I wasn't looking forward to the Super Bowl. I was achingly lonely but so uncomfortable with other people I couldn't bear to be with them for very long. This life I had been so eager to grow up for and take part in was dreary and predictable and utterly joyless. Next year would find me working at the same job, sitting on the same floor, wearing the same old faded blue robe. I had nothing to look forward to. I had no more options.

An hour later I left my teacup on the windowsill and went to bed.

Chapter
Four

We worked only half a day on Christmas Eve. At lunch time the V.D. offices were open to families of employees. The cafeteria was crowded with children and their parents because Santa Claus was arriving there after lunch. I wanted to slip out early but was informed we all had to stay until the head of the company, Edward Van Dyke IV, made his traditional Christmas speech to the masses, after which we would be given our Christmas bonuses. I wandered from floor to floor, sampling eggnog (unspiked) and homemade cookies, until Eddie IV was finished. He gave his speech in the cafeteria, but it was broadcast throughout the building over the PA system, where it reached every employee, even the irreverent ones snorting coke in the bathrooms. When we were officially dismissed, in a little ceremony reminiscent of grade school, I was given my bonus check, resisted an impulse to curtsey, and left for the long holiday weekend.

My bonus was a hundred dollars. It would pay a big chunk of next month's rent, or I could use it to open a savings account. I sat in the car, staring at the check, and felt a little shiver on the nape of my neck, as though my parents were looking over my shoulder. "Save it," my mother said. "Spend it," said my father. "Money can't buy happiness," she warned. "You never know till you try," he said, and I could hear a laugh in his voice. She was right, and he was wrong. He was irresponsible. He never really grew up. But he never quit dreaming, like my mother did. "What the hell," I said out loud, and headed for the mall.

I'd been pinching pennies for so long I hadn't even been to the mall in months. I decided to buy a present for Latanya, and blow the rest on myself. Maybe it couldn't buy happiness, but this hundred was going to buy me a little much-needed, small-scale luxury.

The mall was ghastly, filled with hundreds of last minute

shoppers rudely shoving their way from store to store. I stayed there long enough to buy Latanya a new makeup case and gift wrap and a bow, plus a Christmas card for the Pulaskis and one for Cathy, who was staying in Chicago for the holidays. Except for a brief thank you, I hadn't even written her since she steered me onto the plane nearly four months ago. I fled from the garish displays, past a long line of children waiting to sit on Santa's lap, only to get stuck for twenty minutes trying to get out of the parking lot. I drove to the liquor store and bought myself a bottle of champagne, an Italian red, and a French white. Then I went to the grocery store, and splurged on a porterhouse steak and two cartons of Häagen-Dazs.

On the way home I passed the local Christmas tree stand. I drove past it, then impulsively drove around the block to get back to it. Most of the trees were huge, but there was one tiny pine, small enough to fit on a table top. I haggled with the guy running the place and managed to get it for under ten dollars. I stuffed it in the back of the VW, among the groceries and wine, then drove to Woolworth's to pick up a small stand. I had just enough cash left over for two boxes of ornaments and one string of little blinking lights. It was going to be a real Charlie Brown tree, but it was mine.

That evening I set the tree up in the front window. It took all of ten minutes to wrap it with the strand of lights and dress it in two dozen red, green, and silver balls. I wrapped Latanya's present and put it under the tree. Then I feasted on steak and red wine and ate a whole carton of chocolate ice cream for dessert. I tried to watch TV but it was all cheery Christmas specials. I ended up with the Channel 11 yule log, but turned down the volume so I wouldn't have to listen to "Frosty the Snowman." I sat down with the rest of the wine, watching the video image of burning logs in a TV fireplace. Tomorrow would be a long day. I had told Latanya I was eating with the Pulaskis, and I had told the Pulaskis I was eating with Latanya and her family. I hoped to sleep through most of the day.

By eleven-thirty boredom had penetrated the fine drunk I had given myself. I shut the TV off in irritation and stood watching the lights blink on my pathetic little tree, wishing this long

Christmas Eve would end. The tree looked forlorn without a single decoration in the apartment to keep it company. The air smelled of steak grease and wine, everyday smells, not the fresh-baked aroma of Christmas cookies. I missed the ones my mother made, traditional pressed cookies and toll house cookies, Russian tea cakes and Hungarian kifli, delicate little rolls of rich flaky dough filled with ground walnuts and a hint of apricot. I missed shopping for my parents, and hiding their presents, and even the stupid fight they had every single year about when to put up the outside lights. I missed the thrill of anticipation, of knowing that you'd sleep tonight and wake up to the best holiday of the year, a daylong celebration of feasting and presents and visits with neighbors and other friends.

I grabbed my coat and turned out the lights, stumbled downstairs, and climbed into the car. After fumbling for five minutes with the key I realized I wouldn't be able to drive, so I got out and walked. I ended up in the old neighborhood, drawn by the clear sound of church bells. Midnight mass was about to start at St. Elizabeth's, where Monsignor Toth would say the prayers in English and Hungarian. I stood for a few minutes at the foot of the church steps until my shivering drove me inside.

The church was warm and dark. Only the red sanctuary light glowed over the altar. I stood in the back of the church, behind the pews, and leaned against the wall, listening to the slow tolling of the bell. It stopped suddenly; I heard the murmur of parishioner's voices fade. After a moment of total silence the bell rang again, twelve times for midnight. At the last peal all the church lights came on, the organ sounded triumphantly, and the choir begin to sing "Adeste Fidelis." The whole church was draped in evergreens and banners; poinsettias filled every empty space on the altar. Monsignor Toth stood in the center, blazing in white and gold vestments, the censor smoking in his hand, flanked by altar boys who clutched fragrant beeswax candles.

I hadn't been in the church since my parents' funeral, and not very often before that. They'd insisted that I accompany them to midnight mass each year, but otherwise let me sleep late on Sundays. I stood there now, with my eyes closed against the bright lights and decorations, listening to the music. I felt the way I did after my First Communion, when I walked proudly back to the pew to await the miracle of grace arriving in my soul, and discovered that all I had received was a slim piece of tasteless bread that stuck like paper to the roof of my mouth.

I stayed through the singing, the familiar opening prayers, and Monsignor Toth's standard sermon on putting Christ back in Christmas. I slipped out when the parishioners began to file toward the altar for communion. Time and the cold air were sobering me up. It was Christmas day. It meant no more to me than saying today was Friday. I turned up the collar of my coat and walked home.

In the morning I plugged in the lights on my little tree, and lacking anything else, opened Latanya's present. Then I wrapped it up again and replaced it under the tree for her; she wasn't coming back until Sunday night. Afterwards I watched TV, or stared out the window, or lay in bed, drinking beer or wine. I wished I could sleep away the weekend but I could hardly sleep at all; when the last of the late late movies was over I would finally doze off to the hiss of the radiators as the heat came up.

When Latanya got home Sunday evening, she knocked on my door. She looked surprised when I let her in.

"Going to bed early?" she asked.

"No," I said. I was still in my pajamas and robe; I hadn't seen any point in getting dressed. She looked around the room. There was a little pile of gift wrap and ribbon on the table, an assortment of half-finished TV-dinner trays, and an empty carton of Häagen-Dazs. Beer cans lay wherever I was when I finished them, mostly next to the sofa bed, which lay opened and rumpled.

"Are you all right?" she asked in a puzzled tone of voice.

"I think I'm coming down with something," I lied. "Would you like a beer?"

"No, thanks."

She handed me a plate covered with foil. "Here, Mom made you some cookies."

"Thanks. I didn't know she was so domestic."

"She pretends to be, this time of year. Actually they're not half bad. So how are the Pulaskis?"

"The Pulaskis?"

"Yes — you spent Christmas Day with them, right?"

"Oh, sure, yes, it was nice. Come see my tree."

I plugged in the lights and handed Latanya her present.

"Oh, Ellen, you didn't have to do this," she said, opening it.

"I wanted to."

"Thanks so much." She handed me a box. "Merry Christmas," she said.

I opened my present; nestled in tissue paper was a tiny crystal bird that glittered in the light when I held it in my hand.

"Oh, Latanya, it's so delicate, and so pretty."

"And totally frivolous, therefore very necessary. Hey, come on down to my apartment. You'll never guess what I got from my brother."

"Tell me."

"No, come on down and see."

"No thanks," I said, getting into bed and pulling the covers around my feet. "I'd rather stay here right now."

"Ellen, are you sure you're all right?" she asked, sitting on the edge of the bed.

"Yeah," I said, "It's probably just a bug. Tell me about your present."

"It's a parakeet. A blue one. I've named him Trevor."

"I'll come see him during the week."

"Okay," she said doubtfully. "If you need anything just bang on the floor with a mop handle or something. You want me to take you to a doctor?"

"No," I answered. "I'm sure I'll be fine. And thanks for the bird. I really like it."

"Thanks for the makeup case; my old one is about to fall apart. Come see Trevor tomorrow."

I nodded, and she walked out the door, and the room seemed a little darker, the way it does when a cloud covers the sun.

The next week was an exercise in boredom, because half The Office was on vacation. I had so little to copy I began to wish for work and noise. I polished the glass on the KM9000 until it sparkled like my crystal bird. I watched the second hand travel around the clock face. I couldn't understand why I still had to report for work, why they didn't just close The Office for the week, the way they closed The Plant. I came home each night tired and restless. I stocked up on beer, making good use of the fake I.D. I'd gotten my freshman year at Hardenbergh. Work was so bad that by Tuesday I ate my lunch in the car so I could have a beer with it. It helped me get through the first hour of the afternoon. By Wednesday I had a beer for breakfast, too.

We were released from work the usual time on Thursday, even though it was New Year's Eve. Of course, everyone in the world had plans for the evening except me. I would spend the evening with the bottle of champagne I'd been saving for the occasion, while I watched Dick Clark and New Year's Rockin' Eve on TV. Latanya was already gone by the time I got home. I made myself a tuna sandwich and opened the champagne.

After a couple glasses of bubbly I began to wonder about the Wraith. What was he doing this evening? Could he possibly have a date? No way. Could he be at work, keeping a lonely vigil among the computers so everyone else there could party? Strong probability. Might he, though, be at home? I picked up the phone book. Lots of Pileckis in it, none at this address. I tried information, but his number was unlisted. That figured. I had some more champagne, and thought about knocking on his door. I opened the hall door and listened. Everything was quiet. I shut the door. Maybe I'd wait a while. I took a shower, shaved my legs, trimmed my toenails. I put on clean slacks and a sweater, and had more champagne. I opened the hall door again, and this time walked down as far as Latanya's landing. I still couldn't hear anything. I walked the rest of the way down and stood there for a moment, then knocked. There was no answer, so I knocked again and waited. He wasn't home, or he wasn't answering.

I walked upstairs slowly. I kept looking behind me, as though something or someone might be there. I was getting spooked, being the only one in the house. Back in my apartment, I watched Dick Clark and finished the champagne. Midnight, and the new year, was still an hour away and I had finished the champagne! I rummaged through the kitchen cabinets until I found an unopened bottle of scotch I had brought from home — my parents' home — when I moved here. I never drank it, because I couldn't stand the stuff; I was keeping it for company.

"Company," I said out loud, and giggled at the silly idea. I opened the bottle and poured some in a glass, added ice and water, and sipped it. It didn't taste as bad as I thought it might. I kept on sipping while I danced with Dick Clark. Every few minutes the screen would show the big lit-up apple that would be dropped on a Times Square rooftop at midnight. Everyone on TV was excited. I was drunk.

When the big lit-up apple finally fell, the TV couples kissed and cheered, and I passed out with the lonely comfort of my own hand between my legs.

I woke up shivering next to a puddle of congealed vomit. The front windows were open and the temperature was near freezing. I sat up slowly. My head hurt so much my eye sockets ached. I had thrown up during the night, and opened the windows, but couldn't remember doing it. The apartment looked hideous in the cold grey light; trash littered the floor, spilled food splattered the kitchen cabinets, I couldn't walk without stubbing my toe on a beer can. I took a couple aspirin, drinking directly from the faucet because there wasn't a clean glass in the place. My stomach recoiled when the cold water hit it, but I kept the aspirin down. I closed the windows and checked the radiators. The heat was on but it would be hours before the place was comfortable again. I started to clean up just to move and get warm, but soon began cleaning in earnest. Possessed by my mother's superstition that everything you do on New Year's Day is an omen of the year to come, and revolted by the filth that looked even worse through bloodshot eyes, I got rid of every can, bottle, and TV dinner tray. I cleaned up the puke and the spills. I even threw out the puny little tree, whose needles lay in clumps on the floor because I'd forgotten to give it water. It went in a trash bag, lights, ornaments, and all.

After purging the apartment of every reminder of the past week, I showered, put on clean clothes, and went outside, too restless to stay indoors. The cold air was still and the sky was grey with clouds that promised snow. I decided to drive to the old neighborhood, to wish the Pulaskis a happy new year, but when I turned onto my old street I stopped. No lights were on in their house, but there were lights in the house next door, which used to be mine. I was sure the Pulaskis were there, watching football with the new neighbors. Everything was back to normal for them. I put the VW in reverse.

I ended up driving to Lenape Park. A jogger and a couple of kids walking a big black lab were the only people I saw. I parked the car and started walking. The ground was beginning to freeze hard and uneven. Old oaks and elms stood leafless under the darkening sky. It was late afternoon but too early for the invisible sun to be setting. The sky was a uniform grey that looked close enough to touch. I hoped it would snow soon.

I walked past empty tennis courts, past the small white band-stand, past withered flower gardens where wedding parties posed in the spring and summer. I followed the path to the lake. The water was as grey as the clouds, and nearly as smooth. I walked along the shore until I came to the children's playground, as old fashioned as the rest of the park, just monkey bars and a slide, a couple teeter-totters and some swings, all cold metal and weathered wood, as monochromatic as the sky. I sat down to rest on the thick wooden seat of a swing. My mother had brought me here when I was small, and taught me to swing. "Hold tight and pump your legs," she used to say. "Pump your legs, keep going, higher!" It felt like flying. I used to pretend that the swing would break away and I'd soar, like Peter Pan, over the waters of Lake Lenape to Never-Never Land.

I rocked back and forth, then pushed back with my feet until I was almost standing, with the seat under my butt and my hands on the chains. Then I lifted my feet and swung.

The seat was so low that I couldn't pump properly, with my legs bent back in a neat tuck; I had to splay my feet wide on each stroke so they wouldn't scrape on the ground. I swung higher and higher, then leaned my head back and stuck my legs straight out, coasting back and forth, watching the treetops advance and recede. Then I pumped again, swinging higher to feel the rush of cold air past my head on the backswing, listening to the music of the rusty U-bolts at the top of the chains. The first flakes of snow came down as I swung, and I shouted aloud when I saw them.

They polka-dotted my jacket as I swung forward to meet them, and I held back my head and opened my mouth to catch them on my tongue.

I let the swing coast to a stop, then twisted clockwise until the chains wrapped around each other as far as they could go. I lifted my feet and let the swing spin me in the other direction, swaying as the chains unraveled, stopping for a moment before they wrapped themselves up again and spun me the other way. Then I swung again until I was almost dizzy from the motion of the swing and the snow.

When my feet scraped the ground I sat still, exhilarated and out of breath, watching the transformation of the park from brown to white. I leaned against one of the chains and rested with its cold metal links against my forehead. It was the first time I'd had fun, real fun, since my parents died, and I began to cry, not in sorrow for their deaths, but in relief, because their deaths had not been the end of all joy.

The lights were on in Latanya's apartment when I got home, so I stopped on the landing and knocked on her door. She had a tissue in her hand when she opened the door and she blew her nose after I stepped inside. Her eyes were red and she sounded stuffy.

"When did you catch cold?" I asked, unbuttoning my coat.

"I haven't got a cold," she answered, "I'm allergic to Trevor."

"Oh, no," I said. "What are you going to do?"

"I don't want to give him back to my brother," she said. "It would hurt his feelings." She wiped her nose. "Could you take him?"

"Me? I don't know anything about birds."

"That's okay, he's real easy to take care of. He just needs seed and water once a day, and a change of newspaper now and then. I'd really appreciate it, Ellen, then I could visit him upstairs, and not feel so bad about giving him up." She sneezed. "I can't go on like this. It's driving me crazy."

"Well, okay, if you're sure," I said.

"I'm sure, I'm sure. I'll put his stuff in a bag and carry it up.

You carry Trevor, please."

Trevor was standing on a wooden perch in his cage. His breast was periwinkle blue, his head and back mottled with grey and white stripes. I lifted the cage carefully but he seemed frightened when I moved him, and stepped sideways on his perch until he was as far from me as possible. He looked around with wide little eyes as we walked upstairs. I set his cage on the table and Latanya handed me his belongings.

"Thanks," she said. "I'm going to go back down. I'll visit in a couple days, after my nose clears up. Take care of him, okay?"

"I will. Take care of yourself."

"Yeah. Be sure to cover his cage when you go to bed. The cover's in the bag." She stopped on her way to the door. "Hey, you really straightened up the place. It looks good."

"Yes," I said, and smiled at Trevor. "I decided it was time to straighten up and fly right."

I moved Trevor's cage to the top of the bookshelf, then left him alone for the rest of the night. I figured he'd had enough stress with the relocations, and would be happier if his home stayed in one place for a while. I put the pink cover — Latanya's favorite color — on his cage. He didn't move the rest of the evening.

In the morning I uncovered his cage. He was perched in exactly the same spot, looking small and scared. He had the tiniest eyelashes I'd ever seen. I changed his water and gave him fresh seed, which made him jump from perch to perch, fluttering his wings. A feather drifted out of the cage; I caught it on my palm. It was smaller than a fingernail, dark grey except for a thin white stripe at the edge. It was incredibly soft and probably hell for Latanya, but it didn't bother me at all.

As soon as the stores opened I drove to a pet shop and bought a book about parakeets. I also bought a small mirror to hang in his cage. When I got back, and hung the mirror up, Trevor sidled right up to it. The book said parakeets liked to hear voices, and would imitate them. At first I felt silly talking to a bird, but my voice seemed to soothe him, and soon I found myself having an entire conversation for him. The next day he was much calmer when I gave him seed and water, and I even gave him fresh newspapers to read and shit on.

When I went to work Monday morning I left the radio playing softly so he wouldn't be too lonely. The day was as dreadful
as any Monday, with everyone working full speed once again and
pounds of paper to be copied. But this work day I had someone
waiting for me when I got home. As soon as I got in the door I
said, "Hello, Trevor."

Trevor chirped.

"Trevor! You chirped at me. You never did that before."

Trevor chirped again. I turned the radio off and stood near
the cage. "Trevor is a pretty bird," I said, slipping one fingertip
between the bars of his cage. He looked at my finger suspi-
ciously, but didn't flutter or try to move away. "Good Trevor," I
said, removing my finger. "We'll try again in a little while."

In a few days I was able to open the cage door and put my
hand inside. Then I put one finger out and stroked his breast very
gently. He opened his beak but didn't bite. After a few days of
this I moved my finger down and pressed very lightly on his toes.
He picked up one foot and wrapped it around my finger, then did
the same with the other. Soon he was accustomed to my hand,
and hopped on my finger willingly. One evening, while he was
perched on my finger, I slowly withdrew my hand from the cage.

Trevor flattened his feathers in fear and looked around wild-
ly. "It's freedom, Trevor. A whole apartment to fly in. Well, a
whole studio anyway." But Trevor was not interested. He
flapped clumsily down to the roof of his cage, climbed headfirst
down the side, and hopped in, panting. I shut the cage door.
"One step at a time, Trevor," I told him. "We'll take it one step
at a time."

At lunch the next day I bought a plastic porch affair to hang
on his cage. He chirped over and over when I got home, and ran
back and forth on his perch in excitement. I felt bad about leaving him home alone all day, but if he had another parakeet to play
with he'd stop needing me, and as silly as it seemed I really
looked forward to his company. I opened the cage door, hung the
little porch on it, and kept an eye on him while I made dinner. He
walked to the door with his funny sideways steps, and reached
out for the porch with his beak. He climbed on and sat in the door

of his cage, watching me across the room. I held up my hand and whistled. Trevor chirped, then leapt off the porch and flew, but he'd had little practice and couldn't stay up. He flopped to the floor a couple feet short of me. He was out of breath but didn't look scared, so I sat on the floor and offered him a piece of lettuce. Trevor walked over, pigeon-toed, and nibbled on the lettuce. I put him on my shoulder, and he stayed there all evening.

Despite Trevor's company, I needed to get out of the apartment. At first I spent weekends in the library, browsing through the stacks or attending free lectures, but I found myself craving daylight and fresh air, a change from the browns and greys of pavement and buildings. I began to drive in the country just for the sake of driving, to take narrow, twisting roads for no better reason than to find out where they led. I stopped to read historical markers, or browse in antique shops, or visit a small museum made from a one-room schoolhouse or an old mill.

I discovered Wilson State Park, a rocky hillside with a stream that dropped down in small waterfalls. I'd spend hours climbing the hill to sit on big granite rocks, staring at the water or watching a hawk soar high above me, wishing that I could be circling with him so far above the treetops. Sometimes I'd spend a whole afternoon at the Hunt Mills Reservoir, a big manmade lake set in a ring of hills. After a cold spell parts of the lake froze over, and I laughed to see Canada geese slip and slide across it. As long as I had at least half a tank of gas I'd get deliberately lost, not looking at the map until I got home, when I would mark where I had traveled, while Trevor supervised from my shoulder and nibbled my hair.

I was excited to see signs of spring as early as February. After a thaw, when the top layer of frozen ground turned slippery with mud, I looked for bright green patches of new grass, or a twig with its red buds fattening. I could hear spring, too, in the rush of snow melt through a creek bed, or the rustle of the grass as small creatures passed by. I was filled with anticipation — for what I wasn't sure. Even when the thaw ended, and the countryside was covered with ice again, I was sustained by the knowledge that the season of rebirth and renewal was only a few weeks away.

Chapter Five

On March 21st, I called in sick, because it was Monday, and the sun was shining. It was also my twenty-first birthday. I turned on the radio and Trevor sang with it while I had breakfast. He didn't sing musically, the way a canary sings; instead, he chirped and muttered to himself, rang his bell, and regurgitated seed onto his mirror, which according to the parakeet book was a very sexy thing to do. He wolf-whistled back when I wolf-whistled at him, and said "pretty boy" while I changed his water. I gave him an extra helping of his favorite treat mix and stroked the side of his head with my finger.

"See you later, Trevor," I said before I walked out.

"Piss off," he answered. His vocabulary was growing.

I went outside and took a deep breath. The day was a birthday present in itself — warm enough for just a sweater, with a turquoise sky and the first threads of fluffy white clouds. The city streets were white with ground-in salt, and the last of the snow, plowed into a sooty pile at the end of the street, was already melting in the morning sun. It was a perfect day to play hooky, to be outdoors, to be alive. It had always been my mother's favorite time of year.

I got in the car to go exploring. I had a full tank of gas, a map, a sandwich, and a can of soda. On the way out of town I stopped at the cemetery. I had only been there a few times since the funeral. Once to make sure the headstone had been set in place — Tony Dimeo had paid for it — and once to plant a few crocuses. I wanted to see if they were coming up.

I always shivered driving through the cemetery gates. Just past the fence, on the right, was the oldest part of the cemetery, with huge mausoleums and ornate marble statues. It looked like the set for a slasher movie. On the left were graves marked by miniature headstones — the children's cemetery. These days it was rarely used, but you could walk through there and see a record of the early days of the century, when women had many babies because so few of them lived. The more modern part of the cemetery was further in, past a huge oak tree that was older than any of the headstones. My parents used to drag me here every Sunday after church. We'd visit my grandparents' graves to say a prayer. I said the prayers dutifully but with no feeling; I had never known my grandparents — they were just names carved in granite to me. While my mother changed the flowers I would wander nearby, careful not to step on the graves themselves.

The cemetery held a few more rows than it did in those days. I drove as far as I could and then walked to one of the newer stones, a simple rectangle of polished grey granite, with the family name carved in large block letters. My father's name was on the lower left, with the dates 1948-1987, and my mother's name was on the right, with the same dates. There was enough room in between to put my name, too.

I was glad to see the crocuses, a half-dozen of them, not only up but with fat buds that would bloom before the day was over. Four of them were purple, two yellow. I cleared some stones and dry grass around their slim green and white leaves, then stood up and brushed my hands off. I didn't know what else to do, so I just whispered "Bye-bye" and left.

I took the interstate to get away from Hardenbergh as quickly as possible. After driving for a half-hour I took an exit I wasn't familiar with, and struck off to the northwest. I passed a large horse farm, and pulled over next to one of the fields. I got out and walked over to the fence, to watch the mares and their foals. There were four little ones, leggy and awkward, with short manes that stuck straight up, very punk. One of the brown ones nursed, pretty vigorously it seemed to me, but the mare didn't seem to mind in the least. A dark foal, almost black, was lying on its side, sound asleep. The other two brown ones played with each other, touching noses and dancing stiff legged, until the smaller of the two got frightened and ran for its mother. She stood between the foals with her head lowered and her ears back. The offending foal scooted back to its mother and the two trotted away, the mare tossing her lovely head.

It was so quiet that I could hear the grass tearing under the horses' teeth, until a flock of blackbirds descended with a raucous clamor into the trees on the north side of the field. The trees looked forced into early leaf, so huge was the flock, and still more birds glided in from the south. They blackened the road and the shoulder, so that when I drove off I had to proceed slowly, surrounded by birds flying no faster than they absolutely had to, only inches from the hood of my red beetle.

I was mesmerized. I practically idled forward, so close I could see their tail and wing feathers glitter iridescent in the sun, bronze and purple and green. The hum of their wings and their discordant screeching filled the air; I was part of the flock; I wished Trevor could have been there.

I had lunch on a hillside with a panoramic view of farms in the valley below. I sat on a big chunk of rock and shared my sandwich with a chipmunk, who was brazen enough to creep just out of reach for the crumbs. The air on the hill was fragrant from a small stand of pines. I took off my sweater and leaned back on my elbows, looking up at row after row of puffy clouds, then looking down at their shadows, where a farmer plowed a dark brown ribbon in a quilt of green and tan.

Suddenly, a dark shadow, shaped nothing like a cloud, skimmed over the valley. It rippled toward the hill, a wedge of grey, and I looked up, holding my hand over the sun, to see what made this shadow speeding toward me.

It was an airplane, unlike anything I'd ever seen, with impossibly long wings, slim as a bullet and whiter than the clouds, flying low and fast and aiming straight for me. It was so close I could see the pilot but then it swooped up and over my head. It made no sound except for a whistling noise; in a second it passed over the treetops and was gone.

"What the hell was that?" I asked out loud.

I went back to the car and pulled out the map. In a few minutes, I found the road I was on, and looked beyond it, in the direction the airplane had flown. "There," I said, when I located the airport symbol a few miles north. "That's where I'm going." I started the car and drove off, holding the map against the steering wheel. About twenty minutes later I saw an airport sign, with an arrow pointing left. I turned onto a steep narrow road that curved for another half mile, then turned right at the sign that read "Crosswind Field."

I pulled into a gravel parking lot. A large trailer, like a mobile home, had the word "Office" painted on the side. I parked in front of it and went in. I entered what looked like a living room, furnished a lot like my place in fact, with a couple ratty-looking easy chairs and an even rattier green sofa. A big golden retriever lay on the sofa. It opened an eye and wagged its tail when I walked in. A counter had been set up between the living room and the kitchen, and a large man who looked like Santa Claus stood over the stove, eating out of a pot.

"Sorry to interrupt your lunch," I said.

"No problem," he said, walking over to the counter. "I squeeze in a couple mouthfuls when I can. More than I get to do on weekends. How can I help you?"

"I'm not sure," I said. "I was just having lunch myself when I saw — actually, I'm not sure what I saw. I mean, it was an airplane, a beautiful airplane, but I don't know what kind."

"White, sleek, no engine?"

"Yeah, I guess it was."

"Sailplane," he said. "That's what we fly here. Seven days a week, year round. Can I schedule a ride for you?"

"A ride? For me? Oh no, I was just wondering about that plane, you know?"

He nodded. "It's a perfect day for a ride."

"Really?"

"Couldn't ask for better."

"Umm...how much does it cost?"

"Thirty-five dollars for a twenty minute ride."

"Oh, well, that's kind of a lot for me right now," I said.

He nodded again. "I know how that goes."

I nodded back and looked around. The glass-bottomed counter had two shelves, filled with stacks of books, T-shirts and hats with "Crosswind Aviation" printed on them, bumper stickers that read "Glider pilots keep it up longer." A calendar with a picture of a white sailplane flying along a rocky cliff hung on one wall, and three pieces of cloth — they looked like shirttails — hung on the other wall, next to the door. Each one had a person's name, the word "solo," the date, and another number written in felt-tip pen. The one on top also had a drawing of an airplane, and the words "Keith Simmons cheated death October 10, 1987." I looked from the shirttail back to the man at the counter, who stood with his big hands on the counter top, watching me and smiling pleasantly.

"Do you take checks?" I asked.

"Sure do." His smile deepened. "Make it out to Crosswind Aviation."

I pulled out my checkbook, took a deep breath, and wrote the check. What the hell, I thought, it's my birthday. This'll be my birthday present, from me to me. The phone bill can wait till the end of the month.

I handed him the check and he handed me a ticket. "Go out the door, walk around the office, turn left, and walk all the way down to the end of the runway. Keep close to the trees and you won't get in anyone's way. Ask for Andy when you get down there."

"Thanks."

"Have a good ride," he said, heading back to the stove.

I followed his directions, and walked down the side of a big grass field, with trees on three sides of it. I didn't see a runway. I looked for the white sailplane, but all I saw was a regular airplane at the far end of the field, and something orange behind it. When I got closer I could see a man and a woman standing in front of the airplane, talking. This man looked something like the man in the office, but wasn't quite as big, and he was bald as well as beardless. The woman was a few inches shorter than me, with long white hair she wore in a braid over her right shoulder, and laugh lines at the corners of her eyes.

"Hi," she said as I walked up. "Here for a ride?"

"Yes," I said. "I'm supposed to go with Andy."

She laughed. "I'm Andy. Let me have your ticket."

I must have looked surprised, because she laughed again and explained, "It's short for Andrea, Andrea Mahon. And you're?"

"Ellen Horvath."

She shook my hand. "Nice to meet you, Ellen. This is Herb Armstrong, our tow pilot."

"Hi," I said. Herb just grunted.

"C'mon," said Andy. "Let's go for a ride."

We walked around the tail of the white airplane, which didn't look so white close up. It was splashed with mud and smudged with black streaks along its sides.

"Have you ever been up in a sailplane, Ellen?"

"No, just jets." I didn't want to admit I'd slept through my one and only airplane ride.

"Well, this is a lot more fun. Let me show you how to get in."

She stopped in front of the orange plane that had been partially hidden by the white airplane. This one had no propeller, but otherwise looked nothing like the sailplane I had seen. Its wings were huge, stuck like a thick slab on top of the fuselage, which was tilted awkwardly so that one wingtip rested on the ground. It had a big lumpy belly, like a whale, and the faded paint was chipped off the nose, revealing irregular patches of greenish yellow and dull silver.

"This is it?" I said with dismay. "I thought you said sailplane?"

"This is a sailplane, or you can call it a glider. What's wrong?"

"I thought it would be white — and pretty."

"Oh, you must have seen one of our private pilots. He was flying a beautiful sailplane, but it belongs to him and it only holds one person." She patted the ugly glider gently. "This is a Schweizer 2-33, a training sailplane, and it may not be long on looks but it soars just fine. Believe me, it becomes much prettier in the air. Now, why don't you come over and put your right foot on this little step and your hands on top of the instrument panel, and climb in. Don't even try to be graceful."

I followed her directions, and sure enough, felt like a klutz. "But this is the front seat," I said.

"The best view is from the front," she told me. "Don't worry, I can fly fine from the back. There's a control stick back there, just like the one up front."

She showed me how to fasten the seat belt and shoulder straps, and pointed to a red knob. "Don't touch this until I tell you," she said, "It's how we release from the towplane."

Herb walked over with a yellow rope as Andy climbed in behind me. He bent down with a grunt and hooked on the rope, then straightened up with another grunt and ambled over to the towplane. He climbed in and a few seconds later the propeller whirled twice with a scraping sound, then stopped. Herb spit through the open window and tried again. This time it whirled about five times before stopping. On the third try the engine finally caught. I thought about the shirttail that read "cheated death."

I tried to turn around, but could only swivel my head because of the shoulder straps. "Is it always that hard to start?" I asked.

"The engine's just a little cold," Andy reassured me. I hoped Herb would warm it up well.

"Now we run through our pre-takeoff checklist," she said. "Are your straps tight?"

They were, but I pulled them even tighter while Andy moved the stick forward and back and side to side. I tried to stay out of her way but there was no room to move my legs aside; the cockpit was just wide enough to sit in, and my arms, resting on cracked plastic armrests, touched the sides of the glider.

"How high do we go?" I asked as the towplane started to move.

"Three thousand feet."

"Isn't that awfully high?"

"Not nearly high enough for a glider pilot. Now, I need to tell you that we'll be airborne before the towplane. That's normal. And it's a little bumpy when we're rolling on the ground. Watch your head — I'm going to shut the canopy." It was clear, shaped like the top half of a bubble, so I would have an unobstructed view straight ahead and on both sides. When Andy closed and latched the canopy, the sound of the idling towplane was muffled a little, and the sun quickly warmed us up.

"You can really notice a greenhouse effect in here, can't you?" she asked. "If you're too warm, you can open the air vent once we're moving. The vent's on top of the instrument panel."

The vent, such as it was, consisted of a little black flap that I could swivel open or closed. The glider's few instruments were arranged below it. Andy explained that the altimeter told us how high we were, the airspeed indicator how fast we were going, and the variometer how quickly we were going up or down. A small compass was next to the air vent. It didn't look like enough stuff to me.

The towplane rolled in front of us, dragging the thin yellow towrope behind it. The rope looked a lot thinner than it had when Herb hooked it to the glider.

"Where's the runway?" I asked.

"We're on it."

I looked ahead at the long narrow rectangle of grass, with trees on both sides, the field I had walked down a few minutes before. I'd been expecting a smaller version of Newark International. I watched the towplane roll slowly to a stop ahead of us on the runway. Andy did something with her feet and the pedals near my feet moved forward and back. The towplane's engine roared and it started to roll. I held my breath.

"By the way," said Andy as the glider began to move. "Have you ever been airsick?"

We bumped along the ground, just as Andy had said we would, as the glider righted itself and picked up speed, then suddenly everything was smooth.

"We're flying!" she told me.

The towplane was still rolling on the ground ahead of us, then it lifted off and began to climb. I could see the trees moving past us on either side, but the grass beneath us was just a blur of green. Then it was gone — just like that — magic. A whole valley lay before me, spread out far below. I could see small farmhouses, barns, fields, toy-sized cows and horses; a road was a slim gray ribbon with a matchbox car moving slowly along it. We passed over the car and then it was out of sight, somewhere behind me. Andy was talking — I just realized that she had been describing the scenery, but I hadn't heard a word.

"I'm sorry, what did you say?" I asked.

"I said, taking off from here is almost like launching from an aircraft carrier — the runway ends at a cliff and the ground drops straight down more than four hundred feet." She had to shout a little for me to hear her. "It'll be quieter after we release. The towplane is pretty noisy."

I kept gawking out the window, looking right and left. I could look straight below to watch the ground moving underneath us, or ahead at the towplane, which bobbed up and down in front of us. We bobbed, too, and I gave the shoulder straps an extra tug. They had seemed tight enough on the ground.

"How are you doing?" Andy shouted.

"Fine," I shouted back.

"Almost there. There's going to be a loud bang when we pull the release. Are you ready?"

"Yes."

"Okay, pull the red knob."

"Me?"

"Yes, you! Pull it now."

I pulled, and sure enough, it sounded like a pistol shot. Then — nothing but the soft murmur of the wind outside.

Andy didn't say anything for a minute while I tried to take in the sudden deceleration, the silence. Then, in a quiet voice she said, "Lovely, isn't it?"

"It's beautiful."

We soared over countryside that looked like a postcard. The fields were small squares and rectangles, all shades of brown and green. Houses were smaller than dollhouses. A herd of Angus was an ant colony. Above me, the white clouds hung in puffs with flat grey undersides. We were floating in the blue sky, floating in nothing, detached and silent in a strange craft that was narrower than an armchair.

Suddenly, the sailplane made a whumping noise, with a jolt that I felt through the seat cushion. Andy turned the plane sharply to the left in a circle that made me dizzy. The top of my head felt like a hand pressed on it and when I looked out to the side I was looking straight down. One wing seemed stuck in the ground like the tip of a penknife, and the fields spun around below us. The other wing pointed up, stabbing at the sky.

"How do you feel?" asked Andy.

My heart was pounding and my palms were sweating.

"Funny but okay," I said. "Don't stop."

"All right," she said. "Isn't this great?"

"What are we doing?"

"That bump you felt was a rising air current. We turned toward it and now we're circling to stay in it because it's very narrow. It's taking us up like an elevator, except we're climbing at more than 500 feet a minute. We just gained a thousand feet."

"How high can we go?" I asked.

"Let's see," she answered.

We spun and spun. I couldn't keep track of where we were, or what was beneath us. I held on to the seat cushion, which didn't feel terribly secure, but it was all there was. The fields and houses were smaller and I couldn't see the cows anymore.

"You're one mile high," Andy told me.

A mile high! We were one mile above the hard ground in a plane that had no motor, and we didn't have parachutes, either. We had done what had seemed impossible from down there, not merely floated but actually climbed in the invisible air. We were a mile above our problems. We were cheating death, and I loved it.

The glider stopped turning and we flew straight, but when I closed my eyes I felt like we were spinning the other way.

"Look up," Andy said.

I looked up. We were under a cloud, so close I was sure I could touch it if I opened the canopy. It was massive, dark steel grey, utterly smooth, concave. The edge swirled in white threads alongside us. All I could do was whisper "Wow!"

"It's like a bowl turned upside-down," Andy explained. "We're inside the bowl, actually higher than the edge. The air rises right through the cloud, but we won't go that high."

"How high are we?" I asked.

"We're five thousand, five hundred feet above the ground. The airport is about five hundred feet above sea level, so we're at six thousand feet above sea level. And we climbed over two thousand feet without using an engine."

"Amazing."

"Most people your age say 'awesome,' and in this case they're absolutely right."

"How long could we stay up?"

"In these conditions, all afternoon, but unfortunately we do have to come down sooner. It's going to be bumpy when we fly out from under this cloud."

We were flying straight toward the milky fingers that drifted down at the edge of the cloud. The glider seemed to drop out from under me, and I heard a noise like a beer can being crushed.

"That's the wings you hear," explained Andy, "It's just the metal flexing, and it's perfectly normal. We call it tin-canning."

For a moment we were in the sunlight, so bright I squinted, and then we passed under another massive cloud. This time I felt the glider pushed up. Then we were in the cold shade again. It was like being under a big blanket, but a blanket made of spun ice. I closed the air vent.

"It's about twenty degrees cooler at this altitude," Andy said. "If you're too chilly I can get us down pretty quickly."

"No, I'm fine. I'd like to stay up some more. I wish we could stay up forever."

Andy was quiet for a moment. "Well, we're not exactly busy today, so I guess we can stay up a little while longer."

"Can we do it again, climb up, I mean?"

Andy laughed. "We can sure try."

We flew out from under the edge of the cloud and were jolted once again, as though the cloud was a giant hand that shoved us into the clear blue sky. We flew in the sun's warmth for a few minutes while Andy aimed for another cloud. This time she circled to the right after we slipped under it. Once more I could watch the ground swirl beneath us, or look up to see the cloud grow vast and dark above.

"Fifty-six hundred feet," Andy said with satisfaction. "What a day."

"Isn't it always like this?" I asked.

"I wish," she said. "It's too cold in winter, and usually too hot and muggy in the summer. But in spring and fall, we get days like this, and we can soar all day, just like a hawk. But now it really is time for us to get down."

She flew out from under the cloud, and we floated in the sunshine. I watched the houses getting bigger, and soon could see the ant-like cows again. The cockpit grew noticeably warmer and I opened the air vent once more.

"How would you like to fly it for a few minutes?" Andy suddenly asked.

"Me? I don't know how."

"I'll show you. Hold the stick with your right hand — don't grab it, just caress it. Then push it away a little to go faster, and pull it toward you to slow down."

I held the stick as she told me.

"I'm afraid I'll flip it upside down or something."

"Don't worry about that, you can't. If you want to turn right, just move the stick to the right. To turn left, move it left. I'll work the rudder pedals for you. Go ahead, turn right."

I moved the stick cautiously to the right, and felt the glider tilt over. Andy put her hands on my shoulders.

"See? You're flying it!"

My mouth was dry and my legs were shaking. I was flying! I moved the stick to the right a little more. The right wing tipped down, and the left wing tipped up, then I moved the stick to the left and the glider slowly straightened, but it seemed we were pointed straight at the ground and going far too fast.

"Andy, I need help!" I cried above the noise of the wind. I felt her on the controls, a solid, comforting feel, and let go of the stick.

"I've got it," she said, and the glider pointed up toward the blue sky, and the wind outside quieted once more from a howl to a whisper.

"You did just fine," she told me once we were flying level again. "That wasn't bad at all for your first time. Want to try again?"

"No!" I said quickly. "That was enough for now."

"Okay, it's your nickel."

We flew back to the airport, and I could see the grass runway, with the towplane parked on the side as before, and the office trailer, and my car, a faded red bulge in the parking lot. Now the trees looked like trees instead of brown smudges, and my car grew larger as I watched it. Alice must have felt like this, I thought; she wouldn't see herself get smaller, she'd see everything around her get bigger. We were coming back down to earth, drifting like a leaf, powerless to resist the pull of gravity. Much too soon, we were turning for the last time, aiming for the end of the runway where we had taken off. I heard the landing, rather than felt it — the sound of grass under the wheel and the metal wings booming like thunder as we rolled along the uneven ground. Then we stopped, perfectly balanced, until the left wing reluctantly tilted onto the ground.

Andy got out first and held the front of the glider down so I could climb out more easily.

"Well, we had a forty-five minute ride, but don't tell Marv in the office I kept you up so long. Thanks a lot, Ellen, it was fun."

"Thank you, Andy. It certainly was," I said, and thought, it was more than that. Yet Andy walked back toward the towplane with her hands in her pockets, moving casually. Herb sat in the towplane, apparently napping. How could they be so relaxed?

By the time I walked back to the parking lot I had stopped shaking. It wasn't fear that made me shake, it was adrenaline. Now that I was back on the familiar ground I could start to assimilate what had happened. I had flown an airplane. I had held the control stick in my hand and made it move, right and left, forward and back. I made the glider tilt its wings and soar through the air. I made it fly. I looked back at it, sitting cockeyed on the runway, and realized that Andy had been right. It was a pretty aircraft — no, it was beautiful, the way a lover is beautiful the first time you sleep together. It was really like that, I thought, it was like making love.

I drove home slowly, trying to freeze the sensations in my mind — the smell of warm plastic, the vinyl seat cushion that grew cold as we went up, the feel of the stick in my hands — I went over and over it so the memory would catch in my head like an advertising jingle. I kept looking up at the clouds. There weren't as many of them now. I imagined the last ones were as reluctant to leave the sky as I had been. I had seen wonders — commonplace, ordinary, utterly mundane objects transformed by altitude into rare treasures. How many people saw them like that,

I wondered, so intimate, the countryside reduced to a diorama, Roadside America for an audience of one.

I let Trevor out of his cage as soon as I got home. As always, the first thing he did was fly laps around the apartment, only inches from the ceiling. He terrified me on his first forays, before he had real control. He'd fly madly, faster and faster, until he crashed into a window or misjudged a turn. He'd end up in a heap on the floor, panting like crazy, both of us scared out of our wits. But soon enough he recognized the boundaries of his world, and learned by himself what he had no other bird to teach him. Now he could turn in an instant, swoop up or dive down, land easily on a curtain rod or chair rung. I watched him exercise tonight, envying his ability and admiring his skill. "Do you have any idea what you can do, bird?" I asked him. He landed on top of the kitchen cabinets and chirped at me. He was asking me to join him, and for the first time I realized what I was missing. "I wish I could, Trev, I wish to God I could. But you have to come down to me." I held out my hand and whistled, and an ounce of dive bomber came screaming toward me. He landed lightly and chirped. "Gimme kiss," I said, and held him to my lips. We both made a kissing noise when his little bill touched my mouth. I leaned back on the couch and put my hand on my chest. Trevor stepped off and walked up to my chin to cover it with little bird kisses.

That evening I looked at the brochure from Crosswind Aviation. I got out my bank statement, a month's paycheck stubs, and a calculator. Trevor nibbled the calculator buttons, but when he couldn't pull them off he decided to play with the bank statement instead. He scalloped the edge with his beak while I figured, and left a trail of paper balls on the table. At last I sat back and sighed.

"I can't do it, Trev. No matter how I try to work it out, there's just no way I can afford to fly."

Trevor looked up at me with his dark little eyes and said, "Gimme kiss."

Chapter Six

No one told March it was supposed to come in like a lion and out like a lamb; the last weekend of the month — the first weekend of spring — was overcast and blustery, with the temperature near freezing. I let Latanya talk me into going to New York for the day with her latest, a senior at Lehigh, and his roommate. Latanya had met William at a New Year's Eve party — which she had gone to with someone else — and had been spending a lot of weekends in Pennsylvania ever since.

William and his roommate, Phil, were at our place by 10:00 a.m. and we drove to the train station. Phil was driving so I got in front; Latanya and William cuddled in the back. Phil was a moose; his knees were crammed under the dashboard of the Honda and his shoulders seemed to reach halfway across the car. He was from a coal-mining town somewhere in central Pennsylvania, attending Lehigh on a football scholarship, majoring in history. That's all Latanya had known about him. He had blond hair and green eyes; he wasn't bad looking but he was no Kevin Costner. He was quite a talker, though; by the time our train arrived at Penn Station he had described the entire battle of Gettysburg, inch by inch.

I always enjoyed arriving in New York. The first five minutes in the city, you think it's everything it's supposed to be. Your first impression is of hugeness and speed; you have to crane your neck back to see the skyscrapers, everyone is in a hurry, everything is grey with pavement and concrete and tinted glass except for the bright yellow taxis slaloming past. Nothing is more than a subway ride away — Broadway or baseball, Soho or Central Park, falafel or filet mignon. Whether it's three in the afternoon or three in the morning, the streets are crowded, restaurants are open, the city is alive with musicians, dog walkers, executives, models, grocers, Yiddish grandmothers, mimes; you might see

Christie Brinkley, you might see Mick Jagger.

After five minutes, you wish you could stop one of those taxis; you wish the wind would stop whipping through the canyons of steel and glass; you wish the men would stop undressing you with their eyes; you wish you hadn't seen the bag lady sitting in the trash can, rocking back and forth and shouting gibberish; you wish someone on the subway would make eye contact and then you're afraid when they do; you wish you didn't see the dirt on the bright yellow cabs, the trash blowing in the street, the graffiti on every blank wall, the soot falling from incinerator chimneys, the hookers and the triple-X theaters, the panhandlers, the winos, the pimps.

Neither Phil nor William had been to the city before, so Latanya and I took them to all the places tourists go. We froze on the observation deck of the Empire State Building, we froze on the ferry to the Statue of Liberty, we froze watching the ice skaters at Rockefeller Center. We ate hot dogs in Nedick's for lunch and had dinner in Chinatown. William and Latanya wanted to go to a rock club in the Village, but after we got out of the subway and walked a few blocks I called it quits.

"Maybe you all have the stamina of a polar bear, but I'm freezing my ass off, and it's not going to get any warmer as the night goes on."

Latanya groaned. "It's early! Dancing will warm you up."

"Are we going someplace specific, or are we just walking until we find a place?"

"I thought we'd go to Rock City, but we can stop at a bar on the way to get warm."

"Oh, sure, and do you know any straight bars around here?"

"Uh, I really should get back, too," said Phil, surprising us all. "I have to get up early tomorrow, to study."

"Oh, come on, man," said William.

Phil looked down at his feet. "I have a midterm on Monday."

"Shit," said William.

"I'm on academic probation," Phil explained, apologetically. "If I flunk out I lose my scholarship."

"Aren't you a senior?" I asked.

"Football takes time," he answered. "I had to drop some

classes, and I'm short the credits. I have to go an extra year."

We walked back to the subway with the wind biting our faces.

Latanya and William necked on the train, all the way home, and then necked in the back of Phil's car. Phil was thankfully silent; he must have been all talked out. He walked me to the front door.

"Well, thank you, Phil. I had a nice time. Cold, but nice."

"Me, too," he said. He grabbed me by the arms and gave me a hard, awkward, dry-lipped kiss on the mouth, then he went down the steps without looking back or saying another word.

I shook my head, then hurried into the house and upstairs to my overheated apartment. Tonight I was grateful for the blast of hot air that poured out when I opened the door. Trevor woke up as soon as I turned on the light; I opened his door and he stretched, first the right leg and wing, then the left, while I put up a kettle of water. I started the tub filling while I made tea and undressed, then lay back contentedly in the steaming water to sip my tea and watch Trevor run back and forth on the edge of the tub.

That night I dreamed I was floating over New York City. I soared over the East Side with my arms outstretched, a white scarf draped around my neck, one end of the scarf fluttering in each hand. I flew down the East River and along the Battery, did a figure eight around the towers of the World Trade Center, and aimed for the Statue of Liberty. I circled the torch and then dropped down to the level of the observation deck in the crown. My parents were in there, waving to me. I waved back, circled the statue once more, and then flew west, where the sky was glowing pink and orange with the sunset, only the sun didn't set there, it rose.

I woke up early the next morning because Trevor was making a racket. I had put his cage cover on sloppily, and the morning light reached his perch. He was chattering to the bird in the mirror that hung in his cage. He punctuated his monologue by banging hard on the mirror with his beak, ringing his bell, and hanging upside down from the roof of the cage and flapping his wings so fast it sounded like a bicycle speeding by with a baseball card in its spokes. We had a leisurely breakfast — I a bowl of cereal and Trevor a single cornflake — then I tried to talk myself into spring cleaning. Fortunately, I talked myself out of it easily, grabbed my scarf and gloves and went outside. It was still cold, not the bitter temperature of the previous night but not very spring like, either. The sky was dramatic, cut in half by a solid shelf of white clouds in the east, clear blue in the west. I let the car warm up while I tried to decide where to go. Trevor needed bird seed but it was too early to go to the mall; stores didn't open until noon on Sunday. I dithered around for a good five minutes and then went where I was going to go all along.

Crosswind Field on a Sunday was very different from the sleepy little airport I'd found during the week. The parking lot was nearly full. A picnic table had been set up in a sunny spot next to the office and several people sat there. I wondered why they chose the picnic table instead of the couches inside until I saw their cigarettes. I remembered seeing a big "no smoking" sign in the office. The golden retriever I had first seen lying on one of the couches was stretched out next to the table. A young man drove by in a rusty yellow golf cart. A short rope connected the golf cart to the tail of a sleek white sailplane, like the one I had seen the week before. The letters "CW" were painted on the tail. The near wingtip was held up by a thin, spoked wheel, like a unicycle wheel; the other was held by a heavyset man walking beside the sailplane. He smiled and waved to the group at the picnic table. From the left came the sound of an engine. It got louder and louder and then the towplane flew by, a few feet off the ground, the orange glider behind it. The smokers waved and the person in the front seat of the glider waved back. I watched the two aircraft climb higher and grow smaller, until they were just specks in the clear blue sky.

As I approached the picnic area the dog stood up and walked over to me, her tail waving slowly. I squatted down and let her sniff my hand. She gave me a big, sloppy kiss on the cheek and walked away a few steps, then turned and looked at me. I stood up and followed her. "You must be the official greeter and tour guide," I said. She wagged her tail and walked along, in no great hurry to get anywhere. She led me in the opposite direction from the golf cart and sailplane, past a rundown barn with the word "Shop" painted on the front. We walked along the edge of the woods, and in a hundred yards from the office passed a small, hand-painted sign that read "Trailer Park." Beyond it were a half-dozen white trailers. Each one must have been over twenty feet long. One of them was open, the back wall folded down into a ramp. It was empty except for some rails or tracks on the trailer floor. A number of wooden and metal gizmos, some with little wheels on them, lay in a disorderly group next to the ramp. I had no idea how a glider fit in such a narrow box; it couldn't have been more than five or six feet wide and just as high. Next to it were two flatbed trailers, equally long and narrow, made of metal trusses. They were painted the faded red of Rustoleum primer.

The dog led me past the trailers to a chain link fence that marked the end of the runway. The edge of the cliff was only a few yards past the fence. I looked through the chain links at the valley lying four hundred feet below me. I wished I could remember more of the flight I'd taken the preceding week; the takeoff was just a jumble of impressions, speed and height and motion, the sudden panorama of the valley. I looked back at the runway. This end dipped down slightly; I couldn't see over the rise to the other end. The dog nudged my hand with her nose, and I scratched the top of her head. "Where to now?" I asked her. She wagged her tail and walked along the fence. On the other side of the runway was another band of woods. The dog walked along the edge of the woods until she came to a path. She looked over her shoulder to make sure I was following and trotted onto the path.

The path led through the trees, angling down the side of the hill so no part of it was too steep, although a few times I had to hold onto a tree trunk for balance. I couldn't see any birds but I could certainly hear them, especially one that seemed to shout "teacher, teacher, teacher," each call louder than the one before. Somewhere further in the trees a woodpecker drilled. I heard the annoyed scolding of a squirrel, and would have stopped to look for it, but I didn't want to lose sight of the retriever, whose familiarity with the path let her go much faster than I. The trees were a mixture of hardwoods. Small white flowers grew among the litter of oak, maple, and tulip leaves, and other small green plants were poking up through the rotted brown and grey carpet. As I went down I could hear a brook nearby.

The path bottomed out next to the brook, where the retriever bent her head and took a long drink. The water swirled in a wide curve next to the path. By midsummer it would probably be a muddy flat, with a narrow trickle lazing by. Now it rushed and sparkled over flat rocks. On the other side of the brook was a grassy rise about four feet high, flattening into a newly cultivated field. Emerald whorls of young skunk cabbage dotted both banks of the brook.

When the dog finished drinking she started up another path, which led up the hill. It was a little longer than the first path and climbed steadily. When it broke out of the woods we found ourselves at the end of the runway, where I had taken off from the week before. We got there just as the white sailplane was about to launch. The young man I had seen driving the golf cart held the left wingtip in his right hand, and ran alongside the sailplane as it accelerated. After a few steps he let go, jogged over to the golf cart, and drove toward the office. The retriever loped after him.

I hurried across the end of the runway, looking nervously up and to the right, in case anyone should be landing. The orange glider was parked where I had first seen it. I walked up to it and touched it very gently on the nose, and sighed with frustration. I would have given anything to be able to climb inside and fly it. Thirty-five dollars a lesson might as well be thirty-five thousand. I couldn't imagine ever earning enough to afford lessons.

I continued toward the office, my hands in my pockets. I wasn't used to doing so much walking, and sat down gratefully at one of the picnic tables. I was rubbing my shins when Andy walked by, dressed in jeans and a teal jacket.

"Hi," she said. "Ellen, isn't it? You went for a ride last week."

"Hi, Andy. Yes, I did."

"Come back for another?"

"No, I wish I could but I just can't afford it. I thought I'd come out and watch. It's such a pretty day."

"It sure is. Well, stay as long as you like. Go sit inside when you get cold."

"Thanks."

She walked down the runway toward the glider. A few minutes later the golf cart followed her with a load of customers. I watched when they took off. Andy waved from the back seat. I saw the towplane return for its landing, and the glider followed about ten minutes later. Then they did it again.

All the heat I had generated from walking dissipated and I began to feel chilly, but I was reluctant to go inside. The bright sun felt good on my face, and I didn't want to miss the takeoffs and landings.

"Hey!" someone shouted, off to my right. I looked around, and saw the bearded man who had sold me the glider ride, standing at the trailer door. He was looking my way.

"Me?" I asked.

"Yeah — you want some soup?"

I hesitated only a moment. "Sure, thanks."

I hadn't realized I'd been sitting so long, but at the word soup my stomach began to complain loudly that breakfast was too darn long ago. I'd forgotten to bring lunch.

He told me to walk behind the counter and sit down at the kitchen table. I said hello to the group — two couples — who were sitting on the couch and chair. They were having subs and sodas, watched by the retriever, who was pretending she hadn't eaten in at least six weeks.

"Name's Marv," he said, placing a bowl of soup in front of me. It was thick with chicken, carrots, and noodles; it looked and tasted homemade.

"I'm Ellen. Did you make this?" I asked him.

"Sure did," he said.

"It's great!"

Marv beamed. "Here, have some bread with it."

He handed me a chunk of whole wheat bread, also homemade.

"You made this, too?"

"Mm-hm."

"Are you married?"

He laughed out loud. "No, but I get asked that by every pretty girl who eats my cooking."

I liked Marv. He was one of those big, gruff-looking men who turn out to be surprisingly gentle. His full beard reached past his collar in silver waves. His eyes were deep brown, with laugh lines like Andy's in the corners. It seemed people either laughed or squinted a lot around here.

The group in the lounge area gathered up their trash and headed out the door. "See you later, Marv," said the taller of the two young men.

"Have a good lesson," Marv answered.

When they left, the retriever sat down next to me and stared with her dark chocolate eyes. Her nose followed the progress of my spoon from bowl to mouth; I could almost feel the cross hairs aiming at my hand. "What's her name?" I asked Marv.

"Penny," he answered, "We used to have a male named Sky King, but he died a year ago." Then he asked if I was there for a lesson myself.

"No," I said, breaking up another slice of bread. "I can't afford to."

"Live with your parents?"

"No." I thought that sounded a little curt, so I added, "I live alone. I'm a repro clerk at Van Dyke and Son, in Hardenbergh. It doesn't pay very much."

"What's a repro clerk?"

"Reproduction clerk. I make photocopies."

"All day?"

"All day."

"Hmm," was all he said as he cleared the dishes away.

"Can I help with those?" I asked.

"Nope. This won't take a minute. Have a seat in the lounge if you like."

"Actually, I think I'll go outside again."

"Suit yourself."

Despite the cool air, it was pleasant sitting at the picnic table, watching the glider take off. The roar of the towplane faded to a low hum as it climbed, and when it came back it was idling with a funny putt-putt kind of noise. I liked watching it swoop down and turn sharply, the towrope flapping behind it, then dive steeply and level off just before it touched down. The air was so clear I could see the bright orange glider even when it was quite high. Each time it separated from the towplane I could imagine again the odd feeling of motionlessness, as though someone had stepped on the brakes, and the almost eerie hush of the wind. I watched a lesson in progress, the glider turning first one way and then the other, then flying straight, sometimes flying so slowly it seemed to hang suspended, and then dipping down in a graceful curve. Once it fluttered like a maple seed, spinning toward the ground; unlike the movies, where airplanes that spun always crashed into splinters, the glider merely stopped its fluttering and flew on as though nothing bothered it.

While the towplane was shut off, waiting for the next trip, the airport was peaceful. I watched a hawk soaring along the tree-tops across the runway, its thick wings flexing with every turn. I could hear the soft breeze rustling the twigs of the trees behind me, and the calls of birds. The breeze carried the sweet, muddy smell of early spring. It would be lovely to sit here on warm, summer mornings, to watch robins hunt for worms in the grass, fragrant with mowing and dotted with dandelions and clover, to linger the whole long day, to watch the sun set and the fireflies challenge the stars. Hardenbergh might as well be a million miles away.

The sun had swung low and the chilly air roused me from dreams of summer. I had dozed off at the picnic table, my head on my arms. I stretched and yawned and sighed; it was time to get back to reality. I was buttoning my jacket when Andy and the young man passed by in the golf cart. I got up slowly and walked back to the office, to say good-bye and thank Marv again for lunch. It was warm inside and smelled of fresh coffee. Andy sat at the kitchen table, her feet up on a chair. Marv sat across from her.

"Hi, want some coffee? You must be cold by now," Andy said. "Come on in and sit down." She put her feet down to make room.

"Thanks," I said, glad for an excuse to put off going home.

Marv got me a cup of coffee and rolled down the sleeves of his flannel shirt. "Excuse me, won't you? I'll go help Keith stow the gear."

"Keith is our line boy," Andy explained. "He drives the golf cart, hooks gliders to the towrope, runs wings, things like that."

"I didn't see him last week," I said.

"He only works weekends. He's still in high school."

"Marv makes good coffee."

"Marv is a wonder. He and Herb are brothers. They own this place." She stood up to get the coffeepot. "Marv tells me you were here all day. Refill?"

"No thanks."

She poured herself another cup. "What did you do all that time?"

"Nothing, really. Mostly took a nap. And I went for a walk with Penny — I hope that was okay."

"Sure. You don't look like a vandal to me. What else did you do?"

"I just watched the gliders take off and land. Whatever happened to the white one?"

"Charlie Whiskey? Marv said he called a couple hours ago. He landed in a field about a hundred miles from here. His wife came by for the trailer and left over an hour ago; you must have been asleep when she came. She'll go get him, they'll take the wings off the sailplane and put it in the trailer, and go home. He'll be back next weekend, if the weather is good."

"A hundred miles? This Charlie flew a hundred miles?"

Andy smiled. "His name is Tom Bayard. His sailplane is Charlie Whiskey — C for Charlie, W for Whiskey. Those are the letters painted on the tail. And as for the distance, he was trying to do almost twice that. I told him it wasn't a great day, but it's good practice for him."

I shook my head. "It's a whole different world. I never knew it existed."

She looked at me for a moment. "You'd like to take lessons, wouldn't you?"

I looked down my coffee. A lump of powdered creamer

floated there in a slow circle, with a small contrail dissolving behind it. "Maybe someday."

"You know, Marv and I were talking...Keith is a senior in high school, and when he graduates he's going into the air force. So come June, we're going to be short our line boy. There's no reason why a girl can't be a line boy."

I looked up at her. "You mean me?"

"Why not? We're only talking weekends, and holidays like the Fourth of July. It doesn't pay much — actually it doesn't pay anything, but you get free lessons."

"Oh, Andy!" I couldn't say anything else. My heart started pounding and I felt warm, as though the hot coffee flowed through my veins instead of my stomach. The kitchen was blazing bright all of a sudden.

"You'd work hard for one lesson a day — washing the gliders, untying them and towing them to the flight line, hooking them up, running wings, tying them down at night, helping the customers."

"And I could start in June?"

"You could start this Saturday. We get real busy during the spring and summer. There are more lessons, more rides, more gliders taking off. Keith could use the help, and a day off now and then. He's worked very hard for us for three years. What do you say?"

"Yes! Yes, I'd like to, very much!"

"Good! We'll see you here Saturday morning, eight a.m. sharp."

She leaned forward to shake my hand. "Welcome aboard."

"Oh, Andy, you don't how much this means to me."

She sat back and reached for her coffee cup. "Oh, I think I have a pretty good idea. Maybe even better than you do."

Chapter Seven

"Damn," I swore as my slip knot failed to catch for the fifth time in a row. "Where's a boy scout when you need him?"

"Hold the rope taut," Keith coached patiently, "really taut."

I tried once more, while Keith watched and steadied the glider's wingtip. This time the rope slipped solidly into place with a yank.

"There you go," he said. "Now do one more halfway down, finish off with a couple half-hitches, and we're done tying this bird down for the night."

I struggled again with the rope, but needed only two tries before my knot held. "I'm glad I never took up macrame," I grumbled as we walked toward the golf cart.

"You'll get the hang of it soon, don't worry. You can drive. I'll show you where we park this."

I steered down the side of the runway while Keith sat back and stretched. He was a good-looking guy, with dark hair just long enough to catch in a small ponytail, green eyes, a dynamite smile, no zits. Too bad he was only eighteen.

The evening star was just beginning to glimmer as the sky faded to violet. When I stopped the cart I heard a robin sing softly in the woods. The warm night air was a welcome contrast to last week's bitter cold. It had been a glorious day, the first we'd had of real spring weather. By mid-morning I had tossed my jacket aside and rolled up the sleeves of my flannel shirt. The sun had felt good on my face and arms; I even had a little sunburn on my nose.

I'd learned that the first fine spring weekend brings out pilots by the flock, eager to refresh their rusty skills. The 2-33 was in demand all day and I was kept busy helping passengers buckle their seat belts, hooking up the tow line, and running with the glider's wingtip in my hand until it built enough speed to balance on its own. I helped two private owners put their sailplanes together and learned firsthand just how heavy a fiberglass wing can be. Andy never got a lunch break; she just grabbed a sandwich and took it with her in the 2-33.

I was introduced to a second glider, a small, single-seater called a 1-26. It looked like a little sports car next to the 2-33; its low wings were ten feet shorter and its slim fuselage lay only inches from the ground. It was painted bright yellow, with an orange racing stripe on each side. It was flown by Andy's advanced students and by licensed pilots. Keith, who had gotten his license two years ago, took it up just before the sun went down.

My first lesson had been the last flight of the day. Once more I thrilled at the takeoff, and marveled at the scenery, but this time I paid attention as Andy pointed out the landmarks. She had me take the controls as soon as we released from the towplane, and from that point the flight was nothing like my first as I struggled to turn the glider without letting it roller coaster across the sky. By the time she took over to land I was perspiring and exhausted. I felt as though I'd flown for an hour instead of twenty minutes, but as we rolled the gliders into their tie down positions I regretted having had such a brief flight.

Keith showed me the golf cart's parking spot along the east wall of the shop. The shop had been a barn once; a few stalls had been left standing and were used for storage. The front of the building was kept clear to hangar the towplane, which was already parked there, and the maintenance area filled the back with jigs and jacks and sawhorses. A silver-painted 2-33 fuselage stood in the middle of the floor, held upright by some kind of stand. Wings and tail surfaces lay stacked along the west wall. A glider trailer was parked in the rear behind an assortment of parts, a small motorboat on a trailer, and a cap for the back of a pickup.

Keith demonstrated how to hook the golf cart up to its battery charger, where it would remain overnight. Then we closed and padlocked the doors.

"Whose trailer is that in the back of the shop?" I asked.

"Andy's."

"Is there a sailplane in it?"

"Yeah. Well, it was a long day, wasn't it? How do you like it so far?"

"I like it a lot. Thanks for all your help."

"No problem. Don't worry — you'll do fine. I'll see you tomorrow."

"Aren't you going back to the office?"

"Can't — got a date," he grinned, and turned toward the parking lot.

I watched him go, a little puzzled at the abrupt way he had changed the subject when I asked about Andy's sailplane. Why would Andy leave it in the back of the shop, behind all that junk? It looked as though it had been sitting there for years.

I walked into the office, where Andy, Herb, and Marv were sitting on the couch drinking beer, with Penny lying at Herb's feet. She thumped her tail twice on the floor when I came in. Andy walked into the kitchen and came back with another can of beer. "Here." She handed it to me. "It's Miller time."

"Thanks," I said, and sat down gratefully on the chair to savor that first cold sip. I stretched my legs out and had a bad feeling that I was going to be pretty sore tomorrow morning.

"So, what did you think of your first day? Will you be back tomorrow?" Andy asked.

"You bet," I said with a smile. "I'm pooped but it feels good."

"You too tired to come with us tonight?" asked Marv.

"Where to?"

"The Hoot Owl Bar. It's a couple miles up the road, in Jennytown. We get together there most Saturday nights."

"Sounds good to me," I said. "Thanks for asking."

"This is a class operation all the way," Andy said. "You can follow my car. You coming, Herb?"

"Yeah," he said, "as soon as I log the day's tows."

Marv rode with Andy. It was a short drive to the bar, a small-ish stone building at least 200 years old, with a frame addition that didn't look a day under 150. It looked like a genuine antique on the inside, too, with whitewashed walls and rough-hewn beams in the low ceiling. The long, old-fashioned bar had brass rail at its foot. Any finish the top had once boasted was worn off by bar rags a long time ago. Behind the bar, in the center of the room, was a huge grey owl on a T-shaped wooden perch. I thought it was stuffed until it turned its head to watch as we walked by.

"Hi, Pete," Marv called to the bartender, a burly man with receding black hair. "Meet our new ground crew, Ellen Horvath. Ellen, this is Pete D'Amico. This is his place."

"Pleased to meet you, Ellen," Pete said as he reached over the bar to shake my hand. "What'll it be?"

"Pitcher of draft," Marv answered for me. He and Andy headed for a large table in the back, near a small bandstand. Andy handed me a menu. "It's mostly sandwiches, and soup in the winter. They'll have one hot dish listed on the blackboard behind the bar."

"This is a nice place," I said. "Which came first, the owl or the bar?"

"The bar's been here for over a hundred years," Marv explained. "Pete and his wife, Patti, took it over about ten years ago. They called it Pete's Place until they found the owl. It had been hit by a car one night, right out in front. They took it to a vet to be fixed up, but it'll never fly again, so they got a mascot, called him Butch, and changed the name of the bar."

"Don't you need a permit or something to keep a wild animal?" I asked.

"Mm-hmm. Patti got herself a permit and some training and is now a bird rehabilitation specialist."

"You should see the back yard," Andy added. "It's full of cages. Ask her to give you the tour some time."

A short, dark-haired woman brought over the pitcher, a half-dozen glasses, and a basket of popcorn.

"Patti, this is Ellen Horvath, our new ground crew. Ellen, Patti D'Amico. We were just telling her about your patients."

Patti smiled. "We've got lots of them, too. Just got a golden eagle this week."

"An eagle? Could I see it sometime?" I asked.

"Sure, anytime these folks let you take a break, you come on over. Don't let them work you too hard. So, what can I bring you tonight?"

"We're waiting on Herb," Andy said. "Okay if we order in a little while?"

"Sure thing," said Patti. "Just give me a wave when you're ready."

Herb came in a few minutes later. He brought a man and a woman to the table.

"Look who I ran into in the parking lot," he said.

"Ellen, meet Tom and Katie Bayard," Andy said. "Tom, Katie, this is Ellen Horvath. She's taking over Keith's job."

We shook hands all around and Tom and Katie sat down. I recognized Tom as the heavyset man I'd seen walking with his sailplane the week before. Up close I could see that he had curly blond hair and a Dennis-the-Menace grin. Katie was as different as Laurel from Hardy — she was tall and athletic looking, with a slim face accentuated by long dark hair.

"Charlie Whiskey, right?" I asked Tom.

"That's right." He seemed pleased that I knew. "Although most people call it Cheap Whiskey."

"Do you fly sailplanes, too?" asked Katie.

"I'm taking lessons."

"How many hours do you have?" Tom asked.

"Twenty minutes," I answered.

"Well, congratulations! Hey, Patti! We got a new pilot here — we need a pitcher, put it on my tab."

By the time we finished the second pitcher I had met practically everyone who walked into the Hoot Owl: Jake, who flew a crop duster; Don, who gave lessons in helicopters and was an avid birder; Leo and Marge, local horse breeders and members of the Flying Farmer Association; "Doc" Schmidt, the veterinarian; and after him I lost track. A couple glasses of beer transformed Herb from laconic to loquacious — I had been a little intimidated by him all day; it turned out he had very little to say unless the subject was airplanes. The more animated he became the more I could see his resemblance to Marv, especially in the way his skin wrinkled at the top of his nose, and the mischievous look in his eye as he related a particularly off-color tale, or one in which

Marv was the butt of the joke. I would have known they were brothers even if Andy had not told me so.

Andy looked tiny sitting between them. Like Latanya, she had a fine bone structure and a natural grace, but unlike Latanya, Andy gave the impression of being capable and tough, an airedale instead of an afghan. I was glad to be flanked by Marv and Tom; their bulk made me feel less like a great dane.

A bluegrass band set up on the small stage and put an end to Herb's stories. Tom taught me the two-step and we all danced — even Herb — until the band took a break an hour later. After we sat down I looked at my watch for the first time and saw with a shock that it was after eleven. I still had an hour's ride ahead of me and would have to be up before seven to get back out here on time. I made my farewells and walked out.

Patti caught up with me at the door. "Are you driveable?" she asked, looking up at my eyes.

"Yes," I answered. "I think I just danced most of the beer out of me."

She nodded her head. "Okay. But if you ever overdo it you stay put. You can sleep on our couch, upstairs."

"Thanks, Patti." She gave my arm a squeeze and walked back to the bar.

I stepped outside and took a deep breath of the cool, clean air. I could still feel the pressure of Patti's fingers on my arm. I looked up to where the stars should be white and yellow pin-points, but all I could see were shimmering and blurred splashes of light. You're getting maudlin from all the beer, I told myself. She's a nice lady; she probably cares about all her customers. I sniffed back the sentimental tears and walked to the car, trying not to think about how long it had been since someone, anyone, had touched me. The air had grown chilly enough for me to see my breath. The steering wheel was so cold that I wished I had brought gloves. As I drove away, I could see in the rearview mirror the warm yellow light of the Hoot Owl's windows.

On Sunday morning I helped Tom and Katie rig his sailplane. It was a beauty. The front edge of the wings curved backward in an arc that gave it the appearance of flight even as it sat on the ground. He wanted to launch at 12:30, so they had an early picnic lunch, which they invited me to share. It was an odd combination of foods: chicken on whole wheat and fresh fruit for Katie, three slices of cold pizza for Tom. I opted for half a chicken sandwich and an orange.

"I should change my eating habits just because she's a gym teacher?" Tom said when I looked askance at his pizza.

"The secret of a successful marriage is never to try to change someone," Katie added serenely. "He'll diet when his love handles get too wide for him to fit in the cockpit."

"How long have you been married?" I asked.

"Three years," Tom answered. "We lived together for two years before that."

"We got married after he finished his doctorate," said Katie.

"I didn't realize you had a Ph.D.," I said.

Tom nodded. "I do drugs."

"He develops drugs at JerseyTech," she clarified.

"Enough work talk! This is Sunday. I'm going flying."

I offered to help pick up but Katie shooed me away.

"He wants to fly, you go help him. I can take care of this."

After we towed Cheap Whiskey to the flight line Tom squeezed himself into the cockpit. I thought it wouldn't take many more slices of pizza before he wouldn't fit at all. I handed him the shoulder straps, helped close the tinted canopy, and hooked up the tow rope. Then I walked to the wingtip and signaled the towplane to take up the slack. Herb stopped on my signal and I turned around, scanning the sky all around us for incoming aircraft.

"Pattern is clear," I called to Tom, and he gave me a thumbs up. I lifted the wingtip and waved my free arm in a wide circle, signaling Herb to begin the launch. The towplane pulled the sailplane, so slowly at first I could easily walk alongside, but in a few steps I had to break into a trot and then a run. I let go of the tip and watched Tom's smooth takeoff. The sailplane's wings curved up like a bird's wing in mid-beat. Sunlight glinted off the canopy as they turned. I watched for a moment, feeling a curious satisfaction, then walked off the runway to help Keith and Andy pull the 2-33 into position.

We went back to the Hoot Owl that night, but I didn't stay

long. I wasn't used to so much physical activity; I was hearing from muscles I didn't know I had. I hated leaving, though. I wanted to prolong the weekend, make it last until late at night. But Monday morning would be hard enough to face by itself, let alone with no sleep or a hangover. Besides, I wanted to check up on Trevor. He was molting. He had been dropping feathers for a week, just a couple at first; by midweek it was a flurry and by Friday night the flurry became a dusting. His body needed extra energy to make a new batch of feathers; I planned to buy some molting food at lunch on Monday.

Trevor was mopy when I got home. He stretched and yawned but didn't stir from in front of his mirror, where he stood shoulder to shoulder with his reflection. His breast, normally smooth, looked moth-eaten, with patches of down showing through the flat spots. The floor of his cage was littered with color: short periwinkle feathers from his breast, each with a tuft of white down attached at the base; long wing primaries, shading from gray to violet; stubby grey and white feathers from his back; an infinitesimal bit of iridescent purple fluff from his cheek patches; even one white feather with a round black spot, one of the dotted feathers from either side of his beak. They swirled up in a pastel cloud as I walked by.

"Poor Trevor," I said, "you look lopsided. Maybe you'll lose a dot from the other side."

He was reluctant to leave the cage when I opened the door; I had to put my hand in to retrieve him. Once out he refused to fly, climbing up my arm instead to sit on my shoulder and nestle in my hair. He was holding on so tight I could feel all eight little toenails through my shirt. I scratched his head with one finger.

"Must be the bird equivalent of PMS, huh?" I murmured. "I'm sorry you feel punk — I promise to get molting food tomorrow."

I was just unfolding the sofa bed when the phone rang. "Hello?" I said, the receiver tucked between my ear and my shoulder.

"Uh, hello, Ellen, uh, this is Phil."

"Phil?" I drew a blank for a moment. "Oh, Phil from Lehigh." The Civil War buff. The conversationalist. The great kisser.

"Yeah, uh, how are you?"

"Fine, thank you. I was just getting ready for bed, actually."
I turned down the sheets and sat on the edge of the mattress.

"Uh, well, I'm sorry to be calling so late. I tried all day.
Yesterday, too."

"Sorry, I was out."

"I figured."

I waited.

"Uh, what I'm calling about is to see if you might want to go
out sometime."

I sighed. "Actually, Phil, I've gotten pretty busy lately. I've
got another job, on weekends, and it takes up just about all my
spare time on Saturdays and Sundays."

"Oh. Uh, how about Friday night?"

Hell. Phil was a perfectly nice guy, he just lacked imagination — and chemistry. I knew Latanya would urge me to go out
with him, to stay in practice if for no other reason, but I couldn't
see the sense in dating someone who left you feeling lukewarm,
at best, just for the sake of doing what everyone else did on a
Friday night.

"Gosh, Phil, I'm really sorry but I have to get up awfully
early on Saturday. And I'm usually so tired from being on my
feet all week that I just kind of collapse on Friday nights."

"So, you don't want to go out."

God, he was brilliant.

"No, Phil, I'm sorry but I don't."

"Oh. Okay, well, uh, it was nice talking to you."

No it wasn't, and I hated being so blunt. I said good-bye and
hung up, feeling bad about it. It was so much easier turning down
a sleazeball. Latanya would think I was crazy, saying no to a nice
guy for no reason, except that my free time was suddenly much
less and therefore too precious to waste on a date with no
promise. I lay down, expecting to be up half the night fretting
that I'd committed singles heresy, but I fell sound asleep without
another pang.

The next morning I woke up stiff. Everything hurt — especially the back of my legs and my arms. I got out of bed care-

fully, wishing I could sleep at least six more hours. I wondered if it was going to hurt very much to brush my teeth. A hot shower helped, temporarily, but dressing was a chore. My mood wasn't improved any by knowing it was Monday, and Trevor still felt crummy. He didn't even chirp when I left for work.

I knew work would be a shock after a pleasant weekend outdoors, but I didn't realize how claustrophobic I'd feel once I was back in the all-too-familiar little room with the big copier. I had just hung up my jacket when my supervisor, Moira, gave me the unwelcome news that a crisis was in progress and shit was hitting the fan all over the department. I was to do my bit by making twenty copies of a series of reports dating back more than six months. I made copies all day. I didn't have time to pee all morning and at lunch time managed just enough free time to hit the rest room and grab a sandwich out of a vending machine. It was quarter to six before I could escape.

My favorite pet store was closed on Mondays so I went to my alternate source, a small shop next to the supermarket near my old neighborhood. My head was aching as much as the rest of me and I couldn't wait to get home. I was unlocking the car door when a familiar voice called "Ellen?"

I looked around. Mrs. Pulaski was in the next row of parking places.

"Ellen!" She walked toward me. She looked pulled together, as though she'd come out in a hurry, and I could see she was wearing an apron under her unbuttoned spring coat. "Ellen!" She gave me a hug.

"Mrs. Pulaski, hello, what are you doing here?"

"Oh, wouldn't you know, I ran out of sauerkraut and Fortunato's is closed already. I left Stan watching the stuffed cabbage. Are you coming or going?"

"Going. I had to get something for my parakeet."

"You have a parakeet? I didn't know that. You look tired. Are you working too hard? You need to stop and smell the roses, you know. So how long have you had a parakeet? Come for dinner."

"Thanks, Mrs. Pulaski, I'll have to do that."

"No, I mean tonight. Right now, after I buy the sauerkraut.

We have plenty, and we haven't seen you since Thanksgiving."

"Oh, Mrs. Pulaski, thanks, but I have such a headache, and I worked late. Maybe some other time."

"Tomorrow. Come tomorrow. You have no plans, right, who has plans on a Tuesday night? Come right after work. I'll make pierogies."

"Oh, thank you, but I—"

"No buts," she interrupted. "No buts. It's been too long since we've seen you. I'll make you a good meal for a change, not anything frozen, like you young girls always make for your-selves. Tomorrow, promise?"

"Tomorrow. I promise."

"Good. Oh, my sauerkraut!"

She ran toward the supermarket, the soles of her heavy black shoes clumping on the asphalt. The sound reminded me of the evening of my father's wake, when she and my mother and I walked to the funeral home. I had to lean against the car when I realized that I hadn't thought about my parents — not even once — in two days. For the first time since they died, I had forgotten. I began to wish I hadn't made that promise to Mrs. Pulaski.

I drove to the Pulaskis' after work on Tuesday. I pulled onto the street I'd been avoiding for months. It was still comfortably familiar; I could close my eyes and picture the paw prints in the sidewalk in front of the Giseckis' house; I knew that the third step of the Vargas' porch creaked, that the manhole in front of the Pulaskis' house was home plate on summer evenings. It was the same street, and yet it felt subtly different to be there, perhaps because the Bongiovannis had painted their house green.

I parked in front of the Vargas' and walked to the Pulaskis' so I wouldn't have to pass my old house. I could still see it, of course, as I walked up: the blue porch steps, the white facade, the tiny front yard barely large enough for two pink azaleas, still in winter dormancy. I turned aside at the Pulaskis' and opened the side gate. I knocked once on the side door and stepped in.

The kitchen door was open and Mrs. Pulaski waved me in. She was at the stove, sauteing the pierogies in onions and butter.

The smell made me feel six years old again. She had recently gotten her hair re-blued, and permed, too; it hugged her head in tight curls. She was wearing a grey smock over an aqua knit skirt; I don't think I'd ever seen her in slacks.

"Stanley," she called, "Ellen's here."

Mr. Pulaski came into the kitchen to give me a hug. He was a broad-shouldered man, a couple years older than Mrs. Pulaski and a good two inches shorter. He was balding and beer-bellied, wearing his usual Fruit-of-the-Loom T-shirt and a pair of dark blue work pants. He'd been retired from V. D. for two years, and spent all his time gardening in their back yard.

"You look good," he said. "Got some color in your cheeks. We missed you at Christmas."

"I missed you, too."

"Stan, why don't you give Ellen something to drink."

"Glass of milk, Ellen?" he teased me. I'd always been able to get a can of beer from him, ever since I turned eighteen. He handed me a Miller and led me outside. "Come see my spring planting. I already have the peas in."

We stood on the back porch while he showed me the pea patch, four rows with branches stuck in the ground for the shoots to climb on. He showed me where the spinach would go, the squash, the cabbage, the potatoes. "There's nothing like a new potato, Ellen, boiled fresh from the garden. Some are so small they look like marbles, you don't even have to peel them. Not like the ones in the store, all cut up from the harvesting machines, sprouting and mushy. Well, it'll be September before they're ready. You stop by and we'll have some."

He pointed to a cluster of twigs in one corner of the yard. "My raspberries. And on the other side, concord grapes. For making wine. Old man Bongiovanni and I are going to pool our grapes and make wine in his basement. We'll call it Dago-Polack Red. Or Polack-Dago Red, depending on who puts in the most grapes."

His garden had taken over the whole yard, except for one corner where Mrs. Pulaski's clothesline stood. The side border between his yard and the Vargas' was bordered with a chain-link fence, on which Mr. Pulaski grew climbing roses. Our side was marked with a low hedge. Beyond it was my old yard, mostly lawn, with a row of lilacs at the rear property line. A new swing set had been installed in front of the shrubs.

"I'm thinking about letting that hedge grow, this summer," Mr. Pulaski said.

"Don't you get along with the new neighbors?"

"No, no problems. Actually, we don't see very much of them. They keep to themselves. It's just — not the same."

"Stan! Ellen! Dinner!"

We went inside. Mrs. Pulaski had set the kitchen table, and put in the center an enormous platter of homemade pierogies and links of fresh kielbasa. I was glad to be eating in the kitchen; the dining room would have made me feel like company.

We feasted, and they filled me in on the neighborhood gossip, and soon I was calling them Uncle Stash and Aunt Dot, which I hadn't done since eighth grade. After dinner Uncle Stash went into the living room to watch Jeopardy. He'd become quite a trivia buff since his retirement. I dried the dishes while Aunt Dot washed.

"So are you all right, Ellen?" she asked me. "Really all right?"

"I'm fine," I answered. "I have a job, nothing exciting but it pays the bills. I have a roof over my head, a parakeet that's losing all his feathers; I'm doing okay."

"No boyfriend?"

"No. I've gone out a few times but there's no one special."

"Hmm. If you ever need anything, you know all you have to do is call."

"I know. Thank you. And — thank you for all your help last September. I never really told you how much it meant. I don't think I could have gotten by without all you did."

"That's what friends are for, especially when something so terrible happens. For a young girl to lose her parents like that." She shook her head. "I miss your mother. Like last night, when I ran out of sauerkraut, I would have borrowed a can from your mother. She always had some. Whatever I needed."

"Couldn't you have tried one of the other neighbors?"

"Phooey, you know what a skinflint Mary Varga is, and next

door, well, the Calabreses are nice but they're new, you know?"

"Mmm, but how will you ever get neighborly with them if you don't borrow a can of sauerkraut once in a while?"

"Well, I suppose you're right, but would a woman named Calabrese keep sauerkraut in her kitchen?"

I laughed. "I guess not. Maybe you should run out of tomato paste instead."

"Maybe I will. But it's not the same. Your mom and I went way back. I remember when your parents moved to this neighborhood. My girls were in high school then. They used to baby sit you, remember? I'll tell you, when I was going through the change your mom was all that kept me sane. We used to talk, hanging out our wash; you'd be in school and my girls were grown and your mom and I would talk."

"What about?"

"Oh, women talk, you know. About keeping house, raising kids. It seemed like the world was going crazy then, riots and protests and all those women's libbers."

I smiled. "Didn't you ever go braless?"

"Not me! Time makes them sag enough, no sense hurrying it along. It was just hard for a young woman, keeping house, and all those New York broads — pardon the expression, but they were coarse, you know? — saying it was wrong, everybody should get out of the house and work. So the young women went to work, and afterwards they still have to clean house, and now men don't open car doors for them anymore."

"Is that how my mother felt, too?"

"Oh, I don't know. She loved you, and she never minded the diapers and all. But she always seemed a little, I don't know, not unhappy, but looking for more out of life. You're a lot like her that way, you know. Just like her."

"Me? I never thought I was anything like her. If anything, I think I take after my father."

"Oh, no. Your father was a very nice man, Ellen, but he had no ambition. You have ambition. He was perfectly content to work in The Plant. He could have been a foreman years ago. He finally got it just out of seniority. No, he was nice but your mother should have married a man who was going places."

"But he always wanted more."

"A big win at the track, you mean."

"So you knew all about that, too?"

"Like I said, your mom and I talked. Ellen, all your dad wanted was easy money, quick money, and if he'd ever gotten any he'd've just wanted more. He didn't want to get ahead, make a name for himself. He didn't even want a bigger house or a fancy car. He just wanted things easy. Not to speak ill of the dead, God rest his soul, and I liked him very much, but he was no go-getter. No," she said, as she scrubbed out the sink, "your mom should have married one of those lawyers in The Home Office. She should have married John Cahill."

"John Cahill? The John Cahill who works at V.D.?"

"That's the one."

"Why him?"

She looked up at me and touched her forehead with the back of her hand, leaving a little spot of soap bubbles over one eyebrow.

"She loved him."

"She loved him? When? Not — recently?"

"No, don't be silly. In high school she loved him. He took her to the senior prom. I think he loved her, too. But his parents didn't want him to have anything to do with her. They shipped him off to Europe right after graduation, and then he went away to Princeton or Yale or one of those Ivy League schools."

"She married my father that September."

She gave me a funny look. "That June."

I put the dishtowel down. "I meant that summer." There were some things I didn't want the whole neighborhood to know. "I guess she married my father on the rebound, huh?"

"What if she did? She loved him in the end."

"How do you know, Aunt Dot? How do you know that for sure?"

"I just know, that's all." She finished scrubbing the sink, rinsed her hands, and wiped them on a towel before looking at me. "Ellen, your parents were good people. They loved each other and they loved you. Everything they did was for you."

"Thanks for saying that, Aunt Dot, but I wish I had heard it from them."

"Look, why don't you keep Stanley company in the living room? I'll be out in a minute."

"Sure." I went into the living room, but only to say good-bye. I was starting to feel claustrophobic, hemmed in by familiar sights, old memories, and a new way of thinking about John Cahill, who up to now had been nothing more than a name on an org chart.

I didn't go straight home. I drove to the nearest phone booth, and looked up John Cahill. He lived on Frelinghuysen Avenue, which figured, near the park, in the nicest part of town. I drove along Frelinghuysen until I found the house. It was a pretty house, two stories, with a stone front and two chimneys. My mother could have lived there, if her name hadn't been Toth, if Hardenbergh society had allowed marriage between an immigrant's daughter and the son of a Daughter of the American Revolution.

She had loved him, and he took her to the prom. I wondered if they had made love that night, and when I wondered that I felt goose bumps run down my spine. Was it possible they had slept together, and she had gotten pregnant by him? Was that the reason he had been sent away? Could she have married my father, not just on the rebound, but because good Catholic girls didn't get abortions?

I leaned my head on the steering wheel. It could explain a lot, I thought. My father was a kind man. He could have married her out of kindness, he could have lived with her gratitude. But my mother? Loving someone else, loving me because I was part of him? Was she grateful to my father and relieved because he got her out of a mess, and indebted to him from then on, and in the end, guilty, because she couldn't love him, couldn't repay him for his damned kindness? Was it guilt that made her cry so hard, and call his name? Was it guilt that made her unable to answer me the night of the wake, when I asked her if she loved him?

I sat up and tried to shake the questions out of my head. There was no point in asking, no one was left to tell. John Cahill might not even know. I would never know for sure. And it didn't matter anymore, did it, if I were really a rich man's daughter. I was Ellen Horvath, a repro clerk, with barely enough money to pay the rent, no chance to get out of this town, and no prospects in it. All I had was Trevor, and Crosswind.

Someday, when I was on break, just for the hell of it, I'd go up to the attorneys' offices and take a look at this John Cahill, to see if his face bore anything that showed in my mirror.

Chapter Eight

My life took on a new pattern as I became a Crosswind regular. The old routine from Monday to Friday was as boring as ever, but the rhythm of my week altered as the weekend demanded more of my energy. Until now Saturday and Sunday had been days of oversleeping and aimless wandering, like the drawn-out days of summer when my high-school friends and I would cruise up and down Woodrow Wilson Avenue, endlessly asking "What do you want to do?" and endlessly answering, "I don't know, what do you want to do?" Now I learned that morning is a glorious time when you're up by choice; each weekend I eagerly got up and on the road, without a backward glance or a spare thought for Hardenbergh or John Cahill or the KM9000.

I was never the first to arrive at Crosswind, because Marv and Herb lived there in the trailer, but with Marv in the office and Herb checking over the towplane I seemed to have the gliderport all to myself. It hadn't taken Keith long at all to realize he could sleep an hour later if he let me wash the planes in the morning. I didn't mind. I liked the time alone, before the customers arrived.

Robins and mockingbirds sang as I untied the 2-33. I towed it to the wash area for a quick hose-down and let it dry in the sun while I cleaned the cockpit. When I opened the canopy the smell of the vinyl seats and the plastic sidewalls mingled with the lemon fragrance of the furniture polish that made the canopy gleam. I looked for cracked plastic and loose screws while I plumped the seat cushions and readied the shoulder straps for the first passenger of the day. I towed the 2-33 back to the launch area and sat under the wing for a moment, fingering a blossom of spring beauty while I savored the quiet. Not that I minded the hurry-up atmosphere of a busy day, but something about the morning's promise, all anticipation and blue sky and orange wing, made me feel not just that I belonged here, but that there wasn't any other place to be. Hardenbergh didn't even exist.

At the door to the office Andy waved and I hopped in the golf cart to get her. She never minded walking — it wasn't even a quarter mile — and she often used the time to discuss the upcoming flight with a student. But she waved when we had customers for a demo ride, who not only didn't feel like walking all the way, but who often wore high heels or other improbable shoes more appropriate for a visit to Auntie Em than a gliderport. Andy was great with the customers. She could tell within seconds whether they were confident or scared. With the scared ones she kept up a running conversation about what a wonderful day they had chosen, and what a wonderful ride they would have. She managed to let them know without coming right out and saying so that it was all right to be nervous the first time. "Like losing your virginity," I thought to myself, "but usually more fun."

At the sailplane either Keith or I would help the customer get seated and strapped in while Andy climbed in the back. If Keith was fussing with straps I would hook up the towrope. Then Keith would say something nice like "Have a good flight" while he closed the canopy, and I would hold the glider's wingtip, running alongside as the aircraft rolled, until there was enough air flowing over the wings for Andy to hold them up with the controls. Keith and I would switch roles for the next flight.

I enjoyed working with the students and new customers, but was a little intimidated by the private pilots who had their own sailplanes. They all seemed to be doctors with Jaguars or lawyers with BMWs. Most of them didn't say much to the lowly ground crew, and some looked so serious I wondered if they were having any fun at all. They'd slip into the cockpit with hat, sunglasses, chart, and a calculator, of all things, and twiddle knobs on the instrument panel without cracking a smile. They were very fussy about how I closed the canopy for them and a few doubted my ability to handle a thousand dollars worth of plexiglass, relying instead on Keith or their very patient wives. I didn't understand these women, who seemed content to sit at a picnic table while their husbands soared most of the day. How could they prefer to sit there, smoking and reading romance novels while they waited for their husbands to announce their arrival over the radio? How much more fun it was to fly, or at least to crew, to look up at any sailplane's shadow and to watch every takeoff and landing.

"Those pilots are the 'big boys'," Keith had told me on my first day. "They fly the fiberglass ships, sometimes in contests, sometimes to set records. This is serious fun for them."

"They don't seem to think very highly of 2-33 pilots," I observed.

"Some of them are like that, but Tom Bayard isn't. He remembers when he used to be one of us."

Keith was right. The Bayards were an exception to the "big boy" clique. Tom was always happy to have an extra pair of hands to help assemble his ship, and after he showed me how to hold his canopy without damaging it, he gave me credit for having enough brains to remember the proper technique.

I liked to watch him as he described the day's flight. He had to illustrate every turn of the sailplane with a swoop of his hand, like a puppeteer holding invisible strings. As he grew more and more animated Katie listened to him with a combination of tolerance, amusement, and pride. How lucky she was that she could share his happiness with this very expensive piece of equipment, and how lucky Tom was that Katie didn't seem to mind helping with the heavy wings.

She never complained when Tom was gone for hours. She didn't exactly hang around with the other wives, although she did visit with them, but more often was in the office chatting with Marv, or wandering down to the launch area to visit with me and Keith. Tom and Katie were the only "glass" people to stop in at the Hoot Owl on their way home, and the only ones who made me feel like I belonged on the same runway with them.

On Sunday Tom and Katie showed up during a lull in the flying. A student had cancelled because of the flu and for some reason no customers were waiting for a flight. It was a funny kind of day, overcast with a solid layer of white clouds, punctuated by curly grey wisps underneath, yet Andy and her previous student had stayed up nearly forty minutes. Now we lolled under the orange wing, savoring the fresh air.

"When's your next student due?" Tom asked Andy.

"Not for an hour," she answered.

"Mind if I take the 2-33?"

"Not at all. It's your nickel."

"Great. Mind if I take Ellen with me?"

Andy smiled. So did I. "Be my guest," she told him.

Tom wedged himself in the back seat with some difficulty and I climbed in front. "Why aren't you flying your own ship?" I asked.

"Doesn't look like that great a day," he answered. "I'm not sure it's worth the trouble of assembling and disassembling, with that overcast. But I hate to see a glider sitting idle. Do you mind?"

"Hell, no!"

Tom did the takeoff, as smoothly as Andy did, and once we reached a thousand feet he let me try the tow. I did as badly as ever. I knew where the glider should be in relation to the tow-plane, from having seen Andy put it there, but I couldn't seem to keep it there myself for more than two seconds, even on a dead-calm day. With relief I let Tom take over a few hundred feet later.

"You'll get the hang of it soon enough," he said in a comforting tone as he smoothly brought the glider back into the proper position. "It's one of those funny things — you think you'll never be able to do it, and nobody can even tell you how to, really, but one day you'll see, it'll come to you, just like that."

"That day seems a long way off," I said ruefully.

"It does now. But it'll come. I guarantee it. Besides, you didn't do as badly as I used to when I first started. You're too hard on yourself. This is supposed to be fun!"

In front of us the towplane seemed to jump twenty feet in the air, and three seconds later we did, too. "Lift!" Tom cried, and pulled the release. We were only about two thousand feet above the ground, and I thought he was crazy for releasing so low, but he rolled the 2-33 into a breathtakingly steep bank and we began to climb.

"Son of a gun," he said. "I never would have thought there'd be lift this strong on a day like today. How about that."

I just nodded, none too vigorously because my head was spinning. We continued up in a tight spiral, another one, two, three thousand feet.

"Hey, I didn't mean to be a hog," Tom said. "You want to take it for a while?"

"If I did, I'd probably fly right out of the thermal. I bow to your superior skill."

"You take the next one, then."

To our surprise the soaring air carried us up nearly 6000 feet. Tom began singing in the back seat when we passed through 5200 feet, a nonsense song about being "a mile high, in the sky, we're up a mile in the sky-ul." I turned in my seat to glance back at him. He was grinning broadly.

"Isn't this fun? I always sing when I get this high. Must be lack of oxygen. But I love it, Ellen, I love getting so high when we were so low, and doing it without an engine. All those poor gashawk drivers don't know what they're missing. This is fantastic."

I took over when we reached the top of the lift, and flew straight until I stumbled into another thermal. I turned too soon and lost it right away. Frustrated, I asked Tom to keep flying.

"We'll be on the ground in five minutes if I keep doing this. Besides, you fly so well it's fun for me to sit here and be a passenger for a change."

"Are you sure?" he asked, but he didn't argue as he took the controls and easily brought us back to the thermal. I really did enjoy being released from the responsibility of flying. I loved soaring as much as ever, but lessons were a lot harder than being taken for a ride. I found myself working so hard I didn't have time to have fun, so now I admired the view I was usually too busy to notice, while Tom flew and sang silly songs.

Every flight was different, I realized as I looked out and down. On a sunny day the river gleamed like a silver necklace; today it was as dull as pewter. On a sunny day you could see cloud shadows ripple across the hills, and the brightness that returned as they passed seemed brilliant in contrast. Today was a day of no contrast at all. All the browns were the same shade of brown, and all the greens uniform. Yet the day had a muted beauty, and the diffused light softened the yellow-green spring landscape. I looked up at a white sky patterned with curved fingers of grey and realized that I was more comfortable up here, over a mile above the ground, than I had been anywhere else in the past six months. I belonged here, and everything spread out below me, the farms and hills, small towns and ponds, the river and the runway, looked right, somehow, down there.

We'd been up for three-quarters of an hour when I reminded Tom that we needed to bring the ship back. "Oh heck, you're right," he said. "I was having such a good time I forgot." He pointed the glider toward the airport, but I noticed he didn't open the spoilers or do any maneuvers to get us down even faster. He hung on to every inch of altitude.

"All right, brace yourself," he joked as he began the landing pattern. We touched down gently exactly an hour after we'd taken off.

"What a pilot!" he shouted to Andy as we climbed out. "I'll fly with her anytime." I shook my head and protested that he'd done all the flying.

"I mean it," he said more quietly, to me. "I had fun today, and I'd like to fly with you again."

We shook hands and he went off to find Katie while I attended to Andy and her next student. They had taken off and were still in the air when Tom and Katie returned with Cheap Whiskey in tow. I helped them position it for takeoff and handed Tom his shoulder straps once he was settled in. "You know," he told me as he buckled the straps. "You are going to be a good pilot someday. Believe in yourself and you will be."

"Thanks. And thank you for a wonderful flight."

"My pleasure," he said with a smile, and I closed the canopy for him. A moment later he took off and he didn't return for four hours. By the time he got back Keith and I had put the 2-33 away, so I helped Tom and Katie disassemble their ship.

"Are you ready for the contest at the end of the month?" Tom asked me after the ship was tucked in the trailer.

"I don't know," I said, shaking my head. "I haven't worked here that long, and Keith doesn't know if he'll be able to make it that weekend. No one's even explained to me how the contest works."

"We can talk about it tonight, at the Hoot Owl."

"I won't be there tonight. I have to get up early for work tomorrow, and I need to spend some time with Trevor. I feel bad about leaving him alone all weekend."

"Tom," said Katie, "why don't we have Ellen over for dinner one night this week? You could explain it to her then."

"How about it, Ellen? What's your schedule?"

"I don't have a schedule, exactly."

"How about Thursday?" Katie suggested. "Six-thirty okay?"

"That should be fine. Thanks very much."

"Why don't you give her directions while I pay my bill?" Tom said. He walked toward the office while Katie found a scrap of paper and drew me a map.

They lived in Kilmer, a suburb about halfway between Hardenbergh and Crosswind. I drove there on Thursday after checking on Trevor and changing out of my work clothes, which as usual had gotten full of toner. I left a little early to make sure I found their house while there was still some daylight. I'd never been to Kilmer before. I'd never had any reason to go there.

The drive was pleasant enough, once I got out of Hardenbergh's traffic. Katie's clear directions and map led me on a series of back roads. Just past the town of Kilmer, which was little more than a gas station and a Methodist church, I turned onto a one-way street bordered by huge stone pillars. They looked like old gateposts, and I later found out that's exactly what they were. The development Tom and Katie lived in, Kilmer Farm, had been a prosperous estate until the Depression. It was sold to one developer after another, but nothing much was done with the land until a few years ago, when the interstate was completed. Now the one-way street meandered in carefully designed curves past two-story, Federal-style houses on lots that must have been three or four acres each. Tom and Katie lived three-quarters of a mile in, on the right hand side. Their house was made of brick, with a big bay window in front and a two-car garage built into the side. Daffodils and hyacinths lined the brick walk that led in carefully designed curves to their double front doors. The doors had shiny brass kickplates on the bottom. I began to wish I had brought a bottle of wine or something.

Katie answered the door promptly. She wore pale green

slacks and a matching sweater, with a gold necklace and jade earrings. She was one of those women who always dress neatly — even the jeans she wore to Crosswind were pressed and creased. My own jeans were clean but certainly not ironed, and my blue flannel shirt was rumpled. My right elbow was beginning to poke through the sleeve.

"Hope I'm not too early," I said.

"Not at all, you're right on time. Come on in."

She held the door open while I stepped into the hall. I tried not to act as though I'd never been in a house like this, but it was hard to pull off with a big chandelier hanging over my head and a gleaming wooden staircase curving up to the left. The entrance hall was a full two stories high, and when I looked down I realized I was stepping on real ceramic floor tiles.

"I hope you don't mind eating in the kitchen," Katie said over her shoulder as she led the way.

"Not at all," I answered with relief. I glanced into the dining room as we walked by. The walls were papered in mauve. The hall light reflected off the dark polished wood of a huge china cabinet, in which crystal glasses sparkled as we walked by. The kitchen, in contrast, was blue and white, brightly lit, and as big as my whole apartment. To the side a glass-topped table was set for three, with blue-and-white checked place mats and white china bordered in royal blue. The walls were lined with white cabinets and a large island filled the center of the room. Half of the island was a butcher block, and the other half held six gas burners. I looked around for the rest of the stove and saw two ovens tucked among the wall cabinets. You could cook for the whole Repro department in this kitchen.

Katie motioned me to sit on a stool next to the butcher block. She poured a glass of white wine for me, then took a colander full of fresh asparagus out of the sink. She dumped the stems onto the butcher block and began to cut them into bite-size pieces.

"Will asparagus be okay with you or shall I make something else?" she asked.

"That's fine," I assured her, wondering to myself what fresh asparagus tasted like. I'd only had frozen, and never even made it now that I lived alone. I always bought store-brand bags of mixed veggies or peas, whatever was on sale. "Can I help with something?"

"There's nothing left to do but cut this up, but thanks for offering. Tom's running a little late tonight but he should be home any minute. It's nice to have the company."

I couldn't think of anything else to say, so I smiled and took a sip of wine. It wasn't from a cardboard box, I could tell that right away. "Mm — this is good. What is it?"

"Fumé blanc," she answered, making it sound very French. "So tell me about yourself."

"Um, what do you want to know?"

"Oh, anything. What do you do when you're not at the glid-erport?"

"I work, I take care of Trevor. Not much to tell."

"Trevor's your parakeet, right? He sounds cute. Where do you work?"

"V.D. I make copies."

She looked up at that. "You make copies? What else?"

"That's it."

"All day? Do you like doing that?"

I shrugged. "It pays the bills."

"What do you want to do?" she asked, emphasizing the want. I shrugged again.

"Have you ever thought of going to college?" she asked, scooping the asparagus into a pot.

I looked down at my wine glass. "I went to Hardenbergh. I graduated, actually."

"And?" she prompted.

"I was going on to Trenton State, but then my parents died and I couldn't. It happened last fall."

"Oh, Ellen, I'm so sorry. Here I am asking you twenty questions. I didn't mean to pry."

"That's okay. I don't mind — it's not so hard to talk about anymore. In a way, it's kind of nice to have somebody ask. I mean, it's really strange at Crosswind — everybody's there to have fun, and we all talk a lot about flying, but it seems really hard to get to know people. Do you know what I mean?"

"Do I ever! No one there talks about anything but flying,

which is understandable because it is an airport, after all, and for those of us who work the weekend is our only time for extended recreation. And so the conversation tends to be pretty one-track. Who wants to talk about work on the weekend?"

"Right."

"You have an advantage over me, though, Ellen. You fly."

"What difference does that make?"

She refilled our wine glasses before answering. "You fly. I don't. You know all the arcane secrets of the sky. You know the wonders of the universe, while I, poor mortal, am condemned to a life of ignorance and emotional poverty because I choose to stay on the ground. Isn't that how it goes?"

"Well..."

She laughed. "It's okay, you won't hurt my feelings. I live with a pilot, remember? He's taken me up, and I thought it was very nice, but if I never get to fly again I will still be content. I can live without it. Tom can't understand that, and neither can you. Am I right?"

I had to admit she was.

"So, when we go to Crosswind, all the pilots want to talk about is flying, and since I don't fly, I can't talk much about that, and since the pilots don't do much of anything else but fly, they have little else to talk about. And so the conversation lags. Then the pilots go fly, and when they come back they talk about their flights. And if the weather is bad, God forbid, they talk about other flights they've had, and how they wish they could go flying today, and so on and so on."

"Doesn't that bug you?"

"Surprisingly, it doesn't, because people who have a passionate interest in something become interesting themselves. Not that flying stories can't get boring, Lord knows they can, but I love seeing Tom so happy and so caught up by it all."

"You're the exception, not the rule."

"I know. I've never been much good at 'girl talk.' Besides, much of my happiness comes from Tom's happiness. And it's the same for him. He'll even go to the ballet with me, only partly because he owes me for all the weekends, but also because he likes to share my enjoyment of it."

"Do you dance?"

She smiled ruefully. "I used to. I had to give it up when I was thirteen and hurt my knee. I guess that's how I ended up teaching gym. I had to channel that energy somewhere."

I was startled by a sudden rumbling noise. "Garage door," Katie explained. "Tom's home." She lit the burner under the asparagus and opened the kitchen door.

"Hi, sweetie," she said as Tom bent down to give her a kiss.

He said hello as he strode into the room, looking even bigger than usual in a grey three-piece suit. He looked very nice in it, actually, but it seemed odd to think of this well-dressed man climbing into a glider. He must not have been comfortable, though, because in seconds he'd taken off his jacket, tie, and vest, and looked more like his airport self. Katie poured him a glass of wine and after a few sips he looked even more like his airport self.

"Smells good. What's cooking?"

"I'm steaming some asparagus with garlic and I'm about to grill the tuna, if you'll do the stove," Katie answered. I was trying to figure out how you grill a can of tuna while I watched Tom pull two burners off the stove and substitute a grill, almost like one you'd use outside. Katie brushed it with oil and placed three slabs of dark red fish on it. It took me a moment to realize that I was staring at tuna the way it looks before it gets stuffed into a can.

"Ellen and I were just discussing the idiosyncrasies of airport behavior," Katie explained.

"What do you mean?" asked Tom, looking genuinely puzzled.

"Oh, how no one talks about anything but flying, for example."

"Well, what else is there to talk about at an airport?" he asked, and I don't think he was entirely joking.

"That's what we mean," I said, "assuming you can get anyone to talk to you at all."

"Ah, you've run into the Code," Katie said.

"The Code?" Tom and I asked at the same time.

"Don't you remember, Tom, how it was when we first started going to Crosswind? When you took your first lessons? People were polite but distant — except for Marv of course, he's always a darling. Then you soloed, and they warmed up a bit, because you'd joined 'the club,' but it wasn't until you got your license that you really became a 'full member.' "

"Oh, it's not as bad as that," Tom protested.

"Ellen?"

"It's as bad as that," I said.

"It's not deliberate, Tom," Katie continued. "It's not even something most people are aware they're doing. But people who fly are treated differently from people who don't, and people who prove they take their flying seriously, by sticking around and soloing and getting the license, those are the real pilots, and until they are an airport can be a chilly kind of place, even Crosswind."

Katie was right. I hadn't been able to put my finger on it before, but there was something a little different about how I was treated on that first day when I took my first demo ride, and how I was treated now that I worked there and flew regularly. I began to wonder if my first solo wouldn't be a kind of initiation that wouldn't be completed until I had the license in my hand.

Dinner was simple and elegant and delicious. The tuna, grilled with nothing on it but salt and pepper and a sprinkle of lemon juice, had a delicate flavor unlike any I'd ever had from a can. Fresh asparagus turned out to be slightly crunchy and flavorful, with none of the bitterness I'd often tasted before. Served with freshly baked rolls and more fumé blanc, the meal was a welcome change from my usual fried chicken or hamburger.

After dinner Tom lit a fire in the family room, and we sat on the black leather couch to talk about the upcoming contest. When Katie came in with a tray of coffee and brownies — bought at her school's bake sale, she hastened to say, as though she had to apologize for serving something that wasn't made in her own kitchen — I slipped onto the floor, too paranoid about spilling something on the couch to eat on it.

Tom explained that the contest would be like any other day, just busier. Pilots would be coming to Crosswind from all over the state, and probably Pennsylvania and New York as well. They'd be given a course to follow on the morning of the contest, and would take aerial photographs of various landmarks along the way to prove they'd really flown the whole distance. Whoever got back in the fastest time would win. My job would be no different from any other weekend, just hook 'em up, run the wing, and do that over and over until all the pilots were in the air.

"Herb said that other towpilots would be coming, and we might have two or three tow planes here that weekend. Keith's going to be away at some air force recruitment thing, so I'll be by myself. What if I screw something up?"

"First of all, you won't be by yourself. Andy will help you, or Marv, and a lot of the pilots will have their own crew hook them up and run the wing, so it won't be too hectic for you. Just do it like you always do and you'll make out fine. Besides, the contest isn't until the end of the month, so you have time to get more practiced."

"Are you going to fly in the contest, Ellen?" asked Katie.

"Me? No way," I said. "How could I?"

"Maybe someone could take you in the 2-33," Tom said. "Ask Andy. They usually suspend training that day anyway, so it should be available. Maybe Andy would fly with you."

"Do you think she would?"

"Why not? It would be just as much fun for her. Can't hurt to ask, can it?"

He had a point. I decided to talk to her about it the next weekend. We all carried our cups and plates into the kitchen and I said good-bye, after refusing a second cup of coffee and more brownies and a glass of brandy and an invitation to stay and watch flying videos. I assured Tom and Katie that I really needed to get ready for work the next day and that I would come again for dinner someday soon.

On the ride home I reflected that I'd spent nearly four hours with the Bayards, yet I still knew next to nothing about them, except that they lived in a beautiful home, were gracious hosts, and usually got home from work by six. Once again, we'd talked almost exclusively about flying. Katie was right; it took a long time to get to know pilots, even away from the airport. I thought of how different tonight's dinner had been from dinner with the Pulaskis. Both had been among the nicest evenings I'd spent since my parents died. One started so comfortably but ended with my thoughts in turmoil; this one started a little awkwardly but ended up relaxing and pleasant. One so familiar, one so different. I loved pierogies and beer but had to admit a taste of fresh tuna and fumé blanc now and then would not be a bad deal. I wondered if Tom and Katie knew how fortunate they were, and I didn't mean about their big house and leather furniture. Would I ever love someone so much? Would anyone ever love me even half as much?

Just go with the flow, I told myself, as I parked the Beetle and shut off the engine. I got out and looked around at the shabby houses, so close they practically touched. This is the real world, for me at least, and for now. It had to get better, I thought, watching an elderly black man giving his old mutt one last walk before going to bed. He probably lived in this neighborhood and worked at V.D. all his life, like most of the people in Hardenbergh. Like you will, whispered a cold little voice in my head. Just like you.

Chapter
Nine

Trevor was singing in my dream; not chirping or muttering "Kevin Costner is a hunk," but singing like a canary. I listened, amazed at the new talent my bird displayed, until I realized he was singing not like a canary at all but more like a telephone, and then I woke up a bit more and understood that Trevor was asleep on his top perch but the telephone was singing on the wall. I shuffled over to the wall phone, an off-brand that had the wimpiest of electronic rings, even with the volume turned up high. Whatever happened to good old fashioned black rotary phones with the little bell inside that really rang, I wondered grumpily. I never wake well when I wake suddenly.

"Hello." I leaned against the wall.

"Ellen, it's Andy. How soon can you get here?"

"Andy? What time is it?" I asked, wondering what day it was as well.

"It's 5:30 in the morning. How soon can you get here?"

"Where are you?"

"At Crosswind, of course! Ellen, wake up, please."

"You want me to come out to the airport at 5:30 in the morning?"

"I'd like you to get here as soon as you can. Herb and I will have the 2-33 untied and ready. How soon? Can you make it by 6:30?"

I slid down the wall until my butt hit my heels, and rubbed my eyes. "It'll take me a couple minutes to get dressed. I can be there by seven, I guess. What's going on?"

"I'll explain when you get here, let's not waste time talking. Wear warm clothes — long johns if you have them — and be sure to bring a hat and gloves. It'll be cold up there. See you at seven."

She hung up, and I squatted there for a moment, trying to make sense of our conversation. It was 5:30 in the morning, I was going to the airport, I was apparently going flying, even though I normally flew at the end of the day, after I'd worked for the lesson. I had no idea what was going on.

I got ready as quickly as I could and by ten of six was in the car. Despite a quick but necessary detour to Dunkin' Donuts for a coffee, regular, and two honey dips, I made it to Crosswind in just under an hour.

I had to push the car door open against a strong northwest wind, confirmation that the airport had been aptly named. The sky was pale and almost colorless, half obscured by a great shelf of violet cloud. Andy was outside the office, looking up at the morning sky. Herb was gassing up the towplane. No one else was in sight.

She took one look at the paper cup in my hand and said, "You'd better make a pit stop before we take off." After I did we took the golf cart to the end of the runway, where 42H waited for us. Herb taxied past in the L-19.

"We have no line crew, so the left wing will be on the ground as we begin to roll," Andy cautioned. "Hold the stick to the right to pick it up as we gain speed, but remember there's a 20-knot crosswind from the northwest, so don't let the wing come up too far. Be sure to hold the wing low and use right rudder to hold her straight as we take off."

"Okay, I'll do that," I said, "but why am I flying now instead of at the end of the day?"

"This opportunity is too good to miss." She parked the golf cart next to the runway. Herb pulled into position and Andy hooked us up as soon as I climbed into the front seat.

"We get conditions like this often in early spring, but usually not this strong," she began explaining as we fastened our belts. "The wind is blowing over the Poconos like a stream flowing over a rock, and the 'waves' are reaching us even though we're miles away. We'll tow to 4,000 to see if we can 'catch' one of those waves. If we do, we can get higher than we ever will in a thermal around here. Be sure your shoulder straps are extra tight — it will get pretty bumpy up there."

I went over the takeoff checklist out loud. "Controls free and clear, straps tight, instruments set, canopy closed and latched, dive brakes closed and locked." I looked over at the wind sock, pointing stiffly across the runway. The wind was steady and strong. I'd have my hands full on this takeoff, and I was glad Andy was in the back seat.

I wiggled the rudder and Herb wiggled the L-19's rudder. Its engine roared and we began to roll, awkwardly, with the left wingtip scraping the ground. As we gained speed the wing came up, but I wasn't quick enough; a gust of wind lifted the left wing and the right wing swung down toward the ground. I could feel Andy's firm hand on the stick helping me as I struggled to control the glider. "Stay with it," she told me. "Don't give up now!" We hit a bump and the glider lurched into the air a second before the towplane lifted off. I fought to keep the wings level as we climbed in the turbulence behind the trees, whose tops swirled and bent with the wind. Once we were above the treetops the air became somewhat smoother, and we settled into a series of gentle climbs and descents as I tried, unsuccessfully, to maintain position behind the towplane.

"You're doing fine," Andy encouraged. "Try not to overcorrect."

The tow dragged on, uneventfully and interminably, it always seemed, the towplane never stationary, always slipping out of position no matter how much I willed it to stay in one place for at least a few seconds. I remembered how easy it had seemed on my first couple flights, when Andy flew the tow. She made it look as though the towplane were pasted onto the glider's canopy; I struggled just to keep it in sight. Tom Bayard's words of encouragement about my future towing prowess were no help to me today.

At three thousand feet above the ground, our normal release altitude, I was jolted from my seat so hard my feet jerked off the rudder pedals and my shoulders strained at the straps.

"Are you okay?" Andy asked.

"Yeah," I answered, a little shaken. The glider was pitching and rolling like ship in a storm.

"I'll take it for a minute while you tighten your shoulder

straps," she said. "Your head almost hit the canopy."

The glider settled down, but only a little, when Andy took over. I tightened the straps as much as I could, then looked up to see the towplane rolling to the left. It looked like it was standing on one wing. "Hang on!" Andy shouted, and then we rolled left, too. The horizon bisected the canopy before Andy was able to level off. I glanced at the instruments and saw the airspeed needle swing from eighty to forty and back. I clutched the seat cushion and wished fervently there were something more substantial to hold onto in a glider. Despite the temperature — and it must have been in the low forties at this altitude — beads of sweat gathered on my forehead.

As suddenly as the turbulence began it stopped, and Andy calmly said, "Okay, your turn again."

I took hold of the stick with one hand and wiped my forehead with the other.

"Let's release here," Andy told me.

I glanced to the right to check for traffic, then looked ahead to make sure the rope fell away after I pulled the release. I began a turn to the right but Andy stopped me. "Let me take it for a moment." She pulled the spoiler handle and dove toward the ground, losing two hundred feet of altitude before climbing again. As we leveled out she said, "Okay, you've got it. Turn toward our original heading and fly straight."

I followed her directions. The air around us, so violent a thousand feet below, was absolutely still. There was little noise from the wind; the silence was almost eerie.

I glanced down at the instrument panel. We were at 4,100 feet, flying at 50 miles an hour. The variometer showed us rising at 700 feet per minute.

"Andy, there's something wrong with the variometer."

"What's the matter?"

"It says we're climbing at seven hundred feet per minute."

"We are."

I looked at the altimeter. It read 4,200 feet and climbing. I looked at the ground to check for wind drift. Andy had me check for drift at the start of every flight, by looking straight down to see which way the ground appeared to slide by. That motion told me from which direction the wind aloft was blowing. Today the ground wasn't moving at all.

"Andy, we're not moving. We're hovering."

"Almost. We're flying just as fast as the wind is blowing, so we make no progress over the ground. We're in a mass of very calm air that just happens to be rising like a bat out of hell. Keep doing what you're doing for a while, and then we'll explore."

I wasn't doing much of anything, actually. I was sitting in a glider that wasn't moving. It was as though the air, which usually jostled and bumped the glider like a rude New Yorker, was curiously absent. The glider was rock steady, wings level, with not even the tiniest nudge on either wingtip.

We passed through 5,500 feet. The sun had risen, and long shadows stretched past barns and trees far below us. The temperature on the ground would already be climbing, and daffodils in farmyards would be raising their yellow heads. Penny was probably curled up in the sunny spot on the couch. It was becoming a warm spring day a mile below us. Up here, I pulled my wool hat and gloves from my pockets. "I know it's getting cold," Andy said, "but you need to open your air vent a little to prevent ice from forming on the canopy." I pulled the vent open a crack and lifted my scarf over my chin.

Andy explained that the big cloud above us was called a lennie, short for altocumulus lenticularis. It was a flattish cloud, lens-shaped in cross section, hence the name. It marked the top of a wave.

"That rough air we passed through on the way up is called the rotor," she told me. "It's an area of extreme turbulence under the wave. We try not to fly through it, for obvious reasons. But you can't always tell where it will be."

We continued to climb, through six, seven, then eight thousand feet. Andy didn't talk much, and neither did I. Our flight was as solemn as a church service, but more beautiful, and far more satisfying. We weren't flying through the air, we were part of it. From the ground we'd be a speck, no bigger than a gnat.

I looked out over miles of hills, able to see farther than I ever had before. The Delaware River shone deep blue as it wound past cliffs and wooded hills, one of its islands a yellow-green lozenge upstream of a small patch of rapids. The hills and valleys of Pennsylvania marched north to become the Poconos, the ski resort mountains that helped create this strange wave in the air. Puffs of condensation rose from a cooling tower before being sliced off by the wind I could no longer feel. It was magical.

I glanced at my watch. We'd been aloft less than twenty minutes! We climbed higher, still rock steady, pointed straight into the wind. I couldn't believe it when I saw the altimeter read 10,000 feet. "All right!" I heard Andy say, with excitement in her voice. "What do you think of that?"

I didn't know what to say. I had never experienced anything like this. To be so high, and so still, soaring like an eagle, seeing the morning light from nearly two miles up, the dazzling blue of the river, the deep emerald of a Christmas tree farm, the kelly green of new sod and the warm ochre of a newly harrowed field, looking down — down — at a flock of Canada geese; I took a deep breath of cold, clean air before answering, "It's what I've been looking for." I was happy, really, truly happy, for the first time in months. When I laughed out loud, Andy laughed with me, and gave my shoulder a squeeze.

I looked down at the instrument panel and my happiness disappeared in a hurry. "Andy, we lost it, we're in sink!"

"Shit," she said. It was the first time I'd heard her say that. "Push the stick forward, fly faster, let's get back in before we lose too much altitude."

I held my breath as we flew faster, seeming to make no progress over the ground. After what seemed like hours, but must have been only seconds, the variometer needle began to swing up. We had lost over five hundred feet. We stopped sightseeing and got back to work. Andy showed me how to explore the wave, zigzagging back and forth to see how wide it was, and to find the best lift. We hovered in the strongest lift, but by 11,000 feet could find nothing better than 500 feet per minute up, then 400. By 12,500 feet the lift had diminished to 300 feet per minute. The higher we climbed, the slower we climbed.

"Come on 13," Andy muttered. I tapped the instrument panel, and the altimeter needle jumped a hundred feet. A few minutes later we were at 13,000 feet, looking out at a flattened landscape of toy farms and miniature forests, with Philadelphia jutting over the horizon to the southwest like a tiny Emerald City, and the towers of the World Trade Center, two slim grey matchsticks, marking New York to the northeast.

"My God, Andy, it's better than sex," I told her, and she laughed but didn't disagree. I turned in my seat as much as I could to look at her. Tandem seating had its disadvantages; it was hard to share the experience without eye contact.

Andy looked happier than I'd ever seen her, and she was so cheerful that she'd laugh out loud just because it was a sunny day. That she enjoyed flying was apparent; that she loved it I didn't understand until today. Her eyes sparkled with satisfaction when she grinned at me and gave me a thumb's up. I grinned back, and realized how little I knew about this woman. I had been relieved at and grateful for her no-questions-asked friendliness, which was at once warm and superficial, depending only on one's desire to fly. Friendship was different; it depended only on one's desire to give. I had spent so many months ensconced in numbing solitude I wasn't sure I knew how to give anymore. I hoped I hadn't done such a good job of preventing myself from feeling that I wouldn't be able to anymore. I liked Andy, and this morning I realized how much I wanted to be her friend.

"I hate to break the spell," she said, "but without oxygen we shouldn't stay at this altitude very long, and we do have to get to work this morning. It's time to head back."

Reluctantly, we turned away from the lift and began our descent. Once we passed below 10,000 feet, Andy demonstrated wingovers, diving for speed and then climbing and turning hard, so that we were poised first on one wingtip and then the other. I lost track of up and down and laughed when I got dizzy. Then we leveled off and I practiced turns and stalls, making the glider fly slower and slower until there wasn't enough air flow over the wings to support them, and the glider's nose swung down below the horizon with a stomach-twisting motion that made me fear for my doughnuts and coffee. Much too soon, we were at pattern altitude, and Andy talked me through the only part of soaring I disliked, the landing. It was too much like waking up from a wonderful dream.

When we pushed the glider off the runway, Andy reached behind her seat and pulled out a small gray box. It was sort of egg-shaped, with a window in one end. She handed it to Herb, who looked at it and grunted. "Looks like a good trace," he said, after pushing his cigar stub to one side of his mouth. "Congratulations."

Andy smiled and gave me a hug. "Congratulations," she said. "We just broke the state altitude record for multiplace gliders."

"A record? We set a record?"

"You bet." She turned to Herb. "Let's get that trace off so Keith can use the barograph in the 1-26."

We hurried back to the office, where Herb opened up the barograph, which had been sealed shut with a wire. Inside was a metal drum, with a sheet of paper taped to it.

"The barograph records our altitude," Andy explained. "It scribes the paper with this stylus, and shows how high we've been. We need to submit this as proof of our altitude when we submit the paperwork for the record. See this little notch in the trace? That's when we got off tow — remember how I dove down and then pulled up? We had to do that to prove we were off tow. Herb is our observer, so I let him seal the barograph and open it up. Then he can be sure we didn't tamper with it."

We looked at the thin line that showed our progress up, then a small dip down at the moment when we lost our lift, then our climb to 13,000 feet and subsequent descent. It was odd to see a such an incredible experience reduced to a thin squiggly line.

We handed the barograph to Keith, who had just arrived and was impatient to try a wave flight in the 1-26. Herb put the precious trace in an envelope and locked it in the strong box, so that nothing would happen to it until he had time to complete the proper forms. He followed Keith out the door as Marv walked in with two grocery bags.

"Did you make it?" he asked.

"Sure did," said Andy.

Marv yelled and picked her up and swung her around twice before letting her go. "I knew you would. I knew you would. Gosh darn, and I had to go buy toilet paper instead of being here.

Congratulations, Ellen," he said, giving my hand a hard shake. "How high did you get?"

"13,000 feet," I answered, hardly believing it now that we were on the ground.

"My lord, you ladies didn't just break that record, you smashed it. When did you get off tow?"

"4,000."

"Herb hasn't calibrated the trace yet," Andy cautioned, "but I bet we got close to a 9,000 foot gain."

"That's two records," Marv said, beaming. "Your altitude and your gain. That deserves a party."

Andy laughed. "Let's wait till they're official." She looked out the window as a car pulled up. "There's my first student. C'mon, Ellen, it's business as usual for us."

All that day, part of me stayed at 13,000 feet. I felt like I'd been split in two: one of me was on the ground, greeting customers, running wings, noticing the fresh smell of mint crushed by my feet, admiring the violets scattered in the grass, but one of me was floating in the cold, clear air, looking out and down, fifty miles at a glance. I wondered how many Ellens there were — the peaceful Ellen who stood here, the happy one floating in the air, the dissatisfied one who wished she were still in college, the blank one who worked at V.D., the rootless one who would never know for sure who her father was, the empty one who was orphaned, whose emptiness was being filled in slowly by Trevor, and by Crosswind. How many other Ellens would there be, and would they ever come together?

Overnight the weather changed, and Sunday had no dawn, just a gradual lightening from black to grey. A solid mass of clouds hung low over Hardenbergh and I left the city gladly. The sky was no lighter at Crosswind but the open countryside made up for the oppressive sky. We all dawdled in the office. Herb filled out the paperwork for yesterday's record flight. Keith had not been able to climb as high, but his flight to 11,000 feet was the highest he'd been, and he was happy. After we finished the first pot of coffee, Marv and Herb went into the shop to work on the 2-33 that was in there. They hoped to have it finished and ready to fly in a couple of weeks. Andy was helping Keith study for his commercial pilot exam, so I took Penny for a walk in the woods across the runway. The damp ground smelled good, like a wet flowerpot, but wasn't so muddy that walking was difficult. Penny had fun chasing robins, so much shyer than city birds, and I had fun looking up the spring flora in a field guide. I liked the names of the wildflowers almost as much as the flowers themselves. Daisy-like blossoms of white bloodroot, and toothwort, clusters of four-petaled bells of the palest lilac, sprang up from a carpet of leaf litter and new green vines. Tiny clumps of violets were tucked among the tree roots, and the first Mayapples stood with their leaf umbrellas half folded. Silver dogwood buds stood fat on the tips of branches, and new beech leaves hung like copper against the matte sky.

Penny reached the creek before I did and startled me with a rare bark. I hurried down and saw her standing with her ears back, wagging the tip of her tail uncertainly. Six feet away from her stood a Canada goose, a big bird that looked enormous standing eye to eye with a golden retriever. Its wings were half spread and it hissed at Penny. I called her but when she took a step toward me the goose stepped between us to block her way. I sidled around it, keeping as far as I could. The big bird watched us both, hissing ominously and stretching its neck toward us. I had never seen a goose up close and personal but had no doubt its large bill would make a hell of a welt if it attacked. I came up to Penny slowly, ready to run into the woods if the goose came at us, and took hold of her collar. Penny seemed more curious than afraid, but she backed up when I tugged at her. We retreated up the path until the goose stopped hissing, then I circled back through the woods to get a better look at it. I thought it odd to find a solitary wild goose, especially one that didn't seem sick or injured. I peeked at it from behind a tree and was surprised to find it looking me in the eye. So much for sneaking up on it. It hadn't moved, but had folded its wings and was quiet. I looked all around it, at the stream and opposite bank. I saw nothing but the creek and the grassy bank beyond, studded with violets and skunk cabbage and one brown rock with a small snake draped over it. Then I gasped as I realized that the snake was really the neck of a goose, and the rock was the goose's body. It lay perfectly still, head low, looking right at me and Penny. We sat quietly, and in a few minutes the goose on our side of the creek stepped slowly into the water. It swam across and stepped out, glared in our direction, and then pecked at the grass. Its mate lifted her head, and then reached down to rearrange the nest of twigs beneath her. I watched them for a few minutes, then gave Penny's collar a gentle tug. "Let's leave them alone," I whispered, and we crept away, but both geese saw us move, and they watched us go.

At lunch I told Marv about the goose nest.

"Oh, that's Fred and Ethel," he said. "They've come back every spring that we've been here. They usually have four or five little goslings, hang around for a few weeks, and then disappear just about the time the little ones get big and ugly."

"You wouldn't believe it," said Andy. "They start out so cute, little balls of gold fluff, but in a few weeks their feet are too big and they've lost their down and they turn the color of dirty dishwater."

"We'll have to keep Penny up here for a few weeks," Herb told everyone. "Fred just gets meaner every day until those eggs hatch. Don't want Penny getting bitten, or smacked with those big wings."

"Well," said Marv, "If you're done, Herb, I suggest we get back to the shop and take care of our own bird."

They stood up, and Keith did, too. "Need another pair of hands?" asked Andy.

"Nope," answered Herb. "Got enough as it is."

"It feels like Thanksgiving dinner," I told Andy. "The menfolks go watch football and leave the womenfolks in the kitchen."

She chuckled. "They're not being sexist. Too many helpers get in the way. You'll get your turn, believe me. Then you get to hear Herb's real conversational gifts. He goes 'hmmm' just like a doctor, and says words of wisdom like 'hold this' or 'god damn it, I said phillips head'."

I laughed. "I can hardly wait."

"Well, Ellen, it's pretty obvious we're not going to fly today, so how about we start ground school?"

We cleared the table, and began talking about glider aerodynamics, turns, and stalls. Andy had a way of explaining things that made them easy to understand, and what I'd had trouble comprehending in a textbook was clear when she explained it to me. After an hour and a half she said "That's enough for one day. Why don't we go visit Patti and her baby birds?" I had been looking forward to going there for weeks but had not had the time. We poked our heads in the shop to say where we'd be; Keith said he'd listen for the phone. I didn't think Herb or Marv even heard us. Andy drove her big Suburban and parked behind the Hoot Owl.

The yard behind the bar was filled with large wood and wire cages about seven feet tall and just as wide. There must have been a half dozen, separated by gravel paths. On the back of the Hoot Owl building was a door painted with the silhouette of a bird and the sign "The Owl Center." Andy knocked on it and waited. A moment later a disheveled Patti opened the door and welcomed us in.

"You're just in time for the next feeding," she told us. "My volunteer helper is late today and Pete had to open up."

"I thought you looked tired," Andy said.

"This is our busy time of year," Patti explained to me. "Everyone finds baby birds and brings them over. I wish they wouldn't, because usually the parents are around and everything is fine, but it's hard to tell good-hearted people that sometimes doing nothing is best. And of course, there are genuine orphans — cat got the parents, or they were hit by a car — so we take them all in. But baby birds are always hungry, and we have to feed them every half hour, around the clock, until until they're old enough to fend for themselves. And of course, the big birds outside need attention, too, but not as much as these little ones."

She led us into a room whose back wall was lined with cages, not metal ones with a small door like Trevor's, but wooden crates whose front wall was made of mesh with a wooden frame. Some of the cages had glowing light bulbs in them. Each one contained a collection of tiny, chirping baby birds, some naked, some feathered. She opened one cage and took out a half-pound margarine tub lined with a scrap of terry cloth. Inside, four bright yellow beaks gaped at us. Each beak had a tiny bird attached to it.

"They're all mouth," I said.

"You're right about that," said Patti. "Here's how we feed them: put a little bit of this food on the tip of a teaspoon handle, then give it to them like so." She brought the spoon handle toward the cup, and a little bird gulped at the food.

"What is that stuff?" I asked, eyeing the brown glop that wasn't at all appetizing from my point of view.

"Mostly puppy food, with some egg and vitamins and other stuff. It's for the songbirds. Young hawks and owls get ground quail."

She put the birds back in the cage and brought out another batch, which she handed to me. I looked down at two birds, older than the first group, already feathered in grey fluff, each no bigger than a plum. They were even cuter than Trevor.

"They're mockingbirds. A cat got the mother," she explained, handing another cup of birds to Andy.

"How awful," I said.

"Why?" she asked, passing out spoons. "The cat was just obeying its instincts. It's nature's way."

"Then why go to all this trouble?" Andy asked.

"It's just the way things ended up. We started with owls, trying to undo some of the damage people have done to them, and then we got hawks, for the same reasons, and pretty soon someone knocked on the door with a nest of sparrows. Between pesticides and other pollutants and loss of habitat, we're losing birds right and left, so I figure anything we can do here to help them out is worth it." She put her cup of birds back and got another. She was a lot quicker at this than either Andy or I. "At least, that's how I feel in the fall and winter. This time of year I'm not so sure!"

For the next two hours we had our hands full, literally, feeding the assortment of finches, robins, and sparrows. Patti also had one blue jay, a starling, and a crow.

"I'm surprised you'd save a starling," said Andy.

"Hey, we can't be choosy here. If a good samaritan comes in with a bird and a donation, I'm not going to turn either one away. And once it's here, I have to feed it, even if it is a starling."

"How long do you keep up this nursery?" I asked.

"All spring and summer, because birds raise several broods a year, but this is the busiest time."

When her helper finally arrived, Patti took a break and led us out back. "Our eagle is in this first enclosure. He's almost healed, and we plan to release him next weekend." The eagle had one cage all to himself. He stood on a branch that was stuck across one corner, gripping the branch with powerful looking toes that ended in sharp, curved talons. "Those talons are two and a half inches long," Patti explained. He was a beautiful soft brown color, with gold highlights on his head. He looked at us steadily, with intense eyes. I wondered how high he had flown.

"Over here are our owls," said Patti, "and here are a red-tailed hawk, a broad-winged, and a Cooper's. The other cages hold adult songbirds, pigeons and doves, and ducks."

"And you have all this because of Butch?" I asked, referring to the owl behind the bar.

"He's what got all this started," she said. "I was so upset when he was hit by a car — it's just human stupidity and carelessness that gets them most of the time — and so glad I could help him, that I decided to learn more about bird rehabilitation. I took some courses, did a little volunteer field work, got a permit, and started. At first all we had was the back room, where the nursery cages are now, but we outgrew that and the local Elks club made these outside enclosures for us."

"Where did you get the nursery cages from?" I asked.

"I made them myself one winter."

"You made them?" Patti had handled the infant birds with such tenderness I found it hard to picture her wielding a hammer and saw.

"Oh, you'd be surprised what I can do with a good table saw and a staple gun."

"It's a good thing, too," Andy added. "Pete's downright dangerous with hand tools."

Patti laughed. "He's not exactly a jack of all trades, but he makes great lasagne."

She reached up on one of the cages to bend a piece of loose wire out of the way. Her deft fingers were short and straight, the nails trimmed all the way down and the knuckles a little reddened. Capable hands, ready for anything. I shook my head in wonder that she would do all this — even build some of it — and then wait tables at night.

"And you don't get paid for any of this?" I asked.

"The pay comes when we release a bird, and see it fly away healthy and free. No, this is strictly volunteer. I spend about a quarter of my time fundraising, speaking at dinners and luncheons, going to schools. We just about break even."

"Well, ladies, I have to get back to the nest pretty soon. Can I buy you a drink before the next round of feedings?"

We spent the rest of the afternoon feeding birds. Pete fed us chili, but wouldn't let us pay for it because we were helping Patti. I stayed later than I normally would on a Sunday, because Patti so obviously needed a hand, and before I left I offered to drive out any evening she was stuck for help.

When I got home I saw that Latanya's lights were on. I knocked on her door on my way upstairs. I hardly saw her anymore, now that I was working weekends. She rarely came home week nights earlier than nine or ten at night. She spent most weekends in Pennsylvania, with her boyfriend William, and usually didn't return until Monday morning.

She asked who it was before opening the door, and when she did I could see she had been crying. Even in despair she looked stylish. Her robe was patterned with tiger stripes, and she wore black pajamas. Although dressed for bed she hadn't taken out her gold hoop earrings.

"Latanya? Can I come in? Is something wrong?"

"Sure, come in," she said quietly. I sat down at the kitchen table.

"What happened?"

"William and I broke up this afternoon. I won't be seeing him again."

"Oh, Latanya, I'm sorry. Why?"

"It's the same old thing. Every weekend we fight about it. He wants me to move to Pennsylvania. Just pack up everything, transfer in the middle of the semester, and move myself to Pennsylvania. Now why should I do that?"

"Well, if you care about him, don't you want to be with him

more?"

"Of course I care about him, but I am not gonna give up my career for any man. I'm getting this associate degree in design and then I'm going to New York. New York is where it's at, and Pennsylvania is surely where it ain't. They don't make clothes in Pennsylvania. They don't make anything up there except steel and crayons."

"Why can't you keep seeing him on weekends?"

"Because he wants more than that. He wants to settle down. He hated New York when we went there and refuses to come see me because he has no car, so he wants me to move to where he is so he can keep playing basketball, then we're supposed to get married. He has it all planned. When I'm his wife I won't need a career. I'll have him. Ha! He's so small-town."

She sat down gracefully and tapped her long fingernails on the table.

"Do you know he had all this planned out, and he never asked me? Never asked what did I want, what were my plans. And do you know what he wants to be when he gets out of college? An actuary. Can you see me living the rest of my life with an actuary?"

"Frankly, no. But how did you get so involved when you two are so different?"

"Who talks career plans in bed? It's just — he has these gorgeous shoulders, from playing all that basketball, and for a big tall man he has got some moves. I thought we'd have a good time, that's all, and when I graduated I was gonna say thanks, it was fun, honey, and that was supposed to be that."

"Do you love him?"

She looked at me with disgust.

"Haven't you heard a word I've said? I like him, I like his body, and that's all."

"Then why are you so upset about breaking up?"

"Because," she said, and her eyes filled with tears. "I was going to break up with him, not the other way around."

"Ohhh," I said, finally understanding the problem. "You've never had this happen before, have you? You've always been the one to break it off. Poor Latanya."

I really did feel sorry for her, even though I struggled to keep from smiling. Nothing hurts worse than pride, and rejection sucks, especially when someone beats you to the punch.

"Look," I said, "You need to drown your sorrows. Do you have anything to drink in this apartment?"

"Only Diet Pepsi," she said.

"That'll do," I said. "Pour some out and let's talk girl talk."

She opened a can of soda and filled two wine glasses. We clinked them together and then drank.

"So tell me the truth," I said. "Was he really that good in bed?"

I think women have a special knack for acting silly when they aren't even drunk. Maybe it's left over from the giggle fits we had as twelve year olds, but when you're in the right frame of mind it doesn't take much beyond soda fizz up your nose to bring on the mood. A man watching us would have sworn we were loaded, but we sat in Latanya's kitchen for hours, talking about men and periods and condom brands and how we wet our pants when we were six. By the time I walked upstairs she was feeling a lot better, and had even promised to come with me to Crosswind one day.

Chapter
Ten

Latanya met me at Crosswind on the last Saturday in April, the first day of our weekend contest. She arrived around noon, just before we launched the sailplanes. The runway gleamed with twenty fiberglass ships, so white you needed sunglasses to look at them, with a cluster of colorfully painted 1-26s behind them.

I was hooking up Cheap Whiskey when Latanya strolled by. She wore a pale peach cotton sweater that draped to mid-thigh, skintight white knit pants, and matching peach high-heeled sandals. Her cornrowed hair, cafe-au-lait skin, and graceful carriage — not to mention one-inch polished nails and several pounds of gold jewelry, hardly standard gliderport accoutrements — made even die-hard competitors pause as she glided past. More than one male jaw stood open in her wake.

I was dressed in a faded blue Hardenbergh College T-shirt, and jeans that were muddy at the knees. My feet were encased in rubber shoes and my hair, clean at six o'clock this morning, was matted with perspiration and escaping asymmetrically from the plain rubber band that tried to hold it back. My hands were grimy from putting oil in the towplane and my nails were chipped and uneven.

After Tom took off I flagged Latanya down. I walked up to her half reluctantly, knowing how much I'd suffer in contrast.

"Hi, glad you made it," I said, prepared for her critical designer's eye. I should have known better — my appearance would be low on her list of priorities.

"Why didn't you tell me there were so many men at this place?" she demanded in greeting. "And all the time I thought you were living like a nun."

"Well, there usually aren't, and I pretty much am," I

answered. "I've never seen half of these guys; the rest come out once in a while, put their sailplanes together, and go. I'm just a line 'boy' to them. Besides, a lot of them are married."

"Oh, there's that Catholic training again," she said. "They might not think of you as a line boy — whatever that is — if you wore a tank top and shorts."

"Then I'd have mud on my knees instead of my jeans. How attractive. Let me tell you what's going on. We just launched Tom Bayard, who's our 'thermal sniffer.' He's gone up to see if there's enough lift to start the contest. If he radios that conditions are good, then Andy and I will be real busy for about an hour getting all these sailplanes in the air. Once they're up, they're going on a 125-mile round trip, and whoever gets back fastest wins.

"I'm afraid it's not very exciting to watch. They'll be out of sight most of the afternoon, and some of them may not even make it back. But we'll have a picnic tonight, and you're welcome to stay for that."

"So what can I do in the meantime, if all these fine gentlemen will be out of reach?"

I eyed her outfit doubtfully. "Not a heck of a lot in those shoes, but they can always use an extra pair of eyes at the start gate. That's over there." I pointed to a cluster of lawn chairs. "The starter watches each sailplane glide overhead, and takes down the time as each one passes the start line. Sometimes the sailplanes come across in a cluster, and you can look through binoculars and help keep track of who goes by when."

"I think I can handle that. Lead the way."

I did, with skepticism, since the great outdoors was not Latanya's normal venue, but as I made introductions I could see her turn on the charm, and had no doubt that she would be queen of the gliderport for the rest of the day. When I returned to the launch line Marv was wiping off the nicest lawn chair for her.

It wasn't long before Tom radioed that not only was there lift, but he could see warm front clouds heading our way, and if we wanted to have a contest we had better get going before the clouds moved overhead. His news was unwelcome but not unexpected; the forecast for tomorrow predicted rain. Herb taxied the towplane into position and Andy and I went to work, one of us hooking up, the other running the wing. As Herb had predicted, a club in Pennsylvania had loaned us another towplane and pilot, so we were able to send two aircraft up quickly, and while they were on tow could get the next two ready. In an hour the sky over the airport was filled with aircraft, circling like a gaggle of sea-gulls as they waited for the starter's announcement to begin.

When everyone else was launched, Andy and I had our turn. Andy had been immediately enthusiastic when I asked her if we could fly together this weekend. Now she seemed excited and calm at the same time. I had butterflies. We had no hope of win-ning, and probably would not even finish the sixty-mile course the lower-performing gliders were to fly, but it would be my first flight away from Crosswind. It amazed me even to think of set-ting out on a cross-country flight, with nothing to carry us but skill and luck.

"This will be a real treat," Andy told me as we waited to take off. "I haven't flown away from the airport in years."

"Why not?" I asked.

"Too busy instructing, I guess. Let's go over the chart and review our course one more time."

I looked at the chart, a jumble of symbols showing airports and microwave towers, power lines and roads. Andy would nav-igate while I flew, but she wanted me to have a copy of the chart to follow. Somehow, I didn't think I'd have time to look at it.

I was right. Contest rules required us to release a thousand feet lower than we normally did, and we had to struggle to gain enough altitude to set off on course. By the time we did I was sweating and exhausted.

"We're having fun, are we?" I asked.

"I am," Andy replied, sounding chipper.

I concentrated on my flying, and was shocked a half hour later to look back toward Crosswind and see it far out of reach. The terrain below us was hilly and wooded, with no place to land. I couldn't see any other aircraft; all of the contest ships were far ahead of us. We were alone and far from home. I wasn't sure I liked it.

We struggled on, circling in any lift we could find. The few wisps of cumulus clouds that hung in the sky at noon began to dissipate as a layer of milky cirrus blanketed the sky. The warm front, and its bad weather, was approaching sooner than we had hoped.

"Andy," I said, watching the altimeter needle drift counter-clockwise. "What do we do now?"

"We land," she said, cheerfully. "There's a private strip five miles ahead."

"Can we make it that far?"

"What do you think?" she asked, ever the instructor.

I tried to remember what she had told me about our rate of descent, and tried to work out the math in my head. Two hundred feet a minute down at fifty-two miles per hour, five miles was how many feet? Plus wind speed — or was it minus wind speed? I groaned.

"Can you see this private strip?" I asked her. All I could see were fields and forests.

"It's right off our nose," she answered, and began to hum the theme from Star Wars.

I peered ahead. All I could see were fields and forests.

We were losing altitude steadily. I tapped the instrument panel. The altimeter dropped another hundred feet.

"Andy," I said in what I hoped was a reasonable tone of voice. "We're not going to make it."

"Then speed up," she said, and continued humming.

I pushed the stick forward and our speed rose to sixty.

"Are you sure we're going to make it?" I asked.

"I'm sure," she answered, and continued humming.

"We're not going to make it," I said. A patch of woods lay between us and the next cluster of fields.

"It's just on the other side of the woods," Andy told me. "There's a house and a hangar at one end."

I finally saw the strip, and my heart tried to climb up my esophagus. The strip was cut out of the woods. It didn't look wide enough for a sailplane to land in. I wiped my hands on my jeans, first the right hand, then the left.

"I'd speed up a little if I were you," Andy said calmly. "We're in sink."

I pushed the stick again and listened to the air whistle by.

A moment later Andy said, "I'll take it from here," and I gave up the controls with relief, glad to let her fly the landing pattern. We were much lower than we usually were, and I couldn't look at anything but the treetops rushing under us. I was sure we'd hit them as we turned onto our final approach, but we didn't, and Andy brought the glider to a smooth landing.

When we climbed out of the sailplane I looked past the wingtips. We had only five feet of clearance on each side.

"How did you do that?" I asked in awe.

"Oh, I've been in this field once or twice," she said matter-of-factly. "Let's see if anyone's home."

They weren't, and we had to walk nearly a mile before we found a house where we could call Crosswind. We met a sweet old lady who was delighted to have us use her phone. She gave us a drink of cold well water and the chance to use her bathroom, then introduced us to her chickens and her goats. Andy invited her for a glider ride before we left.

We walked back to the private strip to wait for Herb, who would land there with a tow rope to bring us home. On the way back Andy told stories of some of her other cross country flights.

"One time I landed at a farm where they were having a family reunion," she told me. "I had a wonderful time. It was hours before my crew came. The family had barbecued a whole side of beef, and had so many pies for dessert. They've invited me to every reunion since. One time I landed in a field that had been freshly manured. I won't ever do that again! But the best has to be the time I landed next to a nudist colony. They invited me to use their hot tub."

"Did you?"

"When in Rome..."

"Oh, no, Andy!"

"I have a picture of three of them holding the wing when we took the glider apart. Bare arms and chests above it, bare legs below it. I wish I had taken a shot from the rear!"

We walked in silence for a moment.

"I had no idea you'd done so much," I said. "Why did you stop?"

"Oh, one thing leads to another," she said evasively.

"Instructing takes all my time now. And speaking of which, did I tell you we're thinking of hiring another instructor?"

"No, you didn't."

"The other 2-33 will be finished soon, and we usually get busy in the summer, so we hope to have someone by next month."

We were back at the private strip, and Andy checked the house and hangar one more time to see if the owners had arrived. They hadn't, so we left a note tucked in the screen door of the house and walked back to the glider.

"Could Marv do any instructing?" I asked.

"No. He has the personality for it but poor Marv can't fly. He gets so airsick he's miserable; and when he takes medication to prevent it he falls right to sleep. It's a shame. He loves airplanes so."

"I didn't realize. I just assumed he flew."

"That's because he has aviation in his blood. Their father had been a barnstormer and airmail pilot in the thirties. He met their mother at an air show — she was a wingwalker for another pilot — and bought an airport when she got pregnant with Herb. Their dad trained pilots during World War II, and kept the airport running until the late sixties, until the developers and politicians put the pressure on. He sold the field — I think it's an industrial park now — and they moved to Florida, where he bought another airport. Herb and Marv took over after he died, but they never cared for the climate, and moved back up here eight years ago."

Just then we heard the sound of an engine. Herb came over the treetops, low, and passed over the runway before pulling up into a landing pattern. He cut the power, slipped down onto the field, and parked. We walked over to him.

"May have a hard time clearing those trees," he said, pointing at them with his cigar.

"Let's push the glider as far back as we can," Andy told him. "Then why don't you take Ellen back in the towplane, and come back for me. Not that you weigh a lot, Ellen, but the lighter we are the better chance we'll have for a successful takeoff."

"Maybe we should drive up with the trailer," I suggested.

Herb shook his head. "Should be okay with only one of you

in the glider."

We pushed the 2-33 to the end of the runway, under the shade of the big maple trees. Then Herb climbed in the front seat of the L-19 and motioned me to climb in the seat behind him. I got in awkwardly and buckled the seat belt as he started the engine. I had never been in the L-19 before. It was not luxuriously appointed. The walls were plain metal, painted matte grey, and the seats were black plastic. It smelled of gasoline and hot oil. It was so noisy there was no possibility of conversation, even if Herb had been the talkative type. The airplane accelerated quickly and climbed at a breathtaking angle. I peered out the windows and enjoyed the ride back, which took far less time than the trip out.

When we landed, Herb kept the motor idling and motioned me to get out. I jumped down and ran to get out of the prop wash. When I was clear he taxied away quickly.

I walked up to the cluster of lawn chairs in front of the office. Latanya was still there, sipping a diet soda, in a group of pilot's wives and girlfriends, plus a few chagrined pilots who had not managed to get away from Crosswind. The pilots were drinking beer, talking quietly so they could listen for any radio communications that might indicate someone had landed. Some of the women were chatting about the price of children's clothing. A few were crocheting or doing needlepoint; the younger ones were trying to get a tan. I wondered how they'd been coping with Latanya.

"Hi, how was your flight?" Katie asked with a smile, as she handed me a soda.

"Fun, I guess, although it seemed like a lot of work to me. It must be a lot easier for someone like Tom."

"Oh, he works just as hard as you did, believe me. I sure don't see the attraction. He was nervous all morning, and he's probably out there now, low and mad at himself and sweating, and if he lands out he'll be in a bad mood all night. But if he makes it around, he'll be like a kid on Christmas morning. Then we'll do it all over again the next time."

I looked over at Latanya, who appeared to be getting a lesson in radio operations from Charles St. John, one of the few black pilots who flew with us. She didn't seem to miss me so I sat down next to Katie.

"So, is this any more exciting than our usual weekends?" I asked her.

"Believe it or not, it's very relaxing, and I enjoy the company."

"Really? I didn't think you were the needlework type."

"No, but neither is your friend Latanya, and she seems to be having a good time."

"I was afraid she might not get along with the ladies here."

"Mmm...a few of them were looking daggers at her at first, but she's so charming you can't help but like her."

"She certainly has a way with people," I agreed, then sighed. "If only I could fit into pants like that!"

Katie smiled. "Keep working here and you'll have no problem."

"What do you mean?"

"I'll bet you've lost five pounds since you've been coming here. You have color in your cheeks and you look full of energy. This place is good for you."

Before I had a chance to reply Marv came over, looking worried.

"Where's Andy? I didn't see you land."

"Herb went back to get her. They thought the takeoff would be safer with just Andy in the 2-33. They should be back soon."

"We should have brought the trailer to get you. That's a short, narrow strip you two landed in. If she can't get out, either she or Herb could end up in the trees."

"Don't worry, Marv," I said. "They were pretty confident they'd have no problems."

"Just the same, I'll be over by the radio in case they call." He walked off, still concerned.

"Poor Marv," Katie whispered. "He's got it bad."

"What do you mean?" I whispered back.

"Andy — he's got it bad for her."

"Andy? Marv? Are you kidding?"

"Ellen, open your eyes. The man's in love."

I gaped at Marv. He stood shading his eyes, looking up for

Andy and Herb. "There they are!" he exclaimed. I looked up just as Andy released the rope. A few moments later she landed, while Herb circled the field to let her land first. Marv walked back to the office grinning. Maybe Katie was right.

Later that afternoon Tom returned triumphantly. Not only did he make it all the way around the course, he finished first and won the day. Several of the pilots landed out and soon a caravan of trailers went out to retrieve them. Andy and I put the 2-33 away and Marv started the barbecue grill. We picnicked until the first raindrops fell.

By the time I got home the rain was coming down steadily, and I had no doubt that tomorrow would be dismal. Latanya came home a good hour after I did and knocked on my door. I put Trevor back in his cage before I let her in. He hung upside down from his swing and beat his wings, screaming at me, but I wanted him confined when I opened the door.

"Come on in," I said. She walked in barefoot, holding her sandals in one hand. Her white pants were still spotless.

"Thanks for coming out," I told her. "Did you have an okay time?"

"More than okay," she replied with a smile. "Charles, the tall brother with pretty white sailplane and the red Porsche, lives in New York and tomorrow — assuming it rains and I'm sorry but I hope it pours — we're going to the Guggenheim. He's picking me up here on his way home. He's an architect. He's twenty-nine."

She hugged me. "You work in a paradise, girl. Take my advice and take your pick. Goodnight, Ellen. Goodnight, Trevor."

Trevor wolf-whistled.

Latanya must have been very happy that Sunday because it rained all day. In the morning I went with Marv to the A&P. Even rain, I noticed, and its lack of revenue, couldn't put him in a gloomy mood for long. He put a tape of "La Boheme" in the cassette deck and sang along in a husky voice as he drove. I looked over at him. More than ever he reminded me of Santa

Claus. He was a big man, in a way that had once been muscular but was aging roundly, complete with beer gut straining the buttons of his flannel shirt. His full beard, even curlier from the humidity, blanketed his chest, and his brown eyes glimmered with good humor.

He pulled the pickup into a parking space and turned the engine off. He stretched after he got out of the cab, and reached for the nearest shopping cart. The clerk at the express register looked up and smiled as we walked in. She was a middle-aged woman with graying hair done in the short, sprayed frizz favored by her generation. Marv chatted with her while I tried not to fidget. To me, a grocery store was a place to get in and out of as quickly as possible. Marv made it an experience to relish. He spent 10 minutes in the produce section, choosing California strawberries one by one, checking the grapefruit for spots, "tsk-tsking" over the hard, pale pink fruits the management called tomatoes. "We'll plant some outside the office and have real tomatoes all summer," he told me.

Our progress up each aisle was slow. Marv seemed to know every housewife in Jennytown, and wouldn't pass a fellow shopper without at the least a polite hello, and more usually an update on the kids, the dog, and the car. He picked up a box of oreos — "to cheer us up this afternoon"— and flirted with the girl behind the deli counter as they discussed the merits of imported, low-salt, black forest, and store-baked hams, which she cut just as thin as he wanted. The only thing Marv did quickly was walk past the lobster tank. "I feel sorry for the poor creatures," he said, "even if they have no brains to speak of."

We made a special stop in the pet food aisle to buy Penny a box of dog treats. I picked up a new cuttlebone for Trevor.

Marv picked the slowest checkout line — I'd swear he did it deliberately — and put on his reading glasses to browse the tabloids. He listened avidly to the checker, who was a real Elvis fan and believed the headlines that he had been found alive and well in a drug rehabilitation clinic in Little Rock. Marv started humming "Love Me Tender" as he bagged celery, carrots, and soup bones, whole wheat flour and yeast, Penny's dog biscuits, laundry soap, brown shoelaces, the package of black forest ham, the berries and grapefruit, a copy of *Popular Mechanics*, and Trevor's cuttlebone.

I thought of the huge Pathmark in Hardenbergh, where I usually shopped. It was always crowded with harried-looking yuppies who read grocery lists and used pocket calculators. People shoved your cart aside without saying "excuse me" and the checkers rushed you through without even saying hello. Here, the checker smiled as she handed Marv his change, thanked him for bagging, and laughed when he suggested she come out for a glider ride.

We left the store smiling in spite of the rain, played Trivial Pursuit for the rest of the morning, and spent the wet afternoon in the dry sanctuary of the Hoot Owl.

When I got home I had to park a block away because of all the police cars in front of my building.

"What happened?" I asked the landlady, Mrs. Gadowski, who was standing outside under a black umbrella.

"It's him, the weird one downstairs. They arrested him a few minutes ago and took him away. Now they're searching his apartment, and making a mess, not that it was clean before — you should see the kitchen — but they're really making a mess, and they won't let me in." Indeed, two city policemen were standing at the foot of the porch steps, blocking our way.

"Officer," I said, "I just want to get upstairs to my own apartment."

He looked at Mrs. Gadowski. "She live here?"

"Yes, yes, what are they doing in there?"

He sighed. "Standard procedure, ma'am. You'll be allowed in shortly. Miss, I'd like to get a statement from you. Come up on the porch."

I followed him up the stairs, as relieved as he to get away from Mrs. Gadowski, who could talk longer and say less than anyone I'd ever met. The policeman took a notebook and pen out of his pocket.

"Name?"

"Ellen Horvath."

"Which apartment do you live in?"

"C, on the third floor."

"How long have you lived there?"

"Six months."

"You live alone?"

"No." I paused. "I have a parakeet named Trevor."

He crossed something out. "How well do you know Mr. Pilecki?"

"Not at all, really. We pass in the hall once in a while and say hello, that's all. He works nights."

"All right, miss, that will be all for now. You can go upstairs."

"What's all this about?"

"I'm not at liberty to say, miss."

Sunday night's mystery was Monday night's front-page headlines. My downstairs neighbor, Stanislaus Pilecki, whose first name I hadn't even known, was arrested for computer crime. He'd programmed some sort of computerized "virus" that had bollixed up computers at Hardenbergh College, V. D., and hundreds of other locations. The Wraith was in jail! From the looks of things, he was going to be there for quite a while.

Latanya and I were interviewed by Eyewitness News, and when the Pulaskis saw the broadcast they invited me to dinner again to hear the details. I had no details other than what I'd read in the newspaper, which they had read, too, but they were thrilled to know someone who had actually been on TV. I was not thrilled at all, especially when Personnel sent for me to see if I knew more about my neighbor than I was telling anyone. The next day I was transferred out of Repro — where it was possible I might see confidential documents — into Support Services for the Advertising department. After six months of imprisonment in the copying cubicle, I was given the freedom of a desk in the department reception area, where I tidied magazines, answered the phones, distributed messages and mail, and did very light typing. All this and a pay raise, too. It's an ill wind indeed, I thought, and hoped the Wraith wasn't having too bad a time in the hoosegow.

Still it rained. Each day I'd wake up hearing the gurgle of rainwater down the drainpipes. By Saturday the dampness had penetrated inside. My sheets felt wet, towels refused to dry, the wall calendar began to curl at the corners. I drove out to Crosswind, where everyone sat around the office in a bad mood. Even Marv was subdued by the continued bad weather.

"It's supposed to rain tomorrow, too," muttered Keith.

"Sounds like a good day to go to the movies," Marv said. "We can't paint the 2-33 in this weather."

"We could go help Patti," Andy suggested. "She's up to her armpits in fledglings."

"I'm going to give the towplane an oil change," Herb said without enthusiasm.

Andy and I went to the Hoot Owl to help Patti, and stayed for lunch. When we got back to Crosswind Tom and Katie were outside the office, dressed in matching yellow slickers. Their trailer was hooked up to their car.

"We can't stand the rain anymore, so we're taking the Discus to drier parts," Tom explained.

"He's got contest fever," said Katie. "There's a regional competition in Texas that he's going to enter. Wish us luck."

"Texas? Do you want luck for the contest or the drive down?" I asked. "How long will it take to get there?"

"About four days," Tom said. "We'll take our time and make a vacation out of the trip."

"That's assuming we find a dry spot for sightseeing," Katie added. "The practice day is Friday and the contest starts Saturday, so we don't have to rush."

"We're all hooked up and ready to roll. Get me some fajitas, margaritas, and real barbecue."

"Well, good luck on the way down and once you get there. Drive carefully," I said.

"And fly safely," added Andy. "Excuse me, but I'm going in to dry off."

Katie took my arm as we walked to their car.

"I'll tell you a secret," she said in a low voice. "We just found out this week — but don't tell anyone till we get back. I'm pregnant."

"Katie, congratulations! When?"

"Early November. I'm not going to be much of a crew this summer. Maybe you could help Tom for me?"

"Of course, I'd be happy to."

"Thanks." She smiled. "See you in a couple weeks."

"Bye."

I watched them drive off. They had such a full life, I thought enviously. And now a baby, which was certainly the last thing in the world I would want, but then I wasn't married, with cash to spare and the freedom to take three weeks' vacation on the spur of the moment. I wondered how you got started toward that kind of life?

I hated the thought of being cooped up inside, so once the rain abated to a drizzle I went for a walk in the woods. Penny wisely stayed inside. I had to be careful of the mud; once or twice I slipped on the way down the hill. I was only partway down when I heard a roaring noise. It was a moment before I could identify it as the creek. Eight days of rain had made the peaceful little stream a full-fledged river. It had overflowed its banks and swamped the mud flat where Penny and I liked to peer into the clear water. Today I had to stand in the woods, a good ten feet higher than usual, watching the brown torrents sweep by. It was such a contrast to a few weeks ago, when Penny and the goose faced off on the bank. The goose! I squatted down and peered through the branches. Swirling and foamy, the muddy water raced past, almost to the top of the opposite bank. The eggs must have been swept away by the flood. Fred and Ethel were gone.

I sat down on a piece of deadfall, alternately mourning the goose family and cursing myself for being sentimental. It happens, I told myself, it's nature's way, but I could picture Ethel sitting on her nest of twigs and down, tending her clutch, until the raging water reached up and snatched her children away.

We were a mopy crowd at the Hoot Owl that night, and decided not to show up at Crosswind if Sunday's weather was bad. It was, and staying home made me realize how much the gliderport had become part of my life. For more than a month I had been attuned to a weekend cycle; Monday through Friday was an interruption, a daze of boredom and chores, broken only by Trevor's unceasing perkiness that never failed to make me laugh. He sat on the vacuum hose when I cleaned, and swung on the cord of the iron. He chirped in my ear when I washed dishes, and when I was done would fly onto my hand and stand under the faucet, sipping water and showering, fluffing his feathers and shaking them, spreading his wings and bobbing his head. Afterward he'd sit on his front porch to dry and preen, then fly on my shoulder to kiss my cheek while I studied my soaring manual.

The new job was a relief but no challenge; sometimes I had hours of idleness during which I had to pretend to be busy, in case my new supervisor stopped by.

And so the week dragged on, the clock hands turning ever slower, until interminable Friday, and escape.

I awoke Saturday to a quiet dripping, not the incessant tapping of raindrops. The sky was a shade lighter, and held the promise — at least the hint — of clearing. I dressed eagerly and drove to Crosswind. The runway was too soggy to fly in the morning, but by late afternoon the breeze had dried it somewhat, and we happily untied the 2-33.

I stopped back at the office to use the bathroom. The phone rang while I was in there, and when I came out Marv was sitting at the kitchen table, the receiver in his hand and a bleak look on his face.

"Marv, is anything wrong?" I asked.

He looked up at me with tears in his eyes.

"Tom Bayard was killed this afternoon."

Chapter

Eleven

The swollen creek flowed past me, a few feet below and beyond the fallen tree trunk on which I sat. I listened to the rush of water as I caught my breath, trying not to think of Tom Bayard, who was still alive to me only ten minutes before. But I couldn't get Marv's words out of my head, nor the look on his face, suddenly pale under the tan, as he pulled a wrinkled, yellowing handkerchief out of his pocket to wipe his eyes before saying, "There was a midair collision. The other pilot bailed out safely." He paused, folding his handkerchief. "Tom's cockpit was smashed by the impact. He didn't have a chance."

His voice had faded into a roaring sound that must have been my own blood rushing life through my veins. I had been sitting on the green couch, where I'd collapsed because my legs had suddenly refused to do anything but buckle under me. The walls of the trailer seemed to curve in and out in time with my breathing, making the ceiling swoop down and the floor bow up with the same crazy rhythm, as though the trailer could not decide whether to implode or explode around me.

I stood up as quickly as I could without losing my balance, and shuffled across the room, my arms outstretched like a beggar's. I pushed the door open to the subdued light and moist air of midafternoon, and after nearly falling down the single step to the ground, I took a couple of deep breaths, then I ran hard across the runway without even a glance up for traffic, heading for the forest, to lose myself among the trees. I slid and stumbled all the way down the muddy path until I was forced to stop by the silt-heavy creek, still overflowing its banks at the foot of the hill.

Now here I sat, head down below my knees to stop the dizziness, the nausea, the nightmare.

I don't know how long it was before I could lift my head and breathe normally. I didn't want to move, and so I didn't, not even when I heard the snap of twigs that meant someone was coming down the path.

"There you are," Andy said quietly. She came over and sat down next to me on the log. Out of the corner of my eye I could see that her eyes were red, and so was her nose. She picked at a piece of lichen and said, "I saw you run away from the trailer. I came up to see what was wrong, and Marv told me."

"Katie's pregnant," I said, looking at the creek.

"Damn." She waited a minute and then asked, "Are you okay?"

"I'm fine," I said shortly. "Nothing's the matter with me. Everything's just dandy."

Andy didn't say anything. We sat watching the creek flow by. It would join a river, probably the Raritan, and from there would spill out to pollute the sea.

"Why Tom?" I asked. "Why did it have to be him?"

"He made a mistake," Andy said gently.

"You shouldn't have to die because you made a mistake!"

"This is aviation, Ellen. Small mistakes can be fixed. Big ones can kill. You know the risks."

"I never think about it."

Andy grimaced. "Then I'm doing a lousy job. Ellen, I'm sorry you had to learn it this way. What we do, we do for fun, for pleasure, for beauty, and even for love. For all sorts of wonderful reasons. But we do it knowing the risks. Good pilots face the risks, and do everything they can to minimize them. That's what training and safety are all about."

"Tom was a good pilot," I told her.

Andy picked up a stone, and tossed it into the creek, where it disappeared with a splash and a plop.

She said, "My husband was a good pilot, too."

I looked at her quickly. "Your husband?"

"He was killed in a crash, six years ago. He was a good pilot, every time but the last." She leaned her elbows on her knees. "He was flying in a regional contest, not his first, either. He was a damn good pilot, and had come in second and third enough to want to win badly. It happened in Ohio. His Nimbus had some minor damage from trailering after the last contest, and so he was flying my Cirrus. He was doing well, and leading after the first three days.

"It was hot as hell, that summer, and a couple of people had had problems with dehydration. Contest tasks are long and tiring, and if a pilot doesn't drink enough water he can get physical and mental symptoms that disrupt his judgment and make it hard to fly safely. That day the temperature was pushing a hundred, and though the task wasn't long, there were no clouds to cool off under. The lift was weak and the pilots were working hard to stay up.

"Mike always carried enough water. But that day one of his water bottles started to leak, and halfway through the task it ran out. I asked him if he wanted to land, but he said he felt fine and would press on as long as he could."

She picked up another stone, a grey-green one the size and shape of a bird's egg.

"Another pilot saw the whole thing. This pilot had landed in a field, and he saw Mike overhead, low, and figured Mike would join him. Instead, Mike kept flying, as though he was looking for lift, and as he zigzagged back and forth the pilot on the ground radioed that the field was a good one, and safe to land, but Mike radioed back that he wanted to search for lift a little longer." She dropped the stone and wiped her hands on her pants. "He was having some trouble speaking, and the other pilot realized he was in trouble, and tried to talk him down. When Mike finally understood that he had to land, he was only a hundred feet off the ground, heading straight for a row of trees. The other pilot saw Mike try to turn back toward the field, but he was too slow, and the Cirrus stalled and spun. Mike was already dead when the other pilot reached him."

"Christ, Andy," was all I could say before the tears fell, and a second later Andy was holding me while I cried and cried and cried.

We had only one tissue between us, so I ended up blowing my nose into a maple leaf. "Oh, how gross," I said, tossing the slimy thing away. I took a deep breath and looked at Andy. "I'm sorry."

She looked puzzled. "For blowing your nose or for crying? One follows the other."

I looked up to stop my nose running. "For crying like that. I never met your husband, and I haven't known Tom for very long, but I cried more for them than I did for my own parents. That shouldn't happen."

"I don't think it did," Andy said, and put her arm around my shoulder. "Weren't a lot of those tears really for your parents?"

I nodded as the damn tears welled up again, out of control. "I think I need another leaf."

Andy gave my shoulder a squeeze before she reached up and pulled down a handful of them.

"And who else are you crying for?" she asked.

"Me, I guess."

"We always do. I think mourning is only for the living. What do the dead have to cry about anymore?"

"I guess you're right," I said from behind a leaf.

She gave me a few minutes, and when I couldn't stop crying asked, "What else is there?"

I blew my nose again. "The flying," I said finally. "It was all I had, and now it's ruined."

"Ellen, it's perfectly natural if you feel scared about flying right now..."

"No! That's not what I mean!"

"What then?"

I looked out at the creek again, trying to find the words. "Please don't laugh, but it was like a entering a magic world." I looked quickly at Andy, but she sat soberly, for once not smiling at all. "I mean, it was beautiful and so different, different from my life, my real life, the nine-to-five one, all those hours I spent making stupid copies of stupid reports, and then coming home to — coming back to the apartment, which doesn't feel like my home, because it's all someone else's stuff, and all I have is Trevor." I reached for another leaf. "Not that he isn't sweet, but it's not much of a life, is it? Every time I see Hardenbergh students I think, hey, that was me last year, having fun and nothing to worry about, no rent, no bills — no funerals, no wills, no house sales. No fun.

"And then I found this place. And being in the glider, up there, so far from everything real...I've been living for the weekend. I get through the lousy week because the weekend will be so good, and now...now it's not escape anymore. Now there are mistakes. Now there are consequences."

I'd finally stopped crying, but I still had to hold my head up to stop sniffing.

Andy put one leg up on the log, and held her shin with her hands. "This was the only place you could get away from death," she said.

I nodded.

"Now it's here."

I nodded again.

"Ellen, if you weren't touched by death before your parents died you were lucky, but it was a mistake to think you could hide from it anywhere, especially here. It's corny to say that death is part of life, but it's the unfortunate truth, and there's no place you can go to get away from it. Everyone has to learn to deal with it, and you do, too.

"I have no magic answers for you. I can't make it easy. You're on your own with this one, but you're not alone. If you need it, my shoulder's here to cry on, any time. I mean that. And Marv feels the same way. He's real worried about how you're taking this. We may not be family, but we are friends, and friends help friends. You ask, and we're here for you."

She reached for my hand. Her hand felt warm and strong, even though it was smaller than my own.

"Ready to show Marv you're still in one piece?"

I nodded.

"Good." She released my hand, and stood up, brushing off her pants. "You know," she said with a smile, "you could have picked a drier log."

We walked back to the office. The 2-33 was back in her tie-down spot, resting there as she did every afternoon when the flying was over. The airport was tranquil. Overhead blew a tattered mass of clouds, patches of white jumbled up with the grey, promising the hope of blue sky tomorrow. Behind us, a wood thrush began to carol. It was one of my favorite times of day —

I couldn't decide which I liked better: first thing in the morning, quiet and clean and full of anticipation; the comfortable chaos of midday, full of sun and laughter and warmth; the serenity of evening, when robins sang and the aircraft were tucked in for the night. But it was not yet night, and the peaceful scene that had given me so much joy was tainted with the knowledge of a young man's death.

The office still oppressed me. Marv looked desolate as he alternately wiped his eyes and made phone calls. Herb sat on the sofa, petting Penny and scowling, not reading the months-old copy of *Trade-A-Plane* draped over his lap. Keith, who had arrived just as the rain stopped, was already gone.

"Why don't we close up and go to the Hoot Owl?" suggested Andy. Herb shook his head, Marv said "Maybe later" then continued talking on the phone.

Andy looked at me doubtfully. "Sure, why not," I said without much enthusiasm. "I'll follow you."

We got there during the respite between lunch hour and happy hour. Pete and Patti were waiting for us, and hugged us both. "Marv called," was all Patti said. She looked stricken. Strange how many lives were affected by Tom's death; my parents' death had altered the lives of so few.

We sat down, all four of us, after Pete brought over a bottle of very old bourbon. He poured a generous amount into our glasses and raised his for a toast. "To Tom," he said simply, to which Patti added, "And Katie."

The bourbon was smooth as milk on the tongue but hell on the esophagus. I wouldn't be able to drink much of it and stay sober enough to drive home.

"Where's Katie now?" asked Patti.

"Still in Texas," Andy answered. "The pilot who called us said her parents would be flying out there from San Diego, and will be bringing her home in a day or two.

"What about Tom?" asked Pete.

"Apparently they're having him cremated out there. I guess they'll bring back the ashes."

I had a horrible vision of Tom in a carry-on bag. I took another sip of bourbon.

"Will there be a memorial service here?" asked Pete.

"I don't know — I suppose so," Andy told him. "We didn't get too many details yet."

"Of course not," Patti said, reaching for her hand. "We should have a service. We can come here afterwards. We'll close for the day so it'll be private."

It was all too much. I stood up suddenly, almost knocking over the bourbon that must have cost a day's pay.

"I have to go," I said, steadying the bottle.

"See you tomorrow?" Andy said, with a question in her voice.

"I'm not sure."

I hardly remember driving home. I walked up the stairs slowly, past The Wraith's apartment, where presumably he was holed up, out on bail and awaiting trial. I never saw him anymore. Latanya was out, of course, probably with the Porsche pilot. My steps echoed in the empty stairwell like water dripping from a faucet in the middle of the night. I felt a familiar awful hollowness, as though I were a tree with the heartwood eaten out of it, and nothing left but bark that a good wind would split and blow away; a dullness, as though I were wrapped in layers of plastic film; and the anger that I couldn't explain or get rid of and that in December I had tried to drink away.

I opened the door and Trevor chirped his hello. I smiled a little. No, it wasn't quite the same. It didn't go as deep, for one, and it didn't affect the basics of my life: where I lived, what I did. I let Trevor out of the cage and he did his usual kamikaze act, flying as fast as he could no more than a wingspan below the high ceiling, circling and circling until he flopped, out of breath and satisfied, onto the kitchen table. I pulled a beer from the refrigerator, but after the first cold sip it tasted stale in my mouth, and I dumped it down the sink. I kicked off my shoes and lay down on the couch. Trevor flew over, landing on my chest, and began to nibble the buttons on my shirt. When he got tired of that he walked up and kissed my chin, then he settled in the hollow of my collarbone. I rubbed his head with one finger as the sun set.

The next morning Trevor woke me by nibbling my eyebrows, which tickled something awful. I was still on the couch in yesterday's clothes. I got up, showered and changed, fed Trevor and gave him a shower under the kitchen faucet, then shut his cage while I cleaned the apartment. If Mom could see me now, I thought wryly, as I dusted and vacuumed, washed the kitchen and bathroom floors, washed the windows, rearranged the few books on the bookshelf, and straightened up inside the kitchen cabinets, all two of them. By then the apartment was too hot for manual labor. I turned on the small window fan, which did little except push hot air from one side of the room to the next, and said goodbye to Trevor, then went outside to sit on the porch steps.

I had no desire to go to Crosswind, but I didn't know what else to do. It had become such a part of my life, even on rainy days, that I was at a loss for something to occupy a Sunday afternoon. I finally decided to walk to the park. Maybe I needed a ride on the swings.

I walked slowly past Toth's Hungarian grocery store, which must be the only store in the country to still have clean sawdust on the floor. The left window of the corner store was full of can pyramids, and the right held a long dowel, from which hung thin links of kolbasz, a powerfully garlic-flavored sausage, and slabs of szalonna, the seasoned bacon we used to cook on the barbecue grill in summer. After I crossed Mindszenty Street I passed the convent of the Sisters of St. Elizabeth's Roses, set back from the street and surrounded by an old-fashioned spiked wrought iron fence. The building used to so terrify me when I was a child that I would cross the street to avoid it. A block away was St. Elizabeth's Grammar School, where I had gone from kindergarten to eighth grade. In kindergarten I had been a middling reader, so the teacher placed me in a group of other middling readers, and we went through the next eight years together, the smart kids in the A class, the dumb kids in the C class, and the rest of us in B, stereotyped for life as the result of a reading test we took when we were five. I shook my head at the thought and walked past the high school, where the same thing had happened after the entrance exam, but at least in high school there were students from other grade schools, and the opportunity to make new friends, although none of us ever overcame the stigma of our grade school rankings. On top of that, the kids from my side of town never mixed with the kids who lived beyond the building, on the north side of town. Most of the A-level kids were from the north side, and most of the C's from the south, with an occasional crossover. The A's were preppies, the C's were greasers, and the B's were nerds, unable to afford preppy clothes and too chicken to hang out with the greasers. Graduation from that school was more emancipation than commencement, and I'd never once been back inside.

Beyond St. Elizabeth's the houses changed from small ones with tiny back yards to large homes with spacious front lawns, and room in between for one-car garages. These houses had no front porches, they had patios instead, in back, under the privacy of large maple trees. Some were pseudo-Dutch-colonial, some were split-levels, built during the prosperity that followed World War Two. Most had fireplaces and air conditioning, unheard of luxuries in my old neighborhood. The smallest of these homes was easily twice the size of the house I used to live in. I walked past the biggest houses, up Van Oort Street to the entrance of the park.

What a contrast to last winter's monochrome quietness — today the park was raucous with azaleas and teenagers. The emerald grass was punctuated with flower beds, where the last of the daffodils mingled with the first of the irises; pansies and ageratum edged the borders. Even the shade was colorful under the great oak in the center of the park. It was a huge tree, four or five feet across, with enormous tree-sized limbs, two of them held up by posts to keep them from snapping under their own weight. The mulched area around the trunk was dotted with newly planted impatiens in concentric circles of coral and white.

The small sandy beach was raucous, too, with boom boxes playing conflicting music. Clusters of girls lying on towels eyed groups of boys ostentatiously playing frisbee or volleyball. The playground was full, too, of small children on the teeter-totters and swings, their mothers arrayed on benches or giving gentle shoves to the littlest ones strapped into the baby swings. It seemed half the town was in the park this afternoon. I couldn't find an unoccupied bench, or a tree to sit under that didn't have two or three little boys perched in the branches. I finally found a relatively secluded spot, under a big maple that seemed empty of children. I was wrong. A moment after I sat down I heard a rustling and the thud of little Reeboks next to me. I looked over at the intruder, a small boy eight or nine years old, I guessed, with dark eyes and long lashes a girl would kill for, and dark curly hair, ditto. He wore dirty jeans that had probably been clean this morning, and a faded Robocop tee shirt.

"Hi," I said.

"Hi," he said back, after looking me over for a minute. "My name's Cheech. What's yours?"

"Ellen."

"You sat under my tree," he told me.

"I'm sorry. I didn't know it was your tree."

"That's okay." He began jumping, alternately putting one foot then the other as high up the tree trunk as he could.

"Are you here by yourself?" I asked him.

"No," he answered, still jumping. "My mother's...by the swings...with my sister." He stopped jumping. "She's just a baby. Do you have a brother?"

"No, no sisters, either."

"You're lucky." He squatted down and dug at the tree root with a twig.

"Where do you go to school?" I asked him.

"St. Elizabeth's," he said with a scowl.

"What grade are you in?" I felt like an interrogator.

"Third. I'm nine. My birthday was last week."

"Congratulations. I went to St. Elizabeth's, too."

"Yeah? I hate it."

"I wasn't so crazy about it myself. Let's see, in third grade I had Sister Mary Elizabeth Ferguson."

"She was old. She croaked last year."

I sighed. Andy was right, I couldn't get away from it anywhere. "I'm sorry to hear that."

"I'm not. I heard she was hard."

I didn't know what to say to that. He began to tease a carpenter ant, blocking its way as it tried to climb the tree.

"Are any of your friends here today?" I asked him.

"On Sunday?" He sounded incredulous. "I always have to

be with my family on Sunday. Sundays are boring."

"They can be," I admitted.

"How 'bout you?" he asked. "Don't you have any friends?"

"Yes, yes I do."

"So why aren't you with them? Grownups can do what they want."

"Yeah, well, grownups can be pretty dumb, sometimes, too." I stood up and held out my hand. "It was nice meeting you, Cheech. I have to go now."

He shook my hand. His hand was small and sweaty and warm. "It was nice meeting you, too," he said politely.

"Be nice to your little sister," I called to him as I walked away. Then I laughed. What a dumb, grownup thing to say.

Monday and Tuesday were ominous with sunshine; good weather at midweek could only mean bad for the weekend. Sure enough, by Wednesday afternoon I could see clouds approaching from the south. Andy called that night to tell me the memorial service would be held on Friday evening. She didn't mention my Sunday absence, or ask whether I was coming back.

I went to the service directly from work, driving through a steady drizzle to the small Episcopal church not far from the airport. I arrived a few minutes before the service. Katie stood in the vestibule with an older couple I assumed were her parents, and another older woman I guessed was Tom's mother. I knew his father had died many years ago. Katie looked tired. Her hair was pulled back and tied with a black bow. She wore a black suit with a pearl-colored blouse, and no jewelry other than her wedding band. She smiled and gave me a hug.

"Thanks for coming, Ellen. These are my parents, John and Margaret Whitney, and Tom's mother, Louise Bayard. This is Ellen Horvath. She works at Crosswind, with Keith, the young man I introduced you to before."

We exchanged "How do you do's" and I walked into the church. It was small and dark, lit only by a few candles and the dull translucence of the stained glass windows. I walked hesitantly up the short aisle. Everyone from Crosswind was sitting in one pew on the left. I slipped in next to Marv, wondering if one should genuflect in an Episcopal church. Marv whispered a hello, and I nodded to Andy, sitting between Marv and Herb, and to Keith at the end of the pew. I recognized several Crosswind pilots scattered among the mourners. The small church was nearly full.

At six on the dot Katie and her parents walked up the aisle, in a grotesque parody of a wedding ceremony. When they sat down the minister came out, wearing a simple white vestment. He spoke kindly about Tom, and about Katie, for about ten minutes, then he said a brief prayer and asked everyone to sing Tom's favorite hymn, "Tis the Gift to be Simple." That was all. I couldn't help but contrast this service with my parents' requiem mass, the hymns of sorrow and resurrection, the incense, followed by the torture of the burial service at the grave site. How much more civilized and soothing this service was.

Afterward we gathered at the Hoot Owl, surely the most somber crowd that bar had ever seen, to eat Pete's homemade lasagne. After a little while — which seemed like hours — I went out back. I put up the hood on my raincoat and walked toward the cages. Katie was standing front of the hawk cage. I started to back away but she heard my step on the gravel and turned toward me.

"I'm sorry, I didn't mean to intrude," I said.

"That's all right. I don't mind company — I just needed some air. Share my umbrella?"

I walked up to her. Her face was wet, despite the umbrella, and I felt awkward.

"I was looking at this hawk." She nodded toward a large red tail, which looked miserable and bedraggled. "Even soaking wet it's a magnificent creature."

"Yes it is."

"Tom often talked about hawks. He told me how wonderful it was to circle with one. He said one time a hawk looked over at him, and he felt that it had accepted him as a fellow pilot, a creature of the air. It sounded so spiritual. It must have been a marvelous experience."

"It sounds wonderful."

"I'm sorry I couldn't appreciate it more. I couldn't share the feeling. Tom could describe it beautifully, but no matter how well he told the story, I couldn't know. You could."

"I haven't had flights like that. I'm just a beginner."

"Maybe so, but you still understood better than I ever could, you know that. Tom said he used to enjoy talking to you about flying, because your eyes would light up. He said your eyes got so wide he could see the clouds in them. He really liked you, Ellen. He was looking forward to your solo flight."

"I think that's a long way off, now."

Katie turned to me. "Don't let what happened to Tom change it for you, Ellen. It would break his heart if he knew that something he did caused you to give it up. He would hate that. I know he would. And so would I. You're like that hawk."

"All wet?"

"You know what I mean. It's part of you, like it was part of Tom. You belong here. Don't let Tom's accident get in your way."

"I'll try. I guess I just need some time."

"Don't we all? And speaking of time, I've been out here long enough. Are you going back inside?"

"Yes, I'll walk in with you."

We turned to go back. "What will you do now, Katie?"

"I'm going to stay with my parents in San Diego until the baby is born. I haven't thought beyond that."

"I'll miss you."

"I'll miss you, too. All of you."

When we got back inside I saw Andy sitting at the bar. I sat down next to her.

"Could I ask you a question?"

She looked over at me. "Sure."

"After what happened to your husband, why did you — how could you — "

"Go on flying?" she finished for me. I nodded. "I didn't want to, at first. I didn't want anything to do with it. But deep down, I knew that I still loved it, and Mike would have hated to have me stop flying because of him. After a while, it just seemed the natural thing to do. So I started teaching."

"Why?"

She shrugged. "It gave me something to do. Mike's insurance left me comfortable, so I didn't need a real job — and believe me, you can't make a living at this — and teaching has its rewards. So that's why I do what I do. How about you?"

"Me?"

"Will we see you on Saturday?"

I looked over at Butch on his perch. He stared back at me with bright yellow eyes, still fierce looking, although he would never again know the feeling of the wind in his feathers, the joy of diving at the ground, the pleasure of doing what he was created for. Poor Butch.

"I'll be there," I told Andy.

It felt normal, after all, to be at Crosswind on Saturday morning. It wasn't raining, for a change, although the sky looked threatening. Keith and I pulled the 2-33 over to the hose, and washed off all the dirty streaks left by the rain. We had a busy day, the first flyable Saturday in weeks, and I was fine as long as I kept away from the trailer with the "for sale" sign on it. At the end of the day Keith went for a flight, and came back grumbling about lousy visibility. Then it was my turn.

I hadn't flown in a couple of weeks, but it felt natural and familiar to climb into the cockpit, buckle the heavy nylon seat belts and shoulder straps, and begin the take-off checklist. I closed the canopy and waited for Keith's signal to launch. Takeoff was as exciting as ever, and I loved to feel the speed build up, to hold the stick in just the right place so that at the right speed we would lift smoothly off the ground, a magical moment that I never tired of experiencing. The tow to three thousand feet, which up till now had been a struggle for stability and control, suddenly seemed almost easy, and for the first time I was able to keep the sailplane right behind the towplane where it belonged. I was jubilant, and knew I had passed a major hurdle in my training. I couldn't wait to tell Marv and Keith and — the tears were quick to come when I thought of Tom buying a pitcher of beer because I'd had my first lesson, and the way he encouraged me the day we flew together. How much he would have enjoyed knowing that I had done my first successful aerotow! I pulled the release knob at three thousand feet and turned right, but the fun was gone from this flight. I did everything Andy told me, mechanically, without thought, until the altimeter showed us only a few hundred feet above pattern altitude. I felt myself stiffen as we got lower, and I began to fly badly, hands and feet not paying attention to the brain, or maybe I just switched off the brain. I couldn't concentrate, and my landing pattern was spectacularly imprecise. I tried to shove the glider onto the ground, and was rewarded with a bounce back into the air, which I repeated, until the 2-33 settled to the ground with an ungraceful thud. It seemed as disgusted as I was.

Andy got out first, and waited until I climbed out to say, "The tow was the best you've ever done. Congratulations."

"Now tell me about the landing," I said.

"You know what you did wrong," she told me. "We'll see how you do tomorrow."

Fortunately, when tomorrow came, it rained all day.

Chapter
Twelve

Latanya graduated from Hardenbergh College on the last Friday in May. The commencement exercises were scheduled in the usually practical Hardenbergh way for 6:00 p.m., so no parents would have to take a day off from V.D. to attend. I joined the throng in the auditorium after work.

I hadn't been inside since my own graduation a year ago. Then, I had sat with the other students, naively happy, enjoying the feel of the gown over my T-shirt and shorts, playing with the tassel on my cap, dreading the boredom of a whole summer on the V.D. assembly line but looking forward to the paychecks and weekends down the shore. All my thoughts were of September, and Trenton State, where I would get the big degree that I hoped would be my ticket to — I didn't know what, but I had hoped it would get me out of Hardenbergh and away from V.D. for good.

I tried not to think about it. This was Latanya's day to get her ticket to New York City. She was all packed, ready to move out in the morning. She had already gotten one-fourth of an overpriced sublet in the Village and felt the roaches would be a small price to pay for the chance to do what she really wanted. She grinned all the way as she walked across the dais, shook hands with the president of the college, and received her diploma.

After the ceremony I found her with her parents. Dr. Ellison was a tall man whose hair was beginning to grey at the temples. His wife, nearly a foot shorter than her husband, was gorgeous in the same small-boned way as Latanya, and I could see that Latanya would have no worries about losing her looks in later years. Her mother's silk suit and gold jewelry that definitely did not come from the local five-and-ten were as imposing as Dr. Ellison's steel-grey double-breasted and red power tie.

Dr. Ellison smiled gamely but I knew from Latanya that he

was opposed to her move to New York. I had the feeling that only his innate politeness and his wife's strong will prevented another installment in their ongoing family war. Latanya's mother masked her disappointment more easily than her husband did, and managed to speak cheerfully of Latanya's future plans. She invited me to join them for dinner but I declined, partly because I didn't want to intrude on a family celebration, and partly because I didn't think I was up to facing Dr. Ellison's grim sociability.

We said good-bye privately that evening, after Latanya returned from dinner, because I would be on my way to Crosswind by the time she got up to leave the next morning. She said hello to Trevor, as she always did, and sat on the couch while I uncorked a bottle of champagne.

"That's real champagne," she said in a surprised voice.

"This is a real occasion," I said. "Don't worry, you aren't taking food from my mouth. I got it from Pete, at cost."

We toasted her future, and she unwrapped her present, a box of new pastels.

"Thank you," she said as she hugged me. "I'll think of you every time I draw."

"Just as I'll think of you every time I look at Trevor."

"I finally told my brother he was living up here, so I guess he's officially yours now."

"I'm sorry your brother couldn't be here."

"Me, too. That's med school for you." She shivered. "That's the future my father wanted for me. Uh-uh."

"So you're finally doing it. I'm so glad for you."

"Thanks. But what about you, Ellen? You still need to get out of here, and I don't mean just this apartment. When are you gonna put the moves on one of those cute pilots you see every weekend?"

"I don't know," I sighed. "I don't think I'm ready yet. Besides, no one ever puts the moves on me."

"Because you don't give them a chance. You might as well carry around a brick wall."

"I don't mean to be so unapproachable."

"The hell you don't. Why not join a convent and get it over

with?"

"I need time."

"How much? Have you got it figured down to the minute? 'If Ellen Horvath mourns her parents for eight months, twenty-one days, three hours, thirty-six minutes and forty-two seconds, how many months more does she have to do? Be sure you answer to three decimal places'. Is that what you're telling me?"

I had to smile. "I'm just trying to say that I'm not ready, that's all. I'm still trying to sort some things out."

"Like whether you have any hormones left?"

I poured more champagne and watched the bubbles rise in straight lines to the top of the glass. "You're so self-assured," I said finally. "You know exactly what you want, and you're going for it. You've got a talent and you're developing it. Maybe because of all the fights you've told me about, because you had to explain to your parents, but you have such a clear picture of the next few years. You know who Latanya is and what she needs to become."

I wondered if I would ever have that assured knowledge of who I was. More and more often I found myself thinking about my mother and John Cahill, about who they were and what they meant to each other, and whether I was the result. How could I begin to explain this to Latanya, when I was so uncertain myself? I pushed the thoughts aside to fester in a gloomy corner of my mind, and resolved again to work up the nerve to confront Cahill. Someday.

"Until last fall, I hadn't thought about anything, Latanya. Who I am. What I want. What I need. I'd only gotten as far as what I don't want. I don't want to end up at V.D. all my life, but I don't want to marry somebody just to escape it. I don't want to stay in Hardenbergh and be another working class hunky whose only excitement every day is watching somebody else get rich on Wheel of Fortune. Jesus, turning the letters would be better than that. But I don't know what I want, what I'm good for, because I thought I had plenty of time to worry about that later, after I got out of school — only I got out a lot sooner than I thought I would. I just want to figure things out a little, that's all."

"And in the meantime?"

"In the meantime I'll just schlepp along like I've been doing. Look, I don't want to talk about this tonight. I'm depressed enough because you're moving." I sipped the champagne and felt the bubbles fizz on my tongue. "I promise not to get maudlin or anything, but I want to thank you. You helped me get through a real bad time. And you gave me Trevor." I looked over at him. He was perched in front of his mirror, his left foot curled up under his feathers, and he muttered to himself, or to the parakeet he saw in the mirror, a little bird bedtime story, a mix of words and faint chirps and chewing noises. His eyes were closing and in a minute he would tuck his head under his right wing.

"It's amazing what a difference such a small bird can make. He's company and he depends on me and he's always happy, even when I've had a bad day. Sometimes I think I would have gone crazy if you hadn't given him to me."

"I know."

"Well, I want you to know this, too: if it ever gets bad for you in New York, and you need to talk, day or night, you can call me. And if you ever need to get out of the city for a while, you can come here, any time."

She thanked me with tears in her eyes, and we hugged each other and cried and drank more champagne, and talked about anything to put off saying good-bye. But finally we had to, and when she left my small apartment, it looked emptier than it ever had before.

I felt bad the next morning, knowing I'd be leaving Trevor alone for a couple days. I'd given him extra food and water, and told myself that he couldn't tell time, and wouldn't know I wasn't coming back till Monday, but I still felt like I was abandoning him. But it was Memorial Day weekend, and we were going to be so busy at Crosswind that it made no sense for me to drive home late each night. My venerable car, though reliable so far, was bound to break down some time, and I had no desire for it to happen at night on the interstate, nor did I want to be on the road with the holiday weekend crazies any more than I had to be. So I was spending two nights at Pete and Patti's.

I was glad I did. The weather was fine for a change, and we did lots of flying, and lots of partying each night. On Saturday we had a cookout at the field to which all of Crosswind's neighbors were invited, as well as any farmers or landowners whose field had ever been landed on. Marv called it our public relations cookout. On Sunday we gathered at the Hoot Owl for Keith's farewell party, and I got drunk for the first time in many weeks, thanks to everyone who knew I wasn't driving. They all kept pace with me, though, and we were a sorry sight the next morning. Fortunately, the holiday was a slow day for sightseeing rides, probably thanks to family picnics; those pilots who were our usual customers each weekend generally opted to stay on the ground and hold their heads.

It was a dismal way to spend Keith's last day at Crosswind. Keith, several years away from the legal drinking age, felt fine because the night before Pete had refused to serve him even one beer. He had a one-hour flight while everyone else was recuperating, and obviously relished the results of his clear head, which did little to improve the mood of those who had been grounded by hangovers. He would have been safe if he hadn't said "You can't soar with the eagles in the morning if you hoot with the owls at the Hoot Owl every night." Marv, who had baked the cake Keith was cutting at the time, was the first to smear some in his face. By the time the food fight was over, even Penny had a nose full of chocolate. The picnic area was a shambles and Keith was unrecognizable. He drove off to join the Air Force with blue frosting in his hair.

In addition to Latanya's and Keith's departures, the holiday weekend brought a change in the weather. The dry weekends and long hours of daylight brought back the customers; Marv began to talk again of hiring another instructor to help Andy. We finished painting the other 2-33, bright yellow with rainbow stripes on the tail, and she took her place on the field next to 42H, who now looked shabbier than ever, and was scheduled for a paint job in the fall. Life settled into a routine again, five days of enclosure and boredom followed by two of sunlight and fun, although I couldn't pull into the Crosswind driveway without a twinge of regret for Tom Bayard.

I had so quickly been lulled by the good weather that I was positively shocked, one Sunday at the end of June, to wake up to fog that refused to burn off but only thinned a little into a persistent haze that kept us grounded all morning. We were cleaning up in the shop when I noticed the wasps. One flew past me as I swept the floor, so low I almost hit it with the broom. It flew under Andy's trailer, and was followed by two others.

"Herb," I called. "I think we have a wasp nest in here."

Herb came over from the workbench and looked where I was pointed.

"Hmm," he grunted, his usual reply to any conversational opening. He walked up to the trailer and sidled behind it as far as his belly would let him.

"Yep. They've built it on the back wall."

He squeezed back out and walked through the door. I followed him to the picnic table, where Andy was giving a ground school lesson to one of her students.

"Andy, sorry to interrupt."

"That's okay, Herb," she said, looking up. "We were just finishing up. What can I do for you?"

"There's a wasp nest in the barn, all the way in the back. I'll need to move your trailer to get it out of there. That okay?"

Andy frowned, just for a moment, then shrugged and said, "Sure, Herb, go ahead. Thanks for asking."

Herb nodded once and walked back to the barn. "We'll move the trailer out now, then Marv and I will take care of it tonight. Give them a chance to settle down in the meantime. Go ask Marv to give me a hand."

By the time Marv and I got back to the barn, Herb had moved the air compressor and other pieces of equipment that blocked access to the trailer. "You stand over by the door," he told me. "If we bump the nest by accident they're going to get awful mad in an awful hurry. Be ready to beat feet. We'll be right behind you."

I watched as he and Marv carefully jacked up the trailer and slid a dolly under the tires. Then, with Marv in front and Herb at the rear, they slowly eased the trailer away from the back wall, far enough to turn it around without hitting the nest. Then they jacked it up again, removed the dolly, and let it down. Marv went to get the pickup to tow the trailer with while Herb and I took a closer but cautious look at the nest. It was surprisingly beautiful, nearly two feet across, made of a papery substance laid on in countless swirls, almost like the end papers of old-fashioned books. Wasps flew in and out from the underside in steady traffic.

Soon Marv backed the pickup into the barn and Herb attached the trailer to the hitch. "Where do you want it?" he asked Herb, who answered, "Just haul it out of here for now. Park it out of the way."

"If you pull it up to the hose I can wash it off," I said, noticing the patina of dust and metal filings on top of the trailer.

"We'll have to ask Andy about that," Marv said.

"Ask Andy what?" she asked, walking up to us.

"If I could wash it off," I told her.

She looked at the trailer and nodded. "It sure needs it, doesn't it."

"Okay," Marv said, and drove out.

I followed him over to the wash stand, a square of gravel just big enough to park the towplane on. A faucet was mounted on a two-foot pipe sticking up out of the ground, with a hose attached to it. When Marv unhitched the trailer and drove away I turned the hose on it and used our long-handled brush to scrub away the grime. Andy came over just as I finished, and swept her hand along the side of the trailer, the same way she had caressed the 2-33 on the day of my first flight here.

"Will it pass the white glove test?" I asked her.

"One hundred percent," she answered smiling.

Marv came up to us and whistled. "Sure looks nice to see it gleaming in the — well, I guess I can't say gleaming in the sun today, but it sure looks nice."

We stood looking at it for a moment. I thought about this trailer sitting in the barn for so many years, and decided to let curiosity override tact.

"Andy, I've never seen a Nimbus 2," I said, watching her face. Her smile faded and I knew she was going to say forget it, but before she had a chance Marv said, "Surely it couldn't hurt anything just to show it to her?"

Andy looked at Marv for a long moment. "No, I suppose it

can't hurt," she said, finally. Marv smiled. "I'll move it where there's room."

Once again he fetched the truck, and this time Andy showed me how to connect the hitch. Then she and I climbed in next to Marv for the short drive to the end of the trailer park. It had a new empty spot where Tom's trailer had been; a pilot from Ohio had bought it the week before. When we parked and unhitched Marv handed Andy the key to the trailer. "I've been holding this on my keychain for a long time," he told her. She fingered it for just a moment, then opened the trailer.

As on most sailplane trailers, the entire back panel folded down to form a ramp. Inside was a jigsaw puzzle of sailplane parts. The fuselage was cradled in a dolly that rolled on a small track down the center of the trailer, making it easy for Marv and Andy to bring it out. They rolled it off the ramp and we all looked at the slim fiberglass fuselage that hadn't seen daylight in more than five years. It was pure white, incredibly smooth, with a bullet-shaped cockpit that tapered back to a slim tube at the tail, a slender vertical rectangle with a thin rudder behind it, painted with large black letters: MM. Without the wings or the elevator it looked off-balance, not like a flying machine at all. Andy removed the white flannel cloth that covered the canopy, a single piece of tinted plexiglass hinged on one side and reaching almost to the nose of the sailplane. She opened it up, and we looked in the cockpit. There was no seat inside, just a scooped out area of molded grey plastic behind the control stick. The instrument panel was a sleek half-moon, matte black. It held some equipment I had never seen.

Marv was grinning when I looked up, and I'm sure my mouth was hanging open. Andy looked funny — not upset, exactly, but not thrilled, either. She knelt down next to the cockpit and rested her hand on the side of the fuselage, where the canopy would sit when it was closed.

"It's fantastic," I told her. "Beautiful."

She nodded. "That she is."

"Is this oxygen?"

"Yes. It's called a blinker valve. It blinks open and shut as you breath. Radio," she said, pointing as she spoke, "and this is a flight computer. You punch in what you know about your flight, and it can calculate how much altitude you need to get home. It can even tell you when to fly faster or slower. Lots of things."

"Wow. It looks complicated."

"You get the hang of it pretty quickly."

"It's a big help on a record flight," said Marv. "Or in a contest."

"Well, we sure could have used one in April," I said.

Marv squatted down next to Andy. "Why don't we put the wings on? Let Ellen see how she really looks."

"Please," I said before Andy could object. "We'll be careful."

"I'm sure you will, but — "

Marv put his hand over hers. "Andy, this poor old bird needs some air. Let's put her together."

"I guess I'm outvoted," she said with a sigh.

"Maybe we shouldn't, Marv," I said, feeling guilty for asking, "if Andy doesn't want us to."

"No!" Andy said a little sharply. She took a deep breath. "I'm being silly. There's no reason why we shouldn't assemble it completely. Let's do it."

Doing it was a bit easier said than done, even with three of us. The wings were so long they came out of the trailer in pieces that had to be fitted together to form a complete wing. In half an hour we were all sweating, but we had an assembled Nimbus 2.

It was huge. Head on it seemed small, but from the side it was all wing, a thin, narrow, but long, long wing.

"Almost sixty-seven feet," Andy told me, before I even had a chance to ask. "From a mile up, in still air, she'll glide forty-nine miles."

"Forty-nine to one?"

"That's at 56 miles per hour."

I did a quick calculation. "You mean if you get one thermal to 5,280 feet, this sailplane will stay up for nearly an hour?"

"That's right."

"That's incredible!"

"It is, until you do it." Then she laughed, for the first time since we brought the trailer out. "And even after you do it, it's still incredible."

Marv whispered something to Andy. "Sure," she said, smiling. They opened the canopy. "Hop in," she told me.

"Go ahead," she said as I began to protest. "You can't hurt anything. Just step inside. It's a lot easier to get in than a 2-33."

"Here," said Marv, handing me a folded blanket. "Sit on this. There's no seat cushion — you're supposed to sit on a parachute."

I stepped in gingerly and eased down, almost as if I were in a bathtub. It was like stepping from my Beetle into a Mercedes, or so I imagined, since I had never sat in one and probably never would. Once my butt was on the blanket I stretched my legs out under the instrument panel. Marv helped me adjust the rudder pedals, which were way out in the nose. The stick felt funny to me, more squat and contoured, but in a minute I realized how comfortable it was to hold, and how smoothly it moved.

"Lean back," Andy said. "This is a recliner, not an upright."

I did as she said. It felt very odd to lie back, but the wall of the fuselage was so low I had no trouble seeing over the side. Andy lowered the canopy and it shut with a solid plastic thump. She pushed the nose down and Marv lifted the left wing. "That's how it looks," Andy said with a smile. "And you look good in there."

Her voice was muffled by the canopy. I felt isolated, sealed inside a plastic bubble. It was lonely inside the cockpit, to see everything but hear so little. I couldn't imagine how this ship sounded in the air, but I was pretty sure it wouldn't clunk and rattle and whistle like the 2-33.

They opened the canopy again and I stepped out. "Now it's your turn, Andy," Marv told her.

"Oh, no, not me." She shook her head and waved her hand.

"Why not?" asked Marv.

"It's been too long."

"Isn't that more reason to do it?" I asked her. "What can it hurt?"

She looked at us, clearly reluctant. "What can it hurt?" Marv repeated with a challenge in his voice.

"What indeed," Andy muttered as she walked up to the cockpit and stepped inside. She lowered herself down more gracefully than I had and Marv closed the canopy again. She looked small and uncomfortable but she began to smile as her fingers touched the stick. She put one hand up on the panel and touched each instrument in turn. She set the altimeter to 480 feet, the height of the airfield above sea level, and she set the radio to the glider frequency, 123.3. When Marv lifted the canopy gently she looked up at us with tears in her eyes.

"You look wonderful in there," Marv said in a husky voice.

"You look like you belong in there," I said.

"She does," Marv told me. "Did you know that this lady holds every feminine soaring record in this state? And some of the open records? And that she has every achievement badge awarded in this sport — except for the 1000 kilometer diploma?"

"Oh, Marv," Andy sighed.

I looked at her, wide-eyed. "You have all those records and badges? And you're content to teach here? And fly a 2-33? And hardly ever get above 3,000 feet?"

"Marv, you've got a big mouth," she said, but I didn't think she was really as annoyed as she sounded.

"What's the 1,000 kilometer diploma?" I asked her.

"It's the award for flying over 1,000 kilometers, of course."

"And only a handful of pilots have done it," added Marv. "Doris Grove was the first woman to do it, back in 1980. Only one other woman has done it since. Andy was working on it when she stopped flying for records."

"Did you do any of the records in this sailplane?" I asked.

"Most of them," she admitted.

"Well, then?"

She looked at me. " 'Well then' what?"

"Well, then why not go for it?"

"I don't do that kind of flying anymore."

"You could," Marv said.

"I haven't flown cross-country in years," she said, this time with genuine annoyance in her voice. "Watch it — I'm coming out."

She looked from Marv to me. "Forget it. Don't even think

it. Not interested."

Marv lowered the canopy and shook his head. "I never thought I'd see the day when Andy Mahon chickened out on a challenge."

"I am not chickening out!" she practically shouted. "I just don't want to!"

Marv faced her squarely. Very quietly he said, "Andrea, your husband's death did not diminish your own abilities."

Andy looked stunned. I can't imagine what my face looked like. I'd never heard sweet, tactful Marv say anything so boldly.

"You are the finest sailplane pilot I've ever met, man or woman," he continued in the same quiet voice. "You have more guts than anyone I know, except maybe Herb, and certainly more brains. I would give anything, anything to be able to do what you do, and as much as I appreciate all the fine teaching you do, and I'm proud as hell of you for doing it, it makes me sick to know you're not using all your abilities. You possess a talent that the Lord did not see fit to give me, but if he had, I'd be damned if I'd waste it the way you have all these years."

"I'm scared, Marv," Andy said in a small, tight voice, and the hungry look on her face made me want to cry.

"I know you are, hon," he said, and wrapped his big arms around her, and kissed her on top of the head. I turned as silently as I could and walked away.

I was sitting in the office with a flying magazine, minding the phone, when Marv and Andy came in about a half hour later. Marv was beaming; Andy looked both sheepish and pleased. She sat down next to me on the couch and gave me a brief hug. Marv chased Penny off the chair and sat down.

"You know," Andy began, "Marv acts very accommodating most of the time, but deep down he's a very stubborn man." Marv grinned at us. "He's gotten this idea that I should start flying cross-country again, and he's decided that I should finish getting that last 1000 kilometer diploma. Is that the gist of things, Marv?"

Marv nodded, still grinning.

"So, against my better judgment, and over all my protests, it looks like that's the plan."

"Andy, I'm so glad!"

"Mmm. There's only one problem — a badge attempt like this requires a lot of coordination on the ground, a lot of preparation, a lot of practice, since I'm so rusty at this sort of thing. We could use an extra crew member. You interested?"

"You bet I am! When do we start?"

Andy laughed. "Not so fast — good soaring weather for a flight like this doesn't always happen on a weekend. You may have to take a couple days off from work. Can you do that?"

"Sure, I haven't taken any vacation yet. I've used only one sick day, so I've got lots of time coming." Actually, I wouldn't get any vacation time until I had worked at V.D. for a year, but I wasn't going to miss this.

Andy looked troubled. "I don't want you wasting your whole vacation on something like this. You need time for yourself."

"Andy, I have all the time for myself anybody could possibly want, every evening during the week. It would be a real pleasure to do this. I really want to."

"Okay, thanks. Where's Herb? I want to see his reaction to all this."

"He's gone over to Doc Schmidt's. Doc's going to take care of the wasp nest for Herb. I didn't know Doc was a beekeeper. "

"That's who we get our honey from," said Marv. "Well, since we don't have a tow pilot for a little while we sure won't be flying. What say we start planning in the meantime?"

He went to the file cabinet and rummaged in the back of the bottom drawer. He came back with a plastic folder.

"What have you got there?" asked Andy.

"Your old charts. You threw them out the day you put the trailer in the barn. I fished them out of the wastebasket and have been hanging on to them, sort of."

Andy shook her head. "I can't believe you saved them." She opened the folder. "They're no good, of course, too old. I'll have to get new ones."

"Sure, but the route's already marked. All you have to do is transfer it to a new set of charts."

Andy frowned at the charts.

"What's the matter?" Marv asked.

She shook her head again. "It's not the same. Back then it was new, exciting. It had only been done a few times. Now — I'm not saying it's no achievement, it is, and a big one, but even if I make it, so what? They'll just add my name to a growing list of pilots who've done the exact same flight."

"Isn't she something?" Marv said to me. "The woman hasn't flown cross-country in something like six years, and she complains because a thousand kilometers isn't special enough for her." He lowered his voice to a mock whisper. "Between you and me, she'll be lucky if she does a hundred kilometers on her first try."

"Bet you a six-pack I do."

"You're on." They shook on it.

"So what's been done since the thousand kilometers?" I asked them.

"Well, Tom Knauff and Karl Striedieck have flown over a thousand miles," Andy answered.

"There you are," said Marv with satisfaction. "That's your flight."

"Oh, Marv, be serious," Andy said.

"I am serious. Be the first woman to fly a sailplane more than a thousand miles."

"Marv!" I said. "That's great!"

Andy looked at both of us as though we were nuts.

"Why not?" I asked.

"You want to be first at something, or you want to be in the middle of the pack?" added Marv.

She looked down at the charts in her lap, biting her bottom lip, and then at Marv, who nodded, and then at me. I smiled. She shook her head and threw the charts in the air.

"What the hell!" And we all laughed as the charts fell scattered on the floor.

Chapter
Thirteen

When I arrived at Crosswind the following Saturday, I was surprised to see Marv standing outside the office with a tall, grey-haired man. Customers rarely showed up before nine a.m., especially on Saturday mornings. Domestic duties usually preceded soaring, Marv had explained to me when I started there, which worked out well since soaring was pretty much an afternoon sport.

"Ellen, come on over," Marv called as I got out of my car.

Marv grinned at me. He was a dedicated morning person but today's grin was a bit much, even for him. As I got closer I could see that he had trimmed his beard. It no longer reached down to his shirt pockets in random swirls; now it lay compactly just below his shirt collar, the ends neatly scissored. He had gone from Santa Claus to Hemingway in a week. His work shirt was neatly pressed and his chinos were creased, for God's sake. Next to him, the other man seemed a little rumpled in a polo shirt and faded jeans.

"Ellen, I'd like you to meet Arthur Bauer, our new flight instructor. Arthur, this is Ellen Horvath, our line crew. She's the reason you're finally here."

"Pleased to meet you, Ellen," Arthur said, holding out his hand. "I hear from Marv that you're a real mover and shaker."

"Me? I'm just the line crew, and pretty new at it," I said in a puzzled voice. I shook hands with Arthur and looked questioningly at Marv.

"You underrate yourself," he said. "If it weren't for you Andy wouldn't be flying a Nimbus 2 today."

"Is she? Did she fly it this week?"

"No, we had to inspect it this week and repair a little bit of trailer rash. She wanted to wait until you were here to try it out.

But she's so eager she already has it on the line, and Herb is ready to tow her. Go be her crew."

I ran down to the end of the runway without even saying good-bye to Arthur and Marv, which wasn't the most polite thing to do, but I couldn't wait to see this takeoff. Andy was sitting under the long wing when I got there. She quickly stood up and took my hand.

"I'm glad you're here," she said.

"I'm glad you waited till I got here."

"It's all your fault. I guess I had to wait." She smiled as she looked at the sailplane. "Well, the logbooks say she's ready. I've read and reread the manual and reviewed everything I ever knew about flying glass, so I guess I'm ready, too." She looked at me with one eyebrow lifted. "But I haven't flown this bird in a long time, so don't expect a textbook takeoff."

"Don't worry," I said. "You'll do fine."

She laughed at that. "You have the makings of an instructor! Listen, these wings are longer than you're used to, and they'll flex more on takeoff. Because of that they'll be harder to hold, and I'll need you to hold them steady because these big wings need a bit more speed before they can hold themselves up."

"Okay."

She took a deep breath. "Well, here goes. Help me with my parachute."

I held the straps of the parachute while she slipped her arms through. It looked more like a long briefcase than a parachute to me. It was made of the same blue nylon lots of wallets are made of.

"Where'd you get this?" I asked.

"I've had it for a long time. Herb made a special trip this week to get it repacked for me. I don't know what kind of deal he made with the rigger to have it done while he waited; usually it takes a couple weeks. Marv washed the ship down before he inspected it, after he inspected it, and again this morning. You're all making this a team effort. And now Arthur's here, on such short notice. It means a lot to me. You don't know how much."

"It means a lot to us, too."

We looked at each other for a minute, and then Andy rolled

her eyes. "Get me in the cockpit before I change my mind."

"Speaking of Marv," I said as she climbed in. "He's looking awfully dapper this morning."

She reddened. "I don't know what to make of that."

"Don't you?"

"Last week," she said, looking down at the seat belt in her hand, "well, I guess you saw Marv give me a hug."

"Mm-hmm."

"Well, then he kissed me, too."

"Mmm."

She looked up then. "You're not helping me out here."

"Nope," I said, grinning almost as much as Marv.

"Well, it's been a little awkward around here all week, and then this morning he shows up looking like — I don't know what — and I don't know what to do." She pulled her seat belt tight with a wince. "My God, Ellen, it's been such a long time."

"Are you attracted to him?"

Her face got even redder. "Would you be?"

"If I weren't young enough to be his daughter, I sure would."

"Really?"

"Andy, he's the sweetest man I've ever met in my life. And right now I think there's the heart of a sexy eighteen year old inside that pressed shirt. He sure as hell loves you — even I can see that. And he can cook, too!"

"Oh, lord, I don't know what's worse this morning, Marv or this flight."

"Actually, they both sound pretty good to me." I heard the towplane and looked up. Herb taxied toward us, swung the tail around, and shut the engine down. He got out of the cockpit with a loop of rope in his hand, hooked one end to the tail of the plane, and walked toward us with the rest, playing it out as he did.

"You ready?" he asked.

"All set," Andy said in a grim voice.

"Let's do a radio check when I get back to the tug. I want to make sure we're communicating. Anything you want me to do different up there, faster or slower, you tell me."

"Okay, Herb, and thanks."

He grunted. "Ellen. This is a brand new rope. Thicker,

cause this is a heavy ship. Don't use it on anything but the Nimbus."

"Okay," I said, taking the end of the rope from him. "Look all right to you, Andy?" She looked at it carefully and nodded. "Looks fine. Hook it up."

When I did she asked for a release check. I pulled on the rope while she pulled the release.

"The release works fine," I said, hooking the rope up again. "You're all set."

"Help me with the canopy, please."

I helped guide it down and she locked it in place. Then she moved the microphone boom in front of her face.

"Crosswind tug, glider Mike Mike. Radio check."

"Read you loud and clear, Mama." Herb's voice sounded funny through the speaker but even I could hear it clearly. Andy should have no problem with that, at least.

Andy looked over at me as Herb started the engine and I gave her a thumb's up. She nodded and I walked over to the wingtip, where I stood and swung my arm in the signal for "take up slack." Herb slowly taxied forward until the rope was taut, then stopped to wait for my signal. I looked around for incoming traffic, then called "pattern is clear" to Andy. She smiled, a little weakly, I thought, and gave me the thumb's up. I lifted the heavy wingtip and rolled my arm in a circle, then trotted along as the towplane and Nimbus started to roll. The long wings did flex a lot, bouncing in my hand and making it difficult to hold on, but I did until I couldn't run any faster. I stood in the runway and watched as the two aircraft picked up speed. The left tip of the Nimbus almost touched the ground once but then the big ship was in the air, its huge wings curving upward as they developed lift. That flexible, graceful curve never ceased to impress me. The Nimbus flew steadily behind the towplane and I knew Andy was okay. "Fly safely," I murmured, then I ran for the golf cart so I could get back to the office and listen to the radio.

Marv had already turned it on, of course, the volume all the way up so he could hear it outside the office. He and Arthur stood watching the two aircraft climb. Arthur shaded his eyes with his hand. His bent arm was tanned and muscular. He was in good shape for someone his age, which I guessed was mid-forties. I supposed Marv was in reasonable shape, too, although his shirt buttons were straining above the belt from too much beer and his own good cooking. "Nothing a little horizontal exercise wouldn't help," I thought crassly, and crossed my fingers.

I don't think Marv even noticed me walk up. His eyes were riveted on Andy. He held the microphone in his hand, the cord stretched as far as it could reach out the window.

"Mike Mike off tow," we heard as the two aircraft separated. Andy made a turn to the right, then one to the left. I could see the nose of the sailplane tilt up, and then drop down, as she stalled it.

"Just putting it through its paces," Marv muttered, more to himself than to me or Arthur. We watched as Andy maneuvered, then flew straight, then maneuvered again in an aerial ballet. The ship seemed hardly to descend at all, regardless of what she did. Through turn after turn, it seemed to float forever. Gradually, though, it spiraled down, until finally we heard her call "Mike Mike on downwind." She flew parallel to the runway, at what would be an alarmingly low altitude for a 2-33. She turned to line up with the runway, then flew level, skimming low over the ground like a swallow, and touched down not far from us. She rolled to a stop almost at the office door.

I ran out to the side of the Nimbus and caught the wingtip just before it touched the ground, lowering it gently. Marv strode up to the cockpit, grinning again, and helped Andy lift the canopy. Then he knelt down, took her face in his big hands, and kissed her on the mouth.

"Arthur," I said, "let's walk down the other end so I can show you the 2-33s."

"I think that's a good idea," he agreed with a smile. "I don't think they'll even notice we've gone," he said after we walked a few steps.

"Probably not."

"I didn't realize Andy and Marv were involved."

"It's a pretty recent development."

"I see. Well, they're fine people. I'm glad for them."

I was beginning to like Arthur. My first impression of his

preppy clothes and carefully combed, wavy hair made him seem a little distant, the kind of person you would never call Artie or even Art. He still didn't seem like anything but an Arthur, but the formality didn't exclude friendliness.

"It was great that you could come here on such short notice," I told him.

"Well, now that I'm retired I can do what I want with my time."

"You're retired?" I said with surprise. Despite the greying hair, he didn't look old enough.

"As of January 1. I turned sixty and stopped flying 747s."

Wow, I thought, I hope I look half that good when I'm sixty. "This will be quite a change from 747s, won't it?" I asked.

"This will be a lot more fun than flying 747s," he answered. "I've always flown gliders. I have a vintage LK-10 — that's a World War Two trainer — that I've been restoring all spring. I hope to bring it out here in a couple of weeks. When I do, I'll take you for a ride in it."

"Thank you!"

We had reached the towplane. Herb was standing in front of it, mouthing his cigar.

"Nice landing," he said. "Where's Andy now?"

"Up front with Marv," I said.

"Necking," Arthur added casually.

"Hmm," Herb grunted. He spit.

"Aren't you glad for them?" I asked.

Herb gnawed his cigar for a minute. "Yeah, I guess I am. I'm a bachelor. Always have been. Always will be. But Marv always had a domestic streak in him. If he's happy, I'm happy. Long as it doesn't interfere with business."

I took the hint and untied the 2-33s. Arthur helped me roll them to the runway as the first ride of the day walked toward us. While Arthur and the customer were flying, Andy walked over. Her eyes glittered as she reached out to give me a hug. "Thank you, for everything," she said.

"How was it?"

She spread her hands. "I'd forgotten. I truly had forgotten."

"Are you talking about the flight or your reception when you landed?" I asked with a smile. She rewarded me by blushing again.

"Ellen, that was below the belt."

She smiled too much for me to take that remark seriously. "So, is he a good kisser?"

She flashed a wicked grin at me. "As a matter of fact, he's a damn good kisser."

"All right!" We gave each other a high five. "Now tell me about your flight."

We sat under the wing of 42H and she told me. I'd never seen her look so happy. She had a vivacity that I'd never seen before, which made me realize just how muted her demeanor had been until now. This was the real Andy, this animated woman with the eyes of a teenager contradicting the white braid across her shoulder. I could see in her the same conviction of purpose and desire I had seen and envied in Latanya.

We were interrupted by the arrival of her student. Andy immediately shifted gears and greeted him warmly, then began to explain the day's lesson. I helped them get situated and ran the wing as usual. Once they were airborne I watched them for a few moments, as I always did. I felt oddly maternal about each take-off, concerned as much about the towplane as I was about the glider. The first few hundred feet were critical. A mistake on the part of the glider pilot could kill a towpilot. I always relaxed a little once a tow was several hundred feet in the air.

Arthur's 2-33 landed and I went to assist them, a little mechanically. I kept thinking about Andy, her excitement over the flight, her happiness about Marv. Not that I begrudged either of those things, but I couldn't stop that old hollow feeling, the almost ache of rootlessness I'd felt when my parents died, renewed now every time I wondered if I were truly my father's child. It wasn't as bad as that original, awful anguish — the hopeless, joyless oppression I felt at first. This was more sub-dued, but so quick to show itself that I was afraid it was becoming a permanent part of me. One of these mornings I'd wake up and look in the mirror and see a forty-year-old woman, with thin lips pressed together and turned down at the corners, a dead look in her eyes from all those hours under the fluorescent lights at

V.D., counting the days till retirement but dreading it, too, because what followed would be nothing, nothing at all.

I shook the image out of my head. This morning was warm and sunlit, and I had precious hours ahead to spend with people whose thoughts were far happier than mine.

That evening, at the Hoot Owl, Andy outlined our plans for the Fourth of July. We would take advantage of the long week-end and travel to Pennsylvania, to the site where a thousand-mile-flight would be possible. Herb would remain at Crosswind to work with Arthur, and Arthur's wife Judy would take over for Marv in the office. "Understand we're not trying for the record this time," Andy explained. "It's far too soon and I have a lot of practice to do before I'm ready to try it. But it will give me a chance to fly the Nimbus in that area, to see firsthand what I'm up against. Plus, it will give us a chance to see how we work as a team, you and me and Marv."

"Sounds like fun," I said.

"I hope so. By the way, I don't want you to worry how much it's going to cost. When you crew for me, I pay your expenses. That's part of the deal."

"Thank you."

"Don't thank me until you see where we're staying. It's not exactly the Ritz."

Marv winked at me. "As long as she buys us a steak dinner anytime we have to do a retrieve, who cares where we sleep, right?"

He got up to get another pitcher. Andy and I took advantage of the dry spell to go to the john. When we were washing our hands, Andy said, "Ellen, about the sleeping arrangements, would you mind staying in a room by yourself?" I watched the color deepen in her cheeks. "Marv's asked me to share a room with him. I haven't said yes yet, so if you're uncomfortable — "

"Don't be silly! I'd be disappointed if you didn't stay with him. Honestly, Andy, I think it's great and I'm really happy for you both."

"Oh, lord," she sighed. "I haven't — I've never — Ellen, I'm from a different generation than you. I've never — slept — with anyone but my husband."

"Really?"

She nodded solemnly.

"Uh, did you and your husband ever fool around before you got married?"

She shook her head just as solemnly.

"Welcome to the eighties," I told her. "Lightening will not strike you dead, you will not go blind, and nobody will give a shit about your reputation. Of course, with AIDS around you'll need to be careful."

"Ellen!" she said in a shocked voice. "We're talking about Marv!"

"I only want you to be safe," I said in my most Mrs. Pulaski voice. "Have you discussed birth control at all?"

"I'm a bit past worrying about that," she said dryly.

"Then there's nothing to consider except what to wear. Will it be Victoria's Secret or Frederick's of Hollywood?"

"Pink flannel, most likely. Come on, let's go back. Marv probably thinks we fell in and got flushed away."

I let Andy go back to the table alone so she could get her blushes under control. It was crazy. She was the most capable woman I'd ever met, confident and self-assured, yet here I was, thirty years younger and celibate as a nun, advising her on her love life. I walked up to the bar, shaking my head.

"What's bugging you?" asked Pete.

"Nothing. Just trying to figure out the meaning of life."

"Ha! You get that figured out, you won't need to win a lottery. What can I get you?"

"Nothing, thanks, I'm drinking beer with the rest of the crew. I just came over to say hi."

He filled a glass with draft. "On the house."

"Thanks, Pete. What's the occasion?"

He leaned over the bar. "You tell me. Marv trimmed his beard. I never saw such a thing. And look at that — he's holding Andy's hand. They got something going on?"

"Didn't Marv tell you?"

"Nah — he's too much of a gentleman."

"And because I wear grass-stained jeans I'm not too much of a lady to discuss it?"

"Hey — you're female. Women talk about these things. Besides, I gave you a beer. You owe me one."

I liked Pete. He grew up in an Italian neighborhood in Bloomfield. He talked tough but was as kind in his own way as Marv. I'd bet that after tonight he and Patti would be planning a wedding reception.

"Yeah, Pete, there's something going on."

He snorted. " 'Bout time."

I really was a little uncomfortable talking about people who were sitting only a few yards away. To change the subject, I asked "How's the new bartender?"

"Numbnuts?" he said, glancing sideways at his helper, a thin young man in a Hawaiian shirt. "He's working his way through college, right? Well, he may have brains but he's got no sense. He's been here three weeks and he still can't make an old-fashioned right. Why'd you ask? You looking for a job?"

I laughed. "No thanks. I already have one of those."

"Well, you think about it. If you're ever strapped for cash you can moonlight here."

"You serious? I probably couldn't make an old-fashioned if I tried."

"Maybe not now, but you know how to learn. Unlike some people who may not be working here much longer."

"Thanks, Pete. I'll keep the offer in mind if V.D.'s stock ever goes sour."

"Ha! Not in this century — or the next," he said over his shoulder as he walked away to serve another customer.

No, indeed, I thought, as I drank my beer. V.D. was as solid as a rock — and as far as my life was concerned, was becoming a permanent part of it. On that unhappy thought I went back to interrupt the lovebirds.

When I got home that night a letter was tucked in the door. Someone had written on it "Delivered to wrong address," using a pen that had been sitting for too long; the "D" was all but filled in with a blob of still-gummy ink that smeared my thumb. The return address was Latanya's.

I'd been wondering when I would hear from her. I'd hoped she wasn't the kind of person who always promised to write but never did. Since a phone call was more her style, I assumed she was economizing, which probably meant she hadn't found a job yet.

I opened the letter after letting Trevor out of his cage, and read it while he flew laps around the room. When he got tired he landed on top of his cage and pulled on the hook that held up his mirror. Doing this seemed to be great fun, besides making a hell of a racket.

"Trevor!" I called. He looked up and chirped at me. "Gimme kiss," I said. He made a kissing noise and flew onto my shoulder. I turned my head toward him and he kissed me on the mouth. "Trev, we got a letter from Latanya."

"Piss off," he answered.

"No I won't. Listen to this: 'Dear Ellen, Can you believe I've been here over a month? No luck with a job so far but I am still confident. A month's not such a long time to be looking. Plus half the people I want to see are on vacation. No wonder. I'd get out of this city, too, if I were filthy rich. It's hot as hell. Thank god for air conditioning. Roommates are okay but one is a flake' — Coming from Latanya that says a lot, huh, Trev? — 'and keeps turning on all the lights at three in the morning. Very disruptive to the beauty sleep. We had words this week. She says Charles — with the Porsche, I met him at your airport, remember? — she says he must be a dealer to have a car like that, let alone an airplane. I told her she was racist, and that his airplane wasn't even a real airplane, and how the hell can you transport drugs in a stupid little plane that doesn't have an engine or anything. Can you believe her? Just because she never saw a black man drive a Porsche! (I didn't even tell her about the sailboat. We're going on it next weekend to watch the fireworks.) Maybe that's why she keeps turning the lights on. She is some kind of ignorant, I tell you. Mama came up last week and gave me some money and said not to tell Daddy, but he sent me a check in the mail and told me not to tell Mama! He's coming around. I miss you. Write back. Say hi to Trevor. Love, Latanya. P.S. Have you gotten laid yet?'

"Latanya says hi, Trevor."

"Tanya's cool. Say hi, Trevor. Gimme kiss. Piss off."

"Didn't she ever learn about paragraphs?" I read the letter once more, then tossed it on the formica-topped coffee table. "I don't know, Trevor. I guess it isn't easy for anybody, even when you know what you want."

"Birdseed is for the birds," he said. "Kevin Costner. Gimme kiss. Nice ass. Left rudder. More left rudder. I said more left rudder."

Poor Trevor. I hated the thought of leaving him alone again over the Fourth of July weekend.

"Pete and Patti. Pete and Patti. Patti is a pretty bird."

"Patti — sure, Trevor, that's a great idea! I'll call her tomorrow and ask if she wouldn't mind adding one more to the nest for a couple days. Come here."

I put my finger out and he hopped on. I put my hand close to my face. "Lesson time. You ready?"

He leaned forward and put his beak on my upper lip while I talked. It seemed to help him learn faster.

"Okay, Trev. Pay attention. 'Pattern is clear. Pattern is clear. Pattern is clear.' Say it, Trev. 'Pattern is clear.' "

Trevor was one smart parakeet. It would take only a few more vocabulary lessons before he's say it back to me. It was nice to hear another voice in the apartment, even such a tiny and gravelly one.

I always tired of a lesson before Trevor did. I put him in his cage and covered it up.

"Goodnight, Trevor," I said to him, as I did every night. I picked up Latanya's letter and read it once more before going to bed. I could hear Trevor whispering sweet nothings to the bird in the mirror. "I don't know, Trev," I said out loud when I turned out the light. "Maybe we both need to get laid."

Chapter Fourteen

The tree-covered ridges of central Pennsylvania rolled past the windows of Andy's Suburban in long green waves. I had first seen this landscape almost a year ago, on my way out to Chicago, just before my parents died. We had been driving at dusk, then, and the hills were dark and muted, rising out of patchy ground fog. Today in the morning sun these fossils of ancient, once-towering mountains gleamed like mammoth cabochon emeralds.

Marv drove the car along a narrow valley, no more than a mile or two across. Farms lay on either side of the two-lane highway, the foot-high cornstalks growing right up to the base of the ridge that loomed like a huge green wall over the south side of the valley. Strung along the road were small towns, nothing more than clusters of houses and trailers and small grocery stores, most of them with peeling paint and cockeyed shutters. A faded "Chew Mail Pouch Tobacco" ad, painted many years ago on the side of an old barn, showed daylight through the rotting boards.

Andy, sitting in the center of the big bench seat, was the first to spot our destination. "There's the gliderport," she told us, pointing ahead. I saw a large building of corrugated aluminum, painted yellow, with a day-glo orange windsock on the gable end nearest us. Marv eased the Suburban carefully into the driveway. I admired his skill at towing a trailer; I probably would have clipped the sign that read "Bald Eagle Gliderport." We pulled into the nearest parking place and got out. It felt good to stretch after the long drive. The trip had taken nearly four hours and I was eager to find a rest room.

Marv, Andy, and I had been on the road by dawn so we could arrive in time to assemble the ship and give Andy the whole afternoon to fly. I had dropped Trevor off the night before at Pete and Patti's, where I spent the night. Trevor hadn't been too happy about the ride over. Once in a while I lifted a corner of his cage cover to peek at him, and saw him huddled against the mirror, gripping his perch tightly. I felt bad for him, but knew he'd be happier with Patti's attention during the three-day holiday weekend.

Andy led us up to a homey-looking log cabin with a wrap-around porch facing the runway. Several people sat there on old-fashioned chairs, the metal kind with shell-shaped backs you might see rusting at a yard sale. These had been freshly painted: some were red, some white, and some blue. I half wondered if the paint was in honor of the Fourth, but when I went in I saw the patriotic color scheme everywhere.

The cabin was beautiful inside. The far wall was dominated by a great stone fireplace. We gathered in in front of it on a braided rug between two colonial-style sofas, one covered in red fabric with white flowers, the other in navy blue with white flowers. Comfortable-looking wing chairs covered in the same material were scattered around the room, which seemed to take up most of the first floor. Through picture windows that wrapped around two of the walls I could see the length of the runway. The remaining wall was covered with a topographic map showing the crumpled landscape. I felt like I was in a hotel lobby instead of a gliderport.

"Plush, isn't it?" Andy asked me with amusement.

Before I could answer a blond-haired man not much taller than I am walked out of a small corridor opening into the rear of the room.

"May I help you?" he asked, formally. As he came closer I could see that he had incredibly blue eyes.

"I'm Andy Mahon, and this is Ellen Horvath and Marv Armstrong."

"Yes, you called last week. I'm Rudi Zimmerman. How nice to meet you all. Welcome to Bald Eagle Gliderport." As he spoke I realized that what I had mistaken for formality was actually a German accent. His tone was extremely cordial.

"I haven't been here in several years," Andy said. "It's a pleasure to be back."

"I am glad to hear you say that. Ernst and I enjoy meeting

everyone who flew here before the previous owners retired. We hope you will not find our services diminished in any way. Let me show you where you can assemble," he said, holding the door open for us. "You have picked a wonderful weekend to soar with us. Several of our pilots have already launched and report excellent lift. The forecast for the remainder of the weekend is for strong thermal conditions."

"Any chance of ridge lift?" Andy asked.

"Unfortunately, no, but this is not yet our ridge season, of course."

He led us to a large grassy area in front of the metal building, which turned out to be a hangar. The doors were wide open. Inside, about half the space was empty. Two pristine 2-33s were stashed in the far corners, and a red 1-26 was in front of them. The floor was spotless.

"We have another 2-33, already in the air with a solo student, and Ernst is up in our two-place glass ship with another student. Holiday weekends are a little slow for us, otherwise these gliders would be in the air," Rudi told us in an apologetic tone. "We have a wash pad over here in front of the hangar, and a hose that you can use to fill your wings with water ballast. Do you need assistance assembling your ship?"

"No thank you," Andy told him. "We'll be fine."

"Excellent. You can park anywhere but please do not drive on the runway itself. Let me know when you are ready to launch." He smiled and walked away a few steps, then turned back. "I almost forgot. If you are hungry we have a restaurant on the field, just past the cabin. We call it Runway Seven. There are restrooms in there, and also in the cabin, just down the hall from the lounge. On the second floor of the cabin we have two classrooms which are currently available if you'd like to use them for flight planning. Also on the second floor is the office. When you are ready, Andy, please come upstairs and we will fill out some paperwork. Then you'll be free to soar all afternoon." He smiled again and left.

I must have stared after him with my mouth gaping. Marv chuckled and Andy said, "Quite a place, isn't it?"

I nodded. Marv rolled his eyes and grinned.

"This gliderport was started about twenty years ago by an older couple, Jean and Henry Smith, who'd been involved in soaring since the late thirties," Andy explained as we walked back to the Suburban. "They started with a trailer like ours, and build it up into what you see today. Henry died about three years ago, and Jean sold it to Rudi and Ernst not long afterward. She doesn't live too far from here and I'm told she still stops in every once in a while.

"They obviously have a fine business going. Most of their soaring is done in the fall, winter, and spring, actually, because that's when the wind blows right for ridge lift. A good northwest wind blowing against that big ridge lets a pilot soar all day. So they do a great business in the colder months — that's why there's such a big fireplace — plus they have a brisk mail-order business in pilot supplies. They're doing all right."

"I guess so," I said drily. "Listen, I don't know about you but I have got to find that rest room."

"Okay," Andy said, "but don't take too long. There's lift!"

After my brief detour we pulled the trailer in front of the hangar and assembled the Nimbus. In an hour and a half Andy was in the air. Marv left to check in at the motel and I sat on the porch, rocking slowly and listening for Andy on a hand-held radio. The day was warm and the shade of the porch was welcome. I sipped a cold soda and looked around. The runway was remarkably tranquil, owing to the good lift; practically every sailplane that took off stayed up for hours. There was nothing to do but sit and enjoy the peace and quiet. This crewing stuff was a good deal.

When Marv came back I let him hold the radio. He sat down with a sigh of pure satisfaction. "Can't beat it, can you?" he asked. "Think of all the people who spend this weekend in a city, or stuck in traffic on the way to the shore. All the cars, all the crowds. What more do you need than a comfortable chair, a cool drink, and the company of a fine lady?"

"Are you referring to me or to Andy?"

He laughed. "Two fine ladies, then."

"Thank you."

"Funny how things turn out," he said. "A few months ago —

heck, a few weeks ago — I would never have thought we'd be sitting here today. Andy's all fired up about a new record, and she's doing it in a sailplane that hadn't seen the light of day in years. And we're, well, she and I...." He looked intently at the ridge.

I decided to come to his rescue. "Marv, I haven't had a chance to tell you, but I'm really happy you and Andy are getting together."

"Thank you, Ellen. That means a lot to me."

"Why should it?"

"I guess my generation worries more about what other people think than yours does. Besides, when you care about people, it always matters what they think. It's a kind of validation, I guess."

"Do you have any doubts?"

"No — no," he said in a very doubtful voice.

"Does it feel right to you?"

"That it sure does."

"That's all that matters, then. To hell with anyone who says otherwise. Besides, it feels right to everyone else, anyway."

"It does?" he asked, finally looking me square in the eye.

It was my turn to laugh. "Some things are pretty god damn obvious, Marv."

He chuckled, and then said in a more serious voice, "And what about you?"

"What about me?"

"Have we brought you any closer to what you really want?"

"I don't think I know what that is yet."

"Well, you've got plenty of time to figure it out."

"That's right. I do."

He shook his head. "You have a lot more patience than most people your age. I thought your generation wanted to take the world by storm, do something big, make a dent in things. Make a difference."

"I think that was my parents' generation. Sometimes I think they took all the 'issues' and didn't leave much of anything for us."

"It's been real hard for you, hasn't it, since they died."

"Yeah, well, things are easing up. I have a steady job, at least."

"You still make copies all day?"

"No, thank god! I got a promotion a couple months ago. I'm sort of a receptionist now. They seem happy with my work. My supervisor thinks I have a great future in the clerical department. So I guess I can work there for the next forty years, if I want."

"Job security's not a bad thing to have."

"No."

Marv looked at me sideways, then resumed his scrutiny of the ridge. He was funny about that. Indoors, he'd always look me straight in the eye; outdoors, his eyes always sought whatever happened to be flying at the time. I had gotten used to this split of attention — part of him focused on the sky, part of him intent on the conversation.

We sat quietly, watching a sailplane tracking back and forth hundreds of feet above the ridge top.

"I guess if your work is fairly routine you'll have to find some other way to achieve distinction," Marv said after a few minutes.

"Like what?"

"Up to you...maybe you should break all of Andy's records."

I laughed at that. "Gimme a break, Marv! I haven't even soloed yet!"

"So, first you solo, then you get your license, and then what? Are you going to fly in circles over the airport all the time?"

I shrugged.

"I'll bet Andy would really like it if her records were broken by someone like you. Someone she taught. Someone she cares for. Someone for whom it would mean as much as it did to her."

"Marv, I can't even land right. Especially in a crosswind, and that's all we ever have."

"Nonsense. Andy says you land quite well on Saturdays."

"Very funny."

"It's true. She says you fly better in general on Saturdays. On Sundays you have a little trouble. She thinks you're probably tired by Sunday. What do you think?"

"I think Andy's coming back. Look, isn't that the Nimbus?"

On cue we heard her terse radio message, "Mike Mike ground, Mama coming home."

"I'll go get the tail dolly," I said, grateful to get up and do something, and glad to end a conversation that had turned far too serious for a holiday weekend. Break Andy's records indeed.

Andy made a textbook landing, as always, and clambered out of the cockpit with a broad smile. "Four and a half hours!"

"Where did you go?" I asked her. "You were out of sight."

"I wanted to get at least as far as Altoona, but the lift was so good I made it all the way to Bedford and back."

"Bedford?" I tried to picture it from the charts. "That's southwest of here, right?"

"Right. It's not too far. The round trip was only about eighty miles."

"Eighty miles!" From my point of view it might as well have been eight hundred.

"I was tired from the drive out, or I would have gone farther. Still, that's the longest flight I've done in years. It felt good. Damn good."

Marv walked up to us with a cold soda in his hand. "I'd offer you a beer but the field rules are no booze until after sundown."

"Thanks anyway," Andy said to him with a smile. "Anything wet and cold will taste great right now."

"Shall we put her to bed?" he asked.

"Sure, I'm pooped."

We rolled the Nimbus to the tie down area. No rain was forecast for the evening so we were happy to tie it down for the night and avoid the cumbersome process of disassembly. After the ship was secure Marv and I accompanied Andy to the office to check tomorrow's weather forecast. The office was on the second floor of the cabin, over the pilot's lounge, with the same wraparound view of the runway. Rudi, who was on the telephone, waved to us from behind the counter. The bulletin board was covered with weather information: maps showing the forecast for the next twelve hours and the next twenty-four, a radar summary that showed no precipitation for hundreds of miles around us; an adiabatic chart, a complicated affair with dotted lines, solid lines, slanting lines, crisscrossed lines, temperatures, and altitudes. From this mess, Andy told me, anyone could predict the height of thermals for the day.

"I'll take your word for it," I said.

"You'll do more than that," she said with a grin. "You'll have to know how to do this when you take your written exam. In fact, you'll have to know about every one of these charts and how to interpret them. I can see we'll have to do some serious ground school when we get back."

"Andy, how was your flight?" Rudi asked when he hung up the phone.

"Wonderful! I went down to Bedford."

"Congratulations. And what have you planned for tomorrow?"

"That depends on the weather."

"Tomorrow should be even better than today. We will take a sounding first thing in the morning and should have the thermal index plotted by eight a.m. I'm sure it will be favorable for a long flight."

"Well, if it's better than today I'll plan on it. Thanks, Rudi."

"I am not responsible for the good weather but I am always happy to take credit for it." He smiled at Andy, showing a deep dimple on the right side of his mouth.

"You know, Rudi, with lift like we had today, I'd feel real bad if Ellen didn't get a chance to soar while we're here. Can we schedule her in one of your ships?"

"Oh, thanks, Andy," I said, "but I'm used to being on the ground, you know." Actually, I was dying to fly but was sure the rates at this place would be way over my budget.

"Nonsense. I told you I take care of my crew. My treat."

"I am afraid we're rather booked up for the rest of today," Rudi said, apologetically. "If you can wait until tomorrow, though, I'll be happy to take you up myself."

"Please don't go to any trouble," I said.

"It's no trouble at all. Ernst and I take turns in the office. Tomorrow is my day to fly. Would 12:30 be convenient?"

"That would be fine."

"Good. I'll meet you downstairs."

Andy leaned over the counter and whispered something that

made Rudi's dimple deepen. "Certainly," he said. "Consider it done."

"What was that about?" I asked her on the way downstairs.

"You'll see," was all she said in her most instructorly voice.

We had an early supper in the field restaurant. Runway Seven was a small, narrow place, apparently made from the old trailer that had been the gliderport's first building. A half dozen long tables were arranged in two rows, with seating and service family style to promote sociability. Ernst's wife, Anna, was the hostess and chief waitress, and her mother was the cook. After an excellent dinner of wiener schnitzel we gathered with the other pilots and guests at the picnic tables outside the restaurant, where we were able to drink beer or wine as long as we stayed in the picnic area. A pilot from New York state brought over a guitar and started playing folk songs.

By the time the fireflies winked on, tiredness forced us to leave the sing-along. I almost dozed off on the short ride to the motel. Andy had warned that the local accommodations were less than luxurious so I was prepared for the worst, but the Nittany Nights Motel was clean and comfortable. The bathroom was small and the TV black and white, but the bed was firm and the sheets were clean. I said goodnight to Andy and Marv, whose room I noticed was several doors down from mine. I guessed the motel walls were thin.

The next morning I was awakened by a knock on the door. "Aren't you ready, yet?" Andy asked when I opened it.

"It'll only take me a few minutes to get dressed," I said, not fully awake. "I'll meet you out there in ten minutes."

She was waiting for me when I walked out just nine minutes later, face washed and teeth brushed and far better able to cope with the concept of awakeness. The sun was still behind the ridge and the cool morning air was refreshing. Andy looked lovely in the diffuse light, relaxed and full of energy at the same time.

"Sleep well?" I asked in a casual voice.

"None of your business," she answered, then smiled and gave me a hug. "I haven't been so happy in a long, long time."

"I know. I'm glad. Where's Marv?"

"He went to get gas. In case I land out today, he wants to be prepared."

"I don't know, Andy, if he has so little faith in you maybe you should reconsider this relationship."

"He's being the perfect crew. Pay attention and you might learn something."

Marv was singing when he picked us up. He sang all the way to the gliderport, and continued singing as we helped Andy prepare for the day's flight. He hummed while we checked on the weather, which promised to be excellent. Once Andy was in the cockpit Marv hooked her up himself and gave her a kiss good-bye before closing the canopy. All I had to do was run the wing. She was in the air by 10:30.

"We have two hours before your flight," Marv said. "How about a driving lesson?"

"I already know how to drive, thanks."

"Ah, but can you drive a car that's towing a trailer?"

He had a point. We picked up Andy's trailer and drove to a small shopping mall across the street from where Marv had bought the gas. Since this was Sunday morning the mall was deserted, so we had lots of room to work. We traded places and Marv began to coach me. Forward was no problem, neither were right and left turns, but backing up was another story. The trailer had a mind of its own and never wanted to go in the direction I wanted it to. After an hour I got it to settle down some, but it would take a while before I could back up as smoothly as Marv.

I drove back to the gliderport and did a reasonable job of parking the trailer. After a quick sandwich I met Rudi in front of the office. He was dressed casually today, in a T-shirt and shorts. With his blond hair and mirrored sunglasses he would have looked at home with a surfboard tucked under his arm. Instead, he held two parachutes.

"Hi," I said. "What are those for?"

"Andy thought you might enjoy it if we did a loop or two," he told me.

"I thought you weren't supposed to do that in a 2-33."

"Ah, but we're not going to fly in a 2-33. We're taking the Grob, and it's certified for aerobatic flight."

"So that's what the whispering was about yesterday."

"That was it. Come, follow me."

We walked over to the Grob, a two-place fiberglass sailplane, gleaming white except for a red-striped rudder. It was a big ship, not as long winged as Andy's Nimbus, but heavy and solid looking.

"Have you ever worn a parachute?" asked Rudi.

"Nope."

"Let me help you put it on. You will have to pardon me, this gets a little intimate," he said with a grin as he reached between my legs to pull the straps up. Somehow I didn't think he was the least embarrassed about the situation. He hooked each strap to a clasp at my hips and pulled them so tight I couldn't stand upright, then he pulled the chest strap tight. "I know it is awkward while standing up, but you'll feel quite comfortable when you sit. In fact, we may even have to tighten the straps again once you're seated."

"Thanks, I can probably handle that part myself."

He laughed and showed me how to climb in without leaning on the expensive canopy. The seat belts were different from those in a 2-33. When Rudi saw me fumbling he showed me how they work. "Again, my apologies, but acrobatic planes have an extra belt, called a crotch strap. It hooks like so," he said, demonstrating.

"I'll bet you do that to all the girls," I told him.

"You're right, I do." He knelt beside the cockpit. "Would you like me to explain the instruments?"

"Altimeter, airspeed, compass, variometer," I said, pointing to each.

"I beg your pardon. I didn't realize you flew sailplanes."

"I'm a student of Andy's."

"Then you can do the takeoff. Hold the stick in this position and she'll take off on her own when she's ready."

He climbed in the back seat and the line boy hooked us up. In a moment we were rolling behind the towplane, and then we were airborne. I hadn't flown behind such a towplane before. It was a Pawnee, a low-winged, boxy looking plane with struts above the wings. The air was bumpy and I had a hard time keeping in position. The controls felt different from a 2-33's and I couldn't stop the sailplane from yawing back and forth. Frustration turned to fright when the towplane turned left and pointed straight at the ridge. It grew larger and larger until it filled my field of view. I could see individual leaves on the trees.

"How close is he going to get?" I yelled.

"Don't worry. We haven't hit it yet."

Just as I thought we couldn't possibly get closer the Pawnee turned parallel to the ridge, only a small comfort because the tree-tops skimmed past us at what seemed only inches away. No matter how well we climbed, they were too close for me.

We released at only 2,000 feet. Rudi helped me center the ship in the lift and we circled in the rough air, climbing quickly to more than six thousand feet.

"Let me take it for a few minutes so you can enjoy the scenery," Rudi said. He pointed the sailplane along the top of the ridge and flew straight. I'd never seen anything like it. Ahead of us, the ridge lay like a green spine, rounded and tree-covered and miles long. It sprawled as far as I could see, with a valley on either side and another ridge roughly parallel to it to the south. To the north was a hilly plateau, but my eyes were drawn to the ridge. I couldn't help but look down its length, and wonder what lay out of sight. For the first time I felt a real desire to fly far from the gliderport, to follow that long green line wherever it might lead.

"I wish we could go," I said.

"Go where?"

"Anywhere, out there. Away."

"Let's do it. See if you can get to Altoona."

"Don't we have to land soon?"

"No. We have the ship all afternoon."

"How did you swing that?"

"It's my gliderport. Let's go. I see a beautiful cloud ahead of us. I'll bet you it takes us halfway to Altoona."

I was skeptical but proved wrong. I couldn't believe how little altitude we lost. The sailplane seemed to float forever, if we let it, but Rudi showed me how to speed up between thermals to maximize our cross-country progress.

"How long have you been doing this?" I asked him.

"Instructing, or flying sailplanes?"

"Both."

"I started flying sailplanes when I was sixteen. That was twelve years ago. I've been instructing since I was twenty."

"Where did you learn?"

"In Switzerland. Ernst and I met at a glider club, outside Bern. That's where we are both from."

"Oh! I thought you were German."

"Horrors! Don't ever say that to a Swiss."

"Sorry. Is Switzerland as beautiful as it seems in pictures?"

"More so."

"Then why did you leave?"

"I like America's bigness. Its variety. Its freedom. Switzerland is a little too regulated, too predictable, too safe. It gave me claustrophobia. Do you know what I mean?"

"I know exactly what you mean."

"How so?"

"My job. Safe. Predictable. Stifling."

"Then quit."

"That's easy to say. Quitting doesn't pay the rent."

"Don't you live at home with your family?"

"I have no family."

"I'm sorry to hear that."

I never knew what to say to that remark, so I said nothing. We flew in silence for a while, except for Rudi's gentle corrections of my technique. I had a hard time getting used to the feel of the ship. My timing was off and my turns were sloppy.

"Shall I take it for a few minutes to give you a rest?" Rudi offered.

"Thanks," I said, flexing my right hand.

"It's hard work today. The thermals are strong and rough."

Maybe they were, but when Rudi took the controls the ship settled into smooth, steep turns that took us up efficiently.

"You fly so smoothly," I told him.

"Thank you. You're doing very well, by the way, for your first time in glass. It's quite a change from a 2-33. Don't be too hard on yourself. By the way, have you noticed where we are?"

I looked down. A large city lay below us. "Altoona? Already?"

"That's right. I told you it would be easy. Well, shall we see how quickly we can get back?"

We turned for the gliderport and flew swiftly, stopping to circle only briefly. In a 2-33 it would have taken hours but for the Grob it was a quick flight back. "Now," said Rudi, "It's too rough for much aerobatic flying, but we should be able to do a trick or two. Are you securely belted?"

I pulled each strap even tighter and nodded. Suddenly the ridge was above our heads and the blue sky was below us.

"How do you like flying inverted?" Rudi asked.

"I'm not sure," I said. I couldn't keep my feet on the rudders, and I didn't like the feel of my body straining at the straps. Nothing more than a thin sheet of plexiglass lay between me and the treetops.

"It's a bit disconcerting the first time," Rudi said, rolling upright. "There. Shall we try a loop?"

"Sure," I said, hoping I sounded brave.

My stomach lurched a little as he nosed the ship over. The speed built up quickly and I could hear the wind whistle by, then we pitched up and up and up until the ground passed overhead, then we were pointed straight down and I could feel my cheeks sag and I was pressed into the seat and suddenly it was over.

"That was fun," I said truthfully. "Can we do it again?"

We did. And again. And again. "Can we go inverted again," I asked when I could catch my breath. Rudi rolled the ship and once more I was looking up at the trees. This time it seemed a bit less dizzying but I still held onto my seat cushion as hard as I could. In a few minutes Rudi rolled right side up and did one more loop, then he handed the controls back to me.

"Our pattern can be a little unnerving the first time around. I'll talk you through it, so trust me. We will not hit the trees. It will just look that way."

He was right. We flew the downwind leg right over the ridge. When I looked to the right I thought our wingtip would crash through the treetops. I solved the problem by not looking. I followed Rudi's directions and soon we were lined up on final approach.

"Do you want to land it?" he asked.

"How much does this sailplane cost?"

"About twenty-five thousand."

"It's all yours," I said. He laughed and took over, landing as smoothly as he had flown.

"Thank you for a lovely flight," I said when we got out of the plane and shrugged off our parachutes.

"My pleasure," he said, and we shook hands. "I'll fly with you anytime, Ellen Horvath. You're going to be a fine glider pilot someday." He held my hand a moment longer than he needed to before releasing it and greeting the next customer. I walked back to the cabin with my right hand tingling.

Andy flew for six hours that day, covering three hundred kilometers. She came back elated, and gave us an inch-by-inch report of the flight over dinner, a barbecue hosted by the gliderport. Rudi and Ernst had adopted this country completely, and served a very American meal of hot dogs and hamburgers, potato salad, cole slaw, and a whole keg of beer. After dinner Marv produced a stash of bottle rockets and every male on the field suddenly reverted to childhood. I was watching this display of gross immaturity when Rudi came over and sat down next to me.

"Did you enjoy the picnic?" he asked.

"Very much, thank you. Anna and her mother are wonderful cooks."

"Yes they are."

"Is Anna Swiss, too? She doesn't have an accent."

"Actually, Anna is from Hoboken. She met Ernst in Switzerland when she was in college, doing her junior year abroad. He was a senior. They were married by the end of the school year, and moved to the States. When they heard this gliderport was for sale, they called me and I came over to be a partner."

"And have you a wife?"

"Are you joking? With a whole university full of women on the other side of the ridge?"

"I see."

"Actually, the pickings are not so great as you might suppose.

Most of the women are too young, or too frivolous, or afraid to fly."

"Have you brought any of them out here?"

"Oh yes," he said with a grin. "It's my standard test."

"I see. If they use the sick-sack you know the relationship is doomed."

"Something like that."

"I can't decide whether that's being practical or whether it's more like checking a horse's teeth."

Before he had a chance to counter that Ernst called from the cabin porch.

"Rudi, telephone!"

He grimaced. "Can't you handle it?" he called.

"No, it's for you."

"Damn." He shrugged his shoulders. "That's one disadvantage of owning the gliderport. Excuse me, please."

"Of course."

He walked toward the cabin. Even in the fading light I could see that he had great legs, and I wondered what the small of his back looked like when he took off his T-shirt. "Oh, get real, Horvath," I said to myself. "He's a hunk and he's got the pick of every female on campus. He's just being nice to the customers."

All the same, I thought, remembering how my hand felt when he held it, if he's looking for a levelheaded pilot type, this has possibilities. Definite possibilities.

Chapter Fifteen

When we woke Monday morning the overcast sky made it apparent that this would be no soaring day, so Andy decided to pack up and head home early. We were not the only ones. The gliderport, so festive the night before, was quiet except for instructions given by fussy pilots to their crews as they dismantled their sailplanes. We had just put the last piece of Nimbus wing into the trailer when the first drops of rain fell. We secured the wing and closed up the trailer in the increasing wet, and dashed to the shelter of the cabin porch to wring out our T-shirts.

Inside, the cool, dry air was a welcome change, and I would have been happy to stay there all day, but Andy was loathe to prolong our departure. We trooped upstairs to settle her account and say good-bye.

"I am sorry to see you leave so early," Rudi said. "Everyone is deserting us this morning and we shall have a very lonely afternoon." He shook hands with Andy and Marv and then with me, covering my right hand with his left. "It has been a pleasure to meet you and fly with you, Ellen. I hope to see you again soon. Perhaps we can share a ridge flight together."

"I'd like that," was all I said.

He let go of my hand — a bit reluctantly, unless that was just wishful thinking on my part — and stood casually with his hands in his pockets as we said good-bye and left.

"Funny," Andy said as we reached the cabin porch. "Rudi didn't hold my hand. Did he hold your hand, Marv?"

"Not mine. Did he hold your hand, Andy?"

"All right, cut the vaudeville routine," I said before she could answer.

"Well, we couldn't help but notice," she said sweetly.

"It was no big deal."

"Of course it wasn't," she said.

"Utterly insignificant," Marv agreed.

They had spent only two nights together and already they were playing matchmaker. It was going to be a long ride home.

It was a long ride, and a dismal one in the rain. After we got off the subject of Rudi, Andy stared straight ahead, disappointed to be missing a day of flying, while Marv concentrated on steering us safely through the holiday traffic. With every wet mile that brought us closer to home I grew more and more unhappy. The weekend had been a vacation for me, the first I'd had in a long time. Andy didn't think we'd be back until the fall, when the cool weather brought the northwest winds she needed for an attempt at the record. Down the highway was the old routine, and long evenings in a stifling studio apartment. I fervently hoped for an early autumn.

We outpaced the rain at the Jersey border and pulled into Crosswind under a threatening but still dry sky. Arthur and his wife were surprised to see us so early in the day, but a rumble of thunder punctuating our arrival made them realize why we had cut our trip short. After securing all the aircraft, we exchanged stories about the weekend. Crosswind had done a good business, which made Herb happy; he listened to Andy's stories with a series of appreciative grunts and Penny curled up on his feet. Afterwards we closed up early and caravaned over to the Hoot Owl. Trevor was ecstatic when I walked in; he hopped from perch to perch, chirping loudly, until I opened the cage, then he flew straight to my hand, stretching up toward my face to cover my mouth and chin with little kisses. He was not happy when I put him back and covered him up for the return trip. He banged the mirror angrily and yelled at me in a harsh chattering syllable, a "ch-ch-ch" sound of frustration. Fortunately he quieted down as soon as I lifted the cage and set it in the car. When we arrived home I opened the cage door right away, but he sat inside sulking for a long while. I got the point.

When I walked into work Tuesday morning the door shut behind me with a clang that echoed in my head like a cell door slamming shut in a B-movie. I had no hope of breathing fresh air until lunch time, if you can call fresh the vapors from melting asphalt and car exhaust. My skirt and blouse felt as constricting as a corset and my pantyhose stuck to my sunburned legs. I fidgeted until my break, then escaped the desk for fifteen precious minutes. At the stairwell I hesitated. I could run downstairs for a snack, as I always did, or I could do something I'd been putting off for a long time. I turned toward the bank of elevators and pushed the up button.

The elevator arrived with a discreet opening of doors and I went in. Taking a deep breath I pushed the button for the ninth floor, arriving there too quickly. I hesitated for a moment in the reception area, awed by the plush carpet, the recessed lighting, the reception desk made from real wood instead of painted steel, as mine was. The receptionist eyed me curiously.

"Mr. Cahill's office?" I inquired.

"Down the hall to your right, third door, but he's not in," the receptionist informed me, fingering the beads around the collar of her silk blouse.

"When do you expect him?" I asked.

"He's on vacation. He won't be back until August. Would you like to leave a message?"

"No, no message." I turned back to the elevator with my heart pounding in a confusion of disappointment and relief. It had taken so long to work up the nerve to see him, that now I wanted to get it over with, quickly. Yet I hadn't prepared anything to say, and still didn't know what I could possibly say to him. Hello, I think you might be my father, and I want to see for myself if there's any resemblance? Hello, did you fool around with my mother twenty-one years ago? Mind if I compare noses?

My hand shook a little as I pressed the elevator button. August. A whole month's vacation. I would have to work at V.D. for fifteen years to qualify for a vacation that long. Fifteen years was a big price to pay for four weeks in Lavalette. Of course, a man like Cahill was probably in Hawaii or Cancun, but places like that were out of reach on a clerk's pay. I stepped off the elevator and regarded my work station with dismay. Thin grey industrial carpet underlay the black steel desk, and harsh fluorescent lights glared overhead. The view from the windows, which I could see only when I walked to the rest room, was of dreary downtown buildings, dirty brick facades and tarred roofs. How could I stand fifteen more years of this? I didn't think I could handle fifteen more minutes. Thank god for weekends.

The short post-holiday week seemed much longer than the regular work week. Half the staff was on vacation, and there was scarcely enough work to keep me from looking at the clock every five minutes. I began to borrow magazines from the main reception area on the ground floor, to fill in the time between phone calls. I actually began to look forward to a dint of light typing, just for something to do. How quickly, in contrast, did the weekend zoom by. Despite the onset of summer haze, Crosswind was always busy with students and sightseeing rides. From the moment I arrived until dark, I was active, with scarcely time for a quick sandwich or a bathroom break. Saturday and Sunday evening were a blur of beer pitchers and flying talk on the porch of the Hoot Owl. The only break in the routine came a week after we returned from Pennsylvania. A package was lying on the front stoop when I got home from work, one of those awful squishy bags that spew out grey shreds of fuzz when you tear them open. The return address was Bald Eagle Gliderport. Curious, I opened it right there, and pulled out a purple T-shirt, with a soaring eagle on the front and the words "Bald Eagle Gliderport" on the back. The note that fell down as I opened the shirt was from Rudi: "I couldn't let you go without a souvenir to remember us by. I hope you like the color; I think it will suit you very well. I look forward to your next visit. Regards, Rudi." Well, well, I thought. What do you know about that?

Upstairs, I turned on the window fan and let Trevor out while I showered and changed into the T-shirt and a pair of shorts. Trevor sat on my shoulder while I reread the note. "You poop on my new shirt and I'll put you in the cage," I threatened. "Look what it says, Trev. 'To remember us by'. Us, not me. Minus one point. But 'I look forward,' not we. Plus one point. And what do I do about 'Regards'? Not 'warmest regards' or even 'warm regards', just 'regards'. Very neutral. Very correct. No points there." I rubbed Trevor's cheek feathers thoughtfully, and he fluffed them out with pleasure. "So, is this standard business practice? Andy spent all the money, shouldn't she get the lagniappe? Do you think she got one, too...and Marv? Would he send us all T-shirts? Not very likely, hmm? So what does Emily Post recommend? Am I to send it back in a huff, saying I don't accept gifts from men I hardly know? Nah, too Victorian. Besides, I like the shirt. Do I send a thank you note? I haven't written one of those since the ninth grade. Am I over complicating this? What would you do, Trev?"

He turned his head so I could rub the other side, which of course I did, exposing the little pink oval of his ear. He closed his eyes in satisfaction, and I kissed the top of his head, and decided to sleep on my etiquette problem.

At lunch the next day I bought a postcard with a picture of Lake Lenape on it. I addressed it to Rudi while I ate a tuna sandwich on a bench in the downtown mini-park, and then I got stuck. With only a few minutes left before I had to go back inside, I finally wrote "Thanks for the shirt. Purple's my favorite color. See you when the wind blows." After a brief internal debate I signed it, "Regards, Ellen," slurped on the stamp, and dropped it in a mail box before I could change my mind. I spent the rest of the afternoon worrying that the remark about my favorite color was too personal.

True to her word, Andy began setting aside part of each weekend for ground school. She had several pupils so it made sense for her to combine her tutoring into scheduled classes, held informally at the picnic tables in good weather, and in the trailer during bad. I couldn't get out of these classes, of course, although I didn't see any real point in my attending, since solo was still a long way off. My tow techniques had improved somewhat, to the degree that Andy tortured me with a maneuver called boxing the wake, which meant that I swung the sailplane far to the right, then down and over to the left, and then up again, all without encountering the turbulence of the towplane's prop wash. Although it sounded simple it required a lot of rudder work, and Andy was forever stomping on the pedals to show me that I really didn't have them pressed down as far as I thought I had. Once off tow, I could handle the sailplane well enough, but Andy was becoming more critical. Little slips of grace and coordination that she would have ignored a few months ago were now major flaws to be corrected. Her standards seemed to outpace my skills, making for some frustrating flights, but nothing was more frustrating than the landing pattern. It would be easy, I thought, if only it weren't for that infernal crosswind, and even that I could overcome if it just behaved consistently. But the only consistent thing about soaring seemed to be that no two flights were ever the same. I longed for a "normal" flight, a baseline to start from, but each time I had to land I was more aware of the fickle wind that seemed to delight in tipping a wing up at the worst possible time, or slowing down suddenly so that the sailplane dropped twenty feet with a lurch, or changing direction so that now we were landing downwind when only seconds before we'd had a head wind. And Marv was right, I discovered to my chagrin, I really did fly lousy on Sundays. I think part of me just didn't want the weekend to end, and so resisted every effort at a decent landing on the last flight of the day.

July passed into August with little progress in my skills, hampered now by the poor visibility of the hazy days of summer. Some weekends we couldn't do more than a landing pattern, some not even that. When a week or two went by without a flight, I grew as rusty as if I hadn't flown in months. I sometimes wondered if I were really meant to fly.

At work I got cold feet again, and put off my visit to John Cahill. I just couldn't think of a plausible reason for showing up on the ninth floor, which was an excellent excuse for putting off the whole confrontation. Besides, what would I do if I turned out to be his spitting image? I tried to forget the whole thing, but one night I had a dream that he came out to Crosswind for a glider ride, and Marv told him he had to wait because my parents were on line ahead of him. I woke up at that and spent the rest of the night watching a George Raft movie and Man from U.N.C.L.E. rerun.

I don't know how days that crawl merge into months that fly, but with a shock I turned the page of the calendar and stared at Labor Day Weekend. That weekend had always marked the new year for me, the end of summer and the start of another school year. My internal clock was more tuned in to the beginning of September than to the beginning of January. How fitting, I thought ironically, for my parents to die on that weekend. After work on Friday I bought a pot of rust-colored mums at the florist, and drove to the cemetery. I hadn't been there all summer. I felt guilty when I saw that somebody — probably Mrs. Pulaski — had kept the grass clipped around the headstone, and had planted geraniums. I set the mums down, sorry that I hadn't picked another color that didn't clash so badly with the cherry-red blossoms already there. I stood there for a few moments, thinking, it's been a year, it's been a year, but I couldn't think of anything else, and I had long since given up praying. I walked away, feeling that I ought to be crying, but I couldn't talk myself into it. After all, a year later was the time to stop mourning, I told myself, time to open the blinds and take down the crape and change from black to purple.

At home I spent the evening cleaning violently. In a tribute to my mother I scrubbed everything that sat still for it, even evicting Trevor from his cage, which I took apart and soaked while I moved all the furniture, and even vacuumed under the rugs. The next morning I packed up Trevor and enough clothes for the weekend — excluding Rudi's T-shirt. I hadn't the nerve to wear it at Crosswind just yet. If I'd worn it as soon as I'd gotten it, I could have pretended I'd bought it myself, but now it was too late and would raise all sorts of questions, and teasing I was in no mood for.

The weekend was a disappointment, thanks to the weather, and thanks to the well-intentioned folks who kept reminding me that it had been a year since I lost my parents. I was almost glad to get back to Hardenbergh afterwards, despite Tuesday's return to V.D.

Just before closing that afternoon, one of the ad execs dropped a piece of interoffice mail in the outgoing bin. The envelope was addressed to John Cahill. I stared at it for only a moment before grabbing it and heading for the elevators. On the ninth floor I merely smiled to the receptionist as she covered her typewriter, and walked purposefully to Cahill's office.

He had his back to me. He was putting papers in his attache case, which lay open on the credenza behind his desk, next to a photo of a man and woman and three smiling teenagers. I took a breath and knocked.

"Mr. Cahill?"

He turned around and looked up. "Yes?"

"Um, I'm from downstairs, in Advertising. I thought you might want to have this before the close of business."

"Is it important?"

"Actually, I don't know. I just thought I'd run it up on my way out."

Since the way out was nine floors below, that sounded strange, even to me, but he seemed not to notice.

"Well, thank you, Miss..."

"Horvath. Ellen Horvath."

He didn't bat an eye at the name, of course; it was common enough in this town. "Thank you, Miss Horvath. Goodnight."

"Goodnight."

I walked calmly to the elevator, and waited quite still for it to arrive. It came down from the tenth floor nearly full, and stopped maddeningly at every floor between nine and my own. Finally, I was able to get off. Instead of going to my desk I went into the ladies room. It was, thank god, deserted. I leaned on a sink with shaking hands and looked into the mirror. Not a trace of Cahill's black hair, flecked now with grey, or his ruddy Irish complexion. His face was broad where mine was narrow, with no cheekbones to speak of and a deeply cleft chin completely unlike my own. I remembered the picture on his credenza, the family grouping that showed him a full six inches shorter than his wife, and she was wearing low heels. That would make me taller than he was. My father was a good six feet tall, and there was something in the shape of my mouth that echoed his, and in my nose, too, I could see for the first time, and in the shape of my chin. My eyes and cheek bones were gifts from my mother, but the rest had nothing to do with Mr. John Cahill, and never had.

Numb with relief, I sat down on the orange plastic chair that was standard issue in every V.D. rest room. Still shaky, I reached into my purse for my wallet, and opened it to the photograph I carried, the one of the three of us at Lavallette that I had thrown against the kitchen wall a long year ago. After I'd cleared up the broken glass, I'd cut the picture to fit in my wallet. Looking at my child's features I could see no resemblance to either of my parents, but when I looked up at the mirror I could see them both in my maturing face. Funny how I'd never noticed before.

When I could trust my legs I left V.D. and drove once more to the florist. I bought a pot of white mums this time, and set it down among the geraniums in front of my parents' headstone. I put the rust-colored mums on a bare, unkempt grave a few rows down, and walked back to my parents. So, I thought to myself, we were never the Brady Bunch, or the Partridge Family, but we were the same flesh and blood. I don't care that you got pregnant before you were married. Nobody cares about that anymore. How much simpler it would have been if you had just told me, but we weren't a telling family, were we? There were always things held back, always a reserve. I don't know, maybe it's not fair to say there was no real love among us; maybe there really was, and I just couldn't recognize it. I'm not so good at recognizing things right now. But there was no passion in your lives, was there? No real depth of feeling, like I see in Andy and Marv. I know you made the best of what you had, but you still settled for second best, both of you, and I'm real sorry you did. You missed a lot — we missed a lot because of it, and you sure can't do anything about it now. But I can, and I promise I will. Rest in peace, okay?

Tears flowed freely this time, and it was a relief to let them go. For the first time I felt lighter afterward, refreshed and serene, the way you're supposed to feel after a good satisfying cry. I wiped my eyes with a rumpled tissue. It blew out of my hand before I could stuff it back in my purse, and I chased it irreverently across the graves until a gust plastered it against a headstone and I could pick it up. Another gust followed and I took a deep breath. The air was clean smelling and cool, with a bite that hinted of the coming autumn. It was a northwest wind, blowing harder every minute, the first cold front of the season. I hurried back to my car. If the wind were strong enough Andy would already be packing.

The telephone was ringing as I unlocked the door to my apartment. I ran for it without even saying hello to Trevor.

"Andy?"

"How'd you know it was me?" she asked.

"I've been out in the wind."

"Ah." I could hear the smile in her voice. "Can you get away from work tomorrow?"

"No problem," I said, knowing it would be. Somehow I didn't care.

"Okay. Meet us at Crosswind as soon as you can. We're driving out tonight."

"Be there in an hour."

I hung up the phone and let Trevor out while I called my boss's number. I left a message on her answering machine that I wouldn't be in the next day. Then I changed clothes, threw the essentials in an overnight bag, and made sure Trevor had plenty of food and water. "I'm sorry, Trev," I told him as I put him back in his cage. He hopped from perch to perch anxiously, knowing I wasn't following our nightly routine. "I promise to play with you extra long when we get back." I put his cover on and walked out, feeling like a stinker because his chirps followed me all the way downstairs.

Marv and Andy were waiting for me when I arrived at Crosswind. We stopped for a quick dinner to allow the last of the rush hour traffic to disperse, then headed west without stopping. We would get to the gliderport by midnight at the latest, giving Andy only a few hours to sleep. She'd have to be up before dawn to have enough time for a record flight. She was too keyed up to doze off on the way, which worried me. I didn't like the idea of her making a stressful flight on four hours sleep.

She had already called the gliderport to arrange an early tow, so all we had to do was drop off the Nimbus and go straight to the motel. I thought I was too excited to sleep but Andy's knock at three-thirty roused me from dreams of Trevor and sailplanes. I was still groggy as we assembled the Nimbus in the light of the floods over the hangar door. The wind was strong, even at this hour, making assembly difficult, and we were grateful for Ernst's practiced hands. He was wide awake, apparently used to this predawn process. Even so, we took longer than we'd hoped to get Andy ready for launch, and it was almost six before she took off.

Ernst was philosophical about Andy's chances for success

when he came back from towing her. "I don't mean to minimize Andy's skills, you understand, but she's attempting a difficult flight, with very little recent ridge experience. The ridge can be tricky, especially down as far as she's heading. If the wind shifts direction, or lessens, she can have a hard time. But, each flight is good experience so her efforts will not be in vain, even should she fail to attain her goal today. She'll do it, when the day is right, I've no doubts about that."

"Maybe today is the day," Marv said, loyally.

"Maybe it is," Ernst agreed, as a polite host should.

"Will Rudi be in later?" I asked in as casual a tone as I could manage.

"Ah, no, I am sorry to say. He is in Switzerland visiting his family." Ernst shook his head. "At the start of our busy season, too. Usually he goes in August, when we have our 'doldrums', but his sister is getting married and so he postponed his trip to attend her wedding." He sighed.

So did I.

Ernst offered us coffee, which Marv accepted readily, but I preferred to stay sleepy and stretched out on one of the couches, which I discovered were extremely comfortable. I napped until the climbing sun filled the room.

"How's she doing?" I asked Marv.

"No word since she went out on course. She said she'd call only if she had problems. She wanted to concentrate on her flying and not be distracted by the radio. She's probably turned it off."

I nodded and went for a cup of coffee. I brought one back for Marv and sat down next to him.

"When did you get that T-shirt?" he asked.

I looked down. I'd forgotten I was wearing the Bald Eagle shirt.

"Rudi sent it to me, as a souvenir." I could feel my face get red.

"Uh-huh," was all Marv said.

We waited, reading magazines and soaring books, through the long morning. When we went out to walk to Runway Seven for lunch, we could see and feel that the wind had lessened, a bad omen for Andy. We could only hope that the winds were blowing strongly further south.

About two in the afternoon we got the call. Andy had land-ed near Altoona. She was fine and the Nimbus was undamaged, but her flight was a failure. Disappointed, we consulted with Ernst about the best way to retrieve her.

"She's in Mr. Burke's field," he told us. "Many, many of our pilots have landed there. Mr. Burke is most accommodating. You should have no trouble."

Not only was it an easy trip to find Andy, but to our surprise she was positively elated when we pulled into the field and parked behind the Nimbus.

"What a flight! I learned so much!" she exclaimed, hugging Marv and me at the same time. "I made it all the way to Mountain Grove — nearly three hundred miles — but the lift got weaker as I went south. Finally, I decided discretion was the bet-ter part of valor and turned tail for home. I wasn't sure I could make it back, but I wanted to shorten your retrieve."

"Thanks for being so considerate, love, but don't worry about us. We like driving, don't we, Ellen?"

"Sure we do. Don't even think about us. This beats work-ing, any day."

She entertained us with the details of her flight as we disas-sembled the Nimbus. Things had gone well until a few miles from Mountain Grove.

"When the wind speed dropped, I thought I'd have to land right away. I tiptoed all the way back. It took hours to get this far north."

"You amaze me." I told her after we were packed up and ready to head back. "If I had tried a flight like that, and didn't make it, I'd be depressed or frustrated, yet here you are as happy as if you'd flown the thousand miles."

"Not quite," she said laughing. "But Ellen, don't you know? Attaining a goal is wonderful, of course, but most of the fun comes in the attempt. Trying is everything."

"I'll have to remember that next time I'm landing in a cross-wind."

"You do that," she said, nodding. "And in the meantime, keep your eyes on the weather. We're going to do this again!"

Chapter
Sixteen

"I called you in here today, Ellen, to speak to you about your review, which is coming up in a few weeks," said my boss, Evelyn Pratt. She was a plump woman in her forties, a twenty-year veteran of the Support Services Department. She spent most of her days wandering the floors of the V.D. building, stopping by the work stations of "her girls" at least once a day. She was regular as clockwork, fortunately, so we always knew when to put the magazine away and thread a piece of letterhead through the platen of the typewriter. She invariably asked if we had any concerns and when we said no never failed to wish us a nice day, which always made me want to throw the tape dispenser at her.

Today I sat in her office, a bright orange cubicle filled with pictures from greeting cards, chiefly puppies with big brown eyes and kittens with big green eyes and small children with big blue eyes. They were probably compensatory in some way since Mrs. Pratt had small pale eyes.

"Frankly, Ellen," she continued, "until last month I would have said that you were destined for a rewarding career in Support Services. You were always punctual, you completed your work on time, and your telephone manners are impeccable. With time, and training, which I would have recommended, I have no doubt you could eventually have become an executive secretary, or at the very least receptionist in the Legal Department or on the Top Floor."

I listened politely but without enthusiasm.

"However, I must say that I am quite, quite disappointed with your performance in the past few weeks. Your work is still adequate but you seem somewhat distracted, and I cannot account for your recent excessive absences."

I could account for them, of course, since I was at Bald Eagle

Gliderport with Andy each time. I declined to tell the truth about
this because I had a strong feeling that the truth would not make
Mrs. Pratt happy.

"You have missed four full days of work and been tardy each
day upon your return from your absences. On those days the
quality of your work has suffered; you sometimes answer the
telephone on the second ring and your letters are speckled with
whiteout. What have you to say in your behalf?"

"As I mentioned, Mrs. Pratt, I was called out of town suddenly to assist a very good friend who needed my help on an
urgent personal matter."

"Three times in five weeks?"

"Yes, ma'am."

"Your sense of duty to your friends is commendable, Ellen,
but I must remind you that your duty to The Company must come
first. We have an agreement that you will provide a certain
amount and quality of work for The Company, in return for
which you receive compensation in the form of a regular paycheck and a generous benefits package. You have not been holding up your end of the bargain."

"I'm sorry. I assure you it's a temporary situation."

"Let us hope it is, Ellen, because unless you return to the
quality of work and level of commitment we expect of you, I seriously doubt that we will be able to give you a favorable review."

"I understand."

She looked at me a moment, drumming her fingers on the
manila folder that held all the incriminating evidence of my way-
wardness.

"You know, Ellen, I really don't understand what's happened
here. You're so unlike most of the young girls we hire. You're
not frivolous, you're not boy-crazy, and you don't dress like a —
well, your style of dress is appropriate for the business environ-
ment. You seemed to be altogether a very sensible young
woman, and, I thought, most loyal to The Company."

I said nothing.

She sighed. "I hope you understand the kind of opportunity
we offer here. You have the chance to embark on a fine career
with long-term potential. Nearly one year ago you started on the

path to a secure position in a very prestigious firm. You seem to have strayed from that path somewhat, but it's not too late to return to it. However, you must report for work on time and without these unexcused absences, and you must demonstrate your willingness to be part of the Van Dyke family. Do you understand what I am saying?"

"Yes, Mrs. Pratt, I understand perfectly what I must do," I said, standing up and holding out my hand. She took it in her chubby one and we shook hands. "You don't know how helpful you've been in clarifying the situation for me."

"That's very sensible of you, Ellen. I'm pleased to hear it."

I left her cubicle and walked thoughtfully past the other anonymous cubicles toward the stairs. When I got back to my work station I typed my letter of resignation, effective in two weeks. I folded the carbon and put it in my purse, then signed the original and put it in an interoffice envelope addressed to Mrs. Pratt. She would receive it first thing in the morning.

I closed up shop a half hour early. Walking out the door was a delicious sample of how it would feel to walk out for the last time. I took a deep gulp of the exhaust-filled air in the parking deck and drove home serenely. The presence there of the telephone bill made me falter for the first time. "It makes no sense to quit a perfectly good job, Ellen Horvath," one of me said. "It makes perfect sense to quit a hateful job that fills your purse but empties your soul," another of me said. I told both of me to shut up. In addition to the bill and the usual collection of junk mail was a postcard from Switzerland. "Here on my annual visit. Happy to see family and scenery but hemmed in by the same. Eager to return. Regret to say I hope Andy has not succeeded yet — I still want to soar the ridge with you. Claustrophobically yours, Rudi." I smiled and ran upstairs to tell Trevor.

The next morning, Mrs. Pratt's only reaction to my letter was a brief memo accepting my resignation. She delivered it personally, though, probably just to have the chance to say "I hope you know what you're giving up, young lady."

I smiled and said, "From my point of view I'm gaining a lot more than I'm giving up, Mrs. Pratt." I sounded very convincing.

That evening I drove out to the Hoot Owl. Pete looked pretty harried. He'd hired and fired two bartenders since the time he half-jokingly offered me a job.

"How's it going, Pete?" I asked.

"Same as always," he said, pouring me a beer.

"That job offer still good?"

"You gonna start moonlighting?"

"Actually, I had in mind more of a full-time position."

His eyes got wide. "Did you get laid off or something?"

"I quit."

"Jesus!"

"I can work anytime except weekend days."

"Jesus," he said again. "Sure you can work here, but Ellen, I can't pay you anything like you could make at V.D."

"I didn't make that much. All I need is enough for rent and bird seed."

He looked at me for a long moment, then said, "Five dollars an hour. When can you start?"

"I gave two weeks notice, but I could start right now if you need a hand."

"Days are slower, it'd be easier to train you days. Come in as soon as you're free. After you know the ropes, you can start working nights. You'll get bigger tips. Hey, Patti!"

She came over after depositing two salads at a table near the bar.

"What's up, Pete? Hi, Ellen."

"She quit her job. Gonna work here starting in two weeks."

"Ellen! How nice — but are you sure this is what you want to do?"

I laughed. "Right now I'm only sure what I don't want to do. But I'd rather be here than at V.D. any day — or night."

"I'm glad to hear it."

"Let me ask you something, Patti. Pete's going to want me to work nights, but if it's okay with you, I wouldn't mind coming out here early, to give you a hand with the birds. I know you can't pay me or anything, but I'd sure like to volunteer. It would make me feel like I was doing something really worthwhile for a change. Something that matters."

She smiled at that.

"I know what you mean. I always thought you'd be perfect for it, but I never wanted to ask because of your job. I'd love to have you helping out. It would give me more time for fund raising, too." She gave me a quick hug and a kiss on the cheek. "I gotta run."

I paid for my beer and drove home with a conviction that things were actually going to work out. Working full time at the bar, with tips, should be enough to pay my expenses. I might come out ahead, actually, since I wouldn't have to dress up, saving on dry cleaning bills and the expense of pantyhose. My only real concern was the long commute. Living and working in Hardenbergh had kept my fuel expenses down. Between the Hoot Owl and Crosswind I'd be on the road seven days a week. Not only would my gas bills soar, pun intended, but I was driving a twenty-year old car. Something was bound to break on it eventually. I decided to get a local paper and look at apartment ads.

I hoped for good weather this weekend. Andy and I had had a long talk after her first record attempt. She said my inconsistent flying was due partly to my own attitude, but also because we were doing the same thing over and over, and whether I knew it or not I was getting bored. So she changed the pattern of my lessons to include simulated rope breaks, high-speed spirals, landing patterns from only half the usual altitude. It was almost a game to see how well I handled the unexpected, and more fun than the more routine maneuvers we'd done up till then.

This weekend was no exception. On Saturday Andy released us from tow at 800 feet, over a point from which I easily made a landing by using a right-hand pattern instead of our standard left-hand one. On Sunday she held the spoilers shut. "The spoilers are broken, and you can't open them," she said. "Let's see how well you control your rate of descent without them."

With Andy's coaching I managed to land, but much further down the runway than I was happy about. If she hadn't helped me, I realized, I would have gone right through the fence.

"That wasn't bad," she said, "but you should be able to land in less distance. Let's try it again, and this time, when you slip, slip harder and much earlier."

Slipping was a maneuver that still made me slightly uncomfortable. When I yawed the sailplane sideways, it shuddered and shook from the wind slapping it broadside. That this response was normal did little to make me more confident. On the next flight, though, I let the left wing dip and pushed right rudder as hard as I could, ignoring the complaints of the poor 2-33. To my surprise I did pretty well, and landed in half the distance I'd used before.

"Much better," Andy said with satisfaction. "And on a Sunday, too!"

"This week I have something to look forward to for a change — my last day at V.D."

"Then I can't wait to see how well you fly next Sunday."

I hadn't felt so lighthearted at the end of a weekend since, well, I couldn't remember feeling so good about a Monday morning. Or a Tuesday, or any other day. I smiled each morning because I was that much closer to freedom, and grinned every evening in expectation.

On Friday, some of "the girls" had a cake for me. Mrs. Pratt made a token appearance but stayed only a few minutes on the pretext of some important work she had to do. We were probably equally relieved when she left. One or two of the women in Support Services thought it was great that I had made my escape, but most were bewildered that I should want to leave. My strange choices of soaring, tending bar, and feeding baby birds did little to help them understand. After a while I just ate my cake and let them gossip.

After a brief exit interview and the solemn presentation of my final paycheck, I was free to go. I popped down to Repro to say good-bye to the folks I used to work with, and walked out the door. It closed with its usual loud clang, but this time, I thought, I'm outside the bars.

That evening I called Latanya to give her the news. She was as happy to hear of my unemployment as I was about her finding employment. It had been a real struggle for her, a difficult summer, but thanks to determination and secret donations from her parents, she hung on until she found work. She was at the very bottom of the heap at a small design firm, but she was working in her chosen field. The prospect of a few years "paying her dues" didn't daunt her in the least.

The autumn wind rattling my windows made me call Andy next. Unfortunately, Arthur was down with the flu, and would be all weekend, so Andy had to forego the chance for another record attempt. Two of her flights had been longer, but not long enough, and on the third she had landed in a field so far away we were forced to stop overnight. That resulted in my two-day absence from work, which resulted in my little heart-to-heart with Mrs. Pratt, so privately I dubbed that my freedom flight. I was sure Andy would be frustrated when I saw her Saturday, but she was remarkably unperturbed.

"I'm savoring the experience," she said as we sat in the office. The gusty crosswind outside was too much for our tow-plane, and we were grounded until the wind died down.

"If I completed the record attempt on the first try, what would be left to look forward to? The anticipation is half the fun."

"Maybe so, but I don't know how you can be so laid back," I told her.

"Oh, the impatience of youth," she said with a smile. "Besides, it's good to have a day off now and then. Why don't we head out to the Hoot Owl right now? Let's go raise hell."

The morning after a hard night at the Hoot Owl is never a pretty thing, even less so when the sun gleams down to raise puffy white clouds in a sky of blue crystal. Aspirin and sunglasses helped Andy get through the morning, but all she had to do was sit, while I had to run and push and bend down, none of which made my head feel better. Fortunately, Marv made a pot of homemade beef noodle soup, so thick it was more stew than soup, that worked miracles as a hangover cure. By midafternoon I could actually smile at the customers sincerely.

At three Andy called me over to the sailplane. "Come on, you should go up while there's still some lift. It's fading quickly and I don't want you to miss it."

We had a wonderful flight. I boxed the wake fairly well, and Herb left us in one of the last thermals of the day. With some coaching I managed to gain just over 600 feet, which I promptly lost as Andy put me through the usual drill of stalls, turns, and slips. She was silent as I flew the landing pattern. On final I held the left wing low, to compensate for the crosswind, but used the right rudder to help me track straight over the ground. The touchdown was smooth and quiet.

When the sailplane stopped rolling, Andy stepped out, as she always did, to critique the flight. "I'd like to see you do that again," she said.

"Okay," I agreed, a little puzzled. "What did I do wrong?"

"Nothing." She smiled then. "This time, though, you have to do it by yourself."

"Oh, shit," I think I said as she reached behind me to buckle the rear seat belt around the back cushions, to prevent them from sliding around in her absence.

"Do it just like this last flight and you'll be fine." She waved Herb over. "I'll run the wing for you, for a change."

I was swallowing too hard to answer. This was the day everyone told me I'd look forward to, but all I felt was a mix of fear and shock. My first solo — the first time I'd fly all by myself, no one in the rear seat to help out or take over if I screwed up. My life was in my own hands. It was the ultimate responsibility.

I saw the towplane approach with the clarity of a major adrenaline rush. As Herb taxied up I began my checklist. The controls worked properly. Ballast — I had no ballast. I didn't weigh enough to fly this thing without it.

"Andy," I called. "I need ballast."

"Good for you," she answered, reaching for the twenty-pound bar we kept at the launch area. "I'm glad to see you're doing your checklist."

"What if I had forgotten?"

"I wouldn't let you solo."

She slid the ballast bar into its holder and pinned it down. "There. Have a good flight. And smile. This is supposed to be fun."

I glared at her and continued the checklist, comforted by the predictable routine of it, the rhythm of the words we always used. I closed the canopy with resignation. I was all alone.

"Pattern is clear," Andy called. I looked at her and she

smiled encouragingly. I smiled wanly and felt my hand make the thumb's up signal, almost without my willing it. I took a deep breath and pushed the rudder pedals alternately, my signal to Herb that I was ready to take off. Ready! As if I could ever be ready for this.

With a familiar lurch the sailplane began to roll. As it picked up speed I could feel it sitting lighter on the wheel, and before I expected I was airborne. I focused on holding the sailplane steady. Without Andy's weight — even though she weighed less than I did — the sailplane was so buoyant it wanted to climb immediately. I had to hold it down with both hands on the stick. Then Herb was in the air and we were over the valley. It was a gorgeous autumn afternoon, I knew, but I couldn't take my eyes off Herb for more than a second. I didn't have time to worry about being solo; all my concentration was spent on maintaining position behind Herb. My hands were sweating and I wiped them, one at a time, on my lap. Herb pressed on steadily, turning gently for my benefit. I briefly wondered how many times he'd done this.

So far so good. I kept glancing at the altimeter, now rapidly approaching release altitude. Now a glance around, to make sure no traffic was near, then I pulled the release.

The sense of stopping in midair that resulted from the deceleration, and the utter quietness without the towplane, were so familiar and welcome that I felt my shoulders relax for the first time. I turned the sailplane to the right, according to procedure, then leveled off to check for wind drift. I turned back to the left to point the sailplane into the wind, then realized with a shock that I had nothing to do. Nothing I had to do, that is, although there were plenty of things I could do. Without Andy to guide me, I had perfect freedom to glide anywhere. I could turn, I could descend, I could fly straight. It was entirely up to me. I was experiencing a solitude like I had never known. I felt a sense of peace, and of power.

Scanning for traffic, I looked down at the full flush of autumn color. Far below me, a combine chewed a swath through a corn field. Next to it, drying hay lay in brown windrows on a green field. A herd of holsteins made their way in black and white dots toward a pond. The Delaware River glimmered like a gold necklace in the afternoon sun. On the horizon climbed the piedmont hills, their color fading to grey in the distance. And above me lay the vast blue bowl I soared in, my invisible support, air that I could dance with. Home.

A bump on the butt startled me out of my lyric rhapsody, and a glance at the variometer showed I was in two hundred foot a minute lift. I swung the sailplane into a left turn and saw Crosswind Field spin below me. My wingtip aimed straight at the office as I spiraled above it. I whooped with pleasure to see that I gained altitude with every turn. Not that I rocketed up like the space shuttle, but I was climbing nonetheless. After a few minutes a glass ship slipped under me, and we circled together. The glass bird shone brilliant and white against the green of the runway, the russet and gold of the trees to either side; I knew my own ship would be a dark silhouette to the pilot. As swiftly as it came the glass ship rolled level and sped away, not satisfied with the climb rate of this weak but pleasant thermal. I lost count of the turns I'd made when I realized that my thermal was drifting inexorably downwind, and me with it. Reluctantly, I leveled off and headed back over the gliderport. I turned right and left, and even worked up the nerve to do a gentle stall. I began to plan my landing when I still had a thousand feet to spare. With five hundred feet to pattern altitude I began circling to check for wind direction at the lower altitude. I completed my landing checklist before I had even begun the pattern, then rolled level into the familiar first leg of the rectangular pattern that would bring me back to Crosswind.

Nothing will ever compare to the feeling I had when I turned onto my final approach and knew I had plenty of altitude to make it back, but I had no time for self-congratulations until the sailplane was firmly on the ground and still. Closer and closer the ground came. I corrected for wind drift as I did before, and tracked straight and true over the threshold of the runway. The clipped grass below me sped past in a green blur as I leveled off and let the sailplane float to a touchdown. It stopped rolling nearly halfway down the runway, but I had never intended this to be a spot landing. The left wingtip touched the ground with a light thud.

"I did it!" I shouted. "I did it! I did it!"

By the time I climbed out and closed the canopy, Andy had pulled up in the golf cart with Herb. Marv was running toward me from the office, and four or five people followed him at a more sedate pace. Andy got to me first, hugging me hard. I'm not sure which of us was happier. Herb shook my hand and so did Marv, then he picked me up in a bear hug and swung me around. I was glad I hadn't realized during my landing that I'd had an audience; I would have bounced it for sure. Several pilots came up to shake my hand, some I barely knew. I was inducted into the club. I wasn't just the line crew anymore; I was a pilot.

A tug on my sweater proved to be Marv, pulling out my shirt to cut off the tail. I thought about all the shirt tails in the office, the trophies I had noticed my first day at Crosswind. How I had envied the pilots who'd worn them! He gave the fabric to Andy, who would fill in the date and my name. I couldn't wait to see it hanging on the wall with the others.

I went over and over the flight in my mind, soaring even while I secured 42H in her tie down spot. I floated back to the office, where I picked up my logbook, then Penny and I walked down the path through the woods. The forest was quiet now; no robins sang in the fall. The opaque mass of underbrush was thinning and brown, except for the honeysuckle, still green and rambling. I could see partly through the trees now, to bare areas that would be full of Mayapples in the spring. My feet crunched over a mix of dried leaves and twigs, and every few yards I'd have to untangle my jeans from the red thorns of brambles. When the leaves began to turn I had felt sorry for the woods, and thought the autumn landscape would be mournful, but I saw now that it had a different beauty, in the shape of the tree trunks, and the muted colors. This was a season of rest, not a season of death. There was peace here, not sorrow.

I sat down on my favorite log while Penny looked for crayfish in the stream. It was so shallow at this time of year that her ankles were barely wet. While she rummaged I made my first entry in the "solo" column of my logbook. Twenty-eight minutes looked so small on the page. I flipped through the pages ahead, thinking of how I would soon fill in all the empty spaces, and looked back to my first logged flights, terse little records of achievement that didn't begin to describe what it was really like.

The calls of a flock of geese made me look up. Through the branches I watched their vee formation pass southwest across the sky, changing now from the bright blue of afternoon to evening's violet. Like the geese I had been up there, I had flown there, I belonged there. I stood up, putting my logbook in my pocket, and called Penny to walk back with me. It was time to go to the Hoot Owl, to celebrate, and the only lack would be Tom and Katie. I would write to Katie, to tell her I'd soloed. If Tom was anyplace where he could know I had done it, he'd be smiling at me, even now. I hoped he was still soaring in the Texas sky, banked over in a strong thermal, singing with joy, and climbing, always climbing.

The beer was on me that night, another pilot tradition, like cutting off my shirt tail, which Andy presented to me after everyone toasted my success. Under the date she had written, in tiny block letters, "On this day Ellen Horvath proved you really can soar with the eagles after hooting with the owls the night before."

"We can hang it up tomorrow," she said. "You'll get it back the day you get your rating."

"Which I hope is very soon," I told her. "Six and a half hours and nineteen flights to go."

"And a written test. You should take that soon."

"I will. It'll be good to study something again."

"Have you thought about what you want to do, a few years down the road?"

"No. I feel like everything's just starting for me. I haven't thought beyond tomorrow, and starting work here."

"I just wondered if you would consider getting commercially rated. You could do it within a year of getting your private license. Then you could give rides at Crosswind, and actually get paid to fly sailplanes."

I looked at her. "You know, if you'd said that a few weeks ago I would have laughed, but today, nothing seems impossible."

I ordered another pitcher of draft. Usually I'd be the first to leave the party on a Sunday night, but since I didn't have to report to Pete until 11:00 a.m. I was able to stay. I quit drinking beer and switched to soda long before I had to leave, but Patti still collared me on the way out.

"You sober?" she asked sternly.

"As a judge," I answered. "You know I'm always careful, Patti, I have a long ride home."

"Yeah, I want to talk to you about that. Come with me." She led me outside and around the back. "Pete and I have been talking. We know it's a long way back to Hardenbergh, and as much as you love that old bomb of yours, we're not happy with the thought of you out alone in it every night. What happens if you get a breakdown after closing? You shouldn't be stuck on an interstate by yourself at 3:00 a.m."

"I've thought of that. I plan to start looking for a place close by."

"Well, tell me what you think of this."

She led me to their garage. It was a big building, with room for three cars, and an upstairs I had never been in but knew they used for storage. We walked up the outside staircase that led to the garage loft.

Patti turned on the light. The room was somewhat bigger than my studio, and full of lumber, tools, and bags of bird feed. Two doors on the opposite wall were closed.

"The door on the right leads to a kitchenette, and the one on the left is a bathroom. The plumbing's all hooked up. Always has been. All it needs is a coat of fresh paint and all this junk cleaned out to be an apartment again. I know it's not much, but if you want it, you pay the utility bills and it's yours."

I started to protest but she stopped me. "I can't charge you rent, not with all the work you're going to do here. We can't pay much for tending bar, and I can't pay you a thing for helping with the birds, so we think it's a fair deal. You gonna take it?"

"Oh, Patti!" was all I could say. I put my arms around her. "I can't believe you're doing this. You don't know what this means. But where will you put all your things? I can't inconvenience you like that."

"We planned on building a real workshop anyway, so we'll just do that sooner rather than later. I'm just sorry it's not nicer."

"Nicer! You should see where I live now. It'll be perfect."

"Do you have any furniture?"

"No."

"We have some pieces you can borrow till you get your own."

"Patti, I can't thank you enough, for everything."

"Nonsense. How would I get any sleep nights with you on the interstate? Now, go home. I'll tell Pete it's all settled, and we'll see you in the morning."

We hugged each other and I left. My head was so full of images — from my flight, from the celebration, and now the apartment — that I almost missed my exit. I made it home in one piece and dashed upstairs as quietly as I could. There were new tenants in both lower apartments, a Spanish family on the ground floor in the Wraith's apartment, now that he'd been tried and sent to jail for a year, and a new batch of college students on the second. None of us had really gotten acquainted, although I knew every record album the students had, because I heard them every night. They were especially fond of heavy metal bands.

Trevor was asleep but stretched and shook himself awake when I came in. I watched him fly with new pleasure, knowing a little of the joy he must feel. When he tired and landed on my shoulder I rubbed his head and kissed him, and told him all about my flight. He listened so intently I could almost believe he understood my words.

"Oh, Trevor, it's going to be all right. For the first time in a year, I know that things will work out. I have choices again! Maybe I'll go back to school, part time. Maybe I can be an ornithologist, hmm?" He kissed my nose. "Or maybe I'll get my commercial rating, and get paid to take people for rides. Wouldn't that be fun? Maybe I'll get good enough, someday, to try for some of those records myself, hmm?" He kissed my upper lip. "Maybe I can learn to be a towpilot. Maybe I'll be a great bartender and make tons of money in tips. Maybe I'll get to see Rudi next time we go out with Andy. All these maybes, Trev, all these good maybes!" He kissed my chin. "We have possibilities again, Trev. Lots and lots of possibilities. What do you say?"

"Piss off!"

"I'm not so sure I'm glad I taught you that, Trevor bird. Come on, gimme kiss."

He did.

Three weeks later I moved out of Hardenbergh. I took most of my clothes in one trip, and the rest of my belongings in another, including one whole grocery bag of Trevor's things. I put the cover on his cage and wrapped it with some towels, to protect him against the November wind until I got him in the car. "One last car ride, Trevor, I promise. After this we'll be in our new home."

On the way out of town I stopped at the cemetery. I left the car running to keep the heat on for Trevor, and walked up to my parents' grave. Frost had taken the blossoms of the mums I had put there; the stems were shriveled and brown. The grass was yellowed and the trees were bare, their branches rubbing together in the breeze. Overhead a red-tailed hawk circled under ragged clouds.

I squatted down and cut the dead stems with my pocket knife. I pulled the last of the season's weeds and removed a few crumbling leaves. The grave looked neater; I was sure my mother would be happier now.

I traced the outline of their names with my fingertip. I didn't think I would be back for a long time. Jennytown wasn't that far away, in miles, but there was a big emotional chasm between here and there. Here, was autumn, and everything was dead; there, and in my heart, it was spring.

Gathering up the refuse, I stood up and walked back toward the car. I dropped the dead stems into a trash container, and brushed off my hands. I looked up just in time to see the hawk level off and glide away. She was heading northwest, toward Crosswind. I got in my car, made sure that Trevor was still okay, and drove northwest, to follow the hawk.

Jo Vernon

ABOUT THE AUTHOR

Patricia Valdata is a commercial soaring pilot and instructor who also holds a private single-engine land rating. She is one of the founders and the secretary of the Women Soaring Pilots Association and has been a member of the Ninety-Nines for many years. She is an instructor for the Atlantic Soaring Club at Harford County Airpark in northeastern Maryland. Ms. Valdata co-owns and flies a Pilatus B-4 sailplane.

Ms. Valdata has numerous articles published in *Soaring*, *Women in Aviation* and other magazines. Her poems have appeared in *Main Street*, *Icarus 1995*, *Phoebe: An Interdisciplinary Journal of Feminist Studies*, and her work is forthcoming in *Onion River Review*. Her short story, "Just Like a Hawk," received the 1993/1994 Lincoln Award from the Harris Hill Soaring Corporation. *Crosswind* is her first novel.

When not working on her second novel, Ms. Valdata teaches English at the University of Delaware. She received an M.F.A. in writing from Goddard College in 1991. A native of New Jersey, where she learned to fly sailplanes, Ms. Valdata now lives in Maryland with her husband, Robert Schreiber, and two standard poodles.